Cinnamon Girl
Blues

10/6/18

To Sandy --
Thanks for your
support! I hope you
enjoy the ride.
Peace + blessings
Wilma Brockington

A novel by

Wilma Brockington

ISBN 978-0-9816806-0-6

Publisher: Simply Creative Publishing
               P. O. Box 41162
               Baltimore, MD 21203

Printed in the United States of America

Cover photograph by Microsoft Corporation
Cover design by Wilma Brockington

Beverly Brown, Regina Webster and Sasha Grant met as new employees at a Baltimore insurance company during their new employee orientation session. They quickly became friends and shared in each other's happiness and disappointments. Even after they left the organization to move on to other career endeavors, they continued to share the bond of friendship. Is it possible for them to continue to support each other while trying to overcome their own drama?

Beverly, an entrepreneur and widow, enjoys living life to the fullest. Her bookstore has turned out to be a thriving venture. Although she is still scarred by her now deceased abusive husband, she channels all of her energies into taking The Bookworm to the next level until she discovers that things are not as they should be with her employees and the store's finances.

Regina's life as a wife, mother and administrative assistant keeps her busy. Although she finds her job rewarding and is able to balance her home and work lives, she has one drawback. She works for the manager from hell. When she learns that her manager is leaving to take a job with the U.S. government, she is elated. Her new manager, Ken, proves to be the best manager she ever had until he begins to take a special interest in her and does the unthinkable.

Sasha, a human resources manager, has had more than her fair share of meeting men via chat rooms on the Internet. After meeting Jordan via the Net and becoming romantically involved with him in a long-distance relationship, Jordan suddenly "disappears" off of the face of the earth. As a result, Sasha vows never to become involved with anyone from the Net again. Her best friends Regina and Beverly give her grief with their "I told you so" responses to her Internet dating habits. During a visit at Beverly's bookstore, she meets handsome financial planner, Darrell, who is divorced due to his philandering former wife. While Sasha and Darrell are in the process of getting to know each other, Erika, Sasha's envious former co-worker, enters the picture and wreaks havoc on Sasha and Darrell's lives and relationship.

For my mother, Jean Brockington,
my grandmother, Maria Ferguson, and
my mentor, Terri Dean,
thank you for bringing out the best in me.

ACKNOWLEDGEMENTS

First and foremost, I'd like to thank God for the many blessings He has bestowed upon me. Thank You Lord for comfort, peace and serenity especially when I needed it most.

To my friends who listened to my ideas, painstakingly read my drafts and offered constructive feedback, I can't thank you enough for your patience, encouragement and support. Special thanks to Betty and Michele. Your words of wisdom and inspiration will always be priceless.

To the readers of this book, thank you for taking a chance on me.

Chapter 1

Friends borrow your books and sit wet glasses on them.
-Edwin Robinson

What a difference a day makes! Business is finally booming! I feel that I have finally found success! The Bookworm finally hit a sales high after a lot of blood, sweat, and tears. I knew my business venture would be a risk, but the way I figured it, no pain means no gain. It took more than awhile, but it finally dawned on me that as long as I worked for someone else, I'd never be rich. There is nothing that can possibly replace being your own boss and calling all the shots.

I decided to step out on faith and made the investment of $20,000 into getting a space in downtown Baltimore, buying inventory, and hiring two full-time salespeople. I was more than particular about the location and the inventory. I wanted an eclectic mix of old and mainstream books and other related merchandise to appeal and appease a variety of discerning consumers. Coming up with a name for the store was probably one of the biggest challenges. First, I thought about calling it Beverly's Book Haven. Then I thought about Brown's Reading Room. Either way, I identified my name with my new business venture, but to me, those names were not exciting. I decided to call it The Bookworm because I was often teased from elementary through high school. My classmates labeled me as a bookworm because I loved to read. They also pegged me as the teacher's pet because I raised my hand a lot and seemingly had all the right answers. If only those same classmates could see me now. I can't wait until the next Valley High School reunion. It will give me an opportunity to brag about my success right in front of their faces.

Of course, The Bookworm can't compete with giants such as Barnes and Noble, Borders and Books-a-Million, but I believe I offer something different. I experimented with poetry readings and a coffee shop atmosphere. I did additional advertising to let potential customers know that The Bookworm was fresh and exciting and they should be a part of it. I also had drawings for gift certificates and several book club events.

To my dismay, the grand opening was less than successful. But after four months and $2,000 advertising dollars later, they came. People were actually interested in The Bookworm. I had arranged to have Beverly Jenkins, my favorite romance novelist, come in for a signing for her latest book, *Something Like Love*. I had read *Night Song* and *Vivid* and became totally mesmerized by Beverly's method of combining history with romance set in the late 1800's. I spent many nights cheering on the characters in her books. Her books showed a glimmer of light that romance could be wonderful. I often read her books over and over again as they were able to temporarily take my mind away from reality. The line for Beverly's signing had stretched beyond the front door and around the corner.

When I got back into reading for pleasure, I used it as therapy to get my mind off of my problems with my abusive husband, Carl. Carl started drinking once he lost his job at the telephone company. His drunken state turned him into an oppressive bully. He never hit me, but his verbal insults and treatment were degrading. He accused me of seeing other men behind his back—of course this was not true. I remember the time that Carl, in his drunken state, slipped and fell down the concrete steps on the outside of our home. My nosey neighbors across the street witnessed him fall, tumble, and scrape the side of his face. In a matter of moments, his eye turned black and his upper lip looked as if he had been in a twelve round heavy weight boxing match with Lennox Lewis. The neighbors called 911 because they were *concerned about him.* Never mind they showed no concern for me. I really shouldn't have been surprised. For whatever reason, they hardly ever spoke to me. Ask me if I cared.

When the police arrived, Carl told them I had pushed him down the steps. You won't believe this, but the police actually arrested *me* for domestic violence. I had to call my friends, Sasha and Regina to bail me out. I told them I would kick Carl's ass for real the next time I laid eyes on him. They tried to keep me calm and focused. Regina offered Keith's help to get me a divorce, but Sasha said I should think about it a little longer before making such a hasty decision. What woman in her right mind wants to stay with a man who is abusive? I had more than a few choices, so staying with that fool was not going to be a part of my game plan. I loved him, but I didn't love him enough to allow him to treat me any way that pleased him.

Sasha has a lot to learn about men. She's a great friend, but she can be as dumb as a doorknob when it comes to dealing with the opposite sex. I think she has been watching far too much TV and reading more than her fair share of romance novels. She needs to get back to reality like the rest of us. It's nice to get away from it all temporarily through the written word, but the line has to be drawn somewhere and reality has to take over again.

On the other hand, Regina doesn't realize what a good thing she has with Keith. I would kill to have a man as fine as Keith and two darling children. Sometimes I think she definitely takes him for granted. Keith has given her so much including the opportunity to be a stay at home mom. Hey, I would jump at an opportunity like that and let someone else run The Bookworm. Regina wants to have her cake and eat it too. In this day and time, that's not always possible.

I stayed at Regina and Keith's house after my release from the Women's Detention Center. My visit made me realize how envious I was of their happy home. When I arrived, Tiffani and Tyrique greeted me with their usual hugs and a formal, "How are you doing, Miss Beverly?" Each time I hug Tyrique, his little sticky fingers always stick to the side of my face. He was definitely the chubbier twin and always had candy, cookies or some other sweets every time I saw him. I saw the bewilderment in their eyes as they wondered why I was spending the night. I made the mistake of explaining that I was there on vacation. This just generated even more questions from the two. Finally, Keith rescued me by telling the children it was time for them to get their baths and go to bed.

Those children are so precious. If things had been different, I would have loved the opportunity to have a family with Carl. I guess that was not meant to be. I often wonder what kind of parent I would have been as my tolerance for noise and drama waned as I was getting older. I continuously tell myself there is no use in crying over spilled milk. Every time I witness a child throwing a temper tantrum in the store, I raise my hands and say a "Thank You, Jesus" that I don't have to be a part of that kind of drama.

I ended up staying at Keith and Regina's house for four days. I called my manager to tell him that I had been in a car accident. That bought me just enough time to get my head together without having to provide a doctor's note in order to return to work. The last thing I needed was for someone at work questioning me about my personal life. It amazes me that everybody wants to be in someone else's business instead of minding their own. I wasn't about to allow myself to be the topic of petty office gossip.

Believe it or not, Carl decided to drop his trumped up charges. I immediately moved out of our beautiful split-level ranch house in Randallstown to a one-bedroom apartment in Ellicott City which was convenient to work and local shopping areas. My move solidified my decision that I was not going to take any of Carl's nonsense any longer.

I had worked so hard to be a perfect wife for Carl. I wanted to give him children, but it was not meant to be. After three miscarriages, my gynecologist informed me that I had no chance of bringing a child to a full term. This devastated me. Carl was even more devastated. To him I was not worthy of being his wife. That's when the abuse really began. It started initially with little snide remarks here and there. Then he became more combative. One time, he even called me a stupid bitch in public. I couldn't believe it. The man that I loved and promised to spend the rest of my life with did not respect me as a woman, let alone a person with feelings.

When I first met Carl, he came to my house to install an additional telephone line. I decided to get an additional line because my friends and family often complained that my phone line was busy. Unfortunately, digital subscriber line service was not available in my area. I often worked at home and had to conduct research via the Internet. I watched Carl as he worked to make sure he was following my specifications, as I wanted none of the wiring showing. He confidently told me that it would not be a problem.

It was a very warm July day and I could not help but notice the little beads of sweat which had formed on Carl's forehead. Carl's chestnut complexion and his very handsome face caught me off guard. What I noticed even more was the definition of his bulging biceps. I guess all of that physical work he was required to do was keeping him in tiptop shape. I estimated him to be about six feet two inches tall. His enormous hands and feet really stirred my imagination—you know what they say about men with big hands and feet. Don't think of me as a flirt, but at that moment, he could have wired me up. I had to get myself together, so I stepped away for a moment into the kitchen. I decided to grab a bottle of water from the fridge and offer it to him to perhaps break the uncomfortable silence between us.

Carl graciously accepted the water, but said he would drink it after he finished working. As he worked, we chatted. I initiated conversation by asking him how long he had been with the telephone company. I became bolder and asked him about his personal life. He stated that he was unattached and didn't have any kids. That sent my mind into a tailspin, as it had been a while since I had dated. After Carl finished the job, I thanked him and signed the premise work invoice. I know I stepped over the line a bit, but I asked Carl if he would like to meet me for lunch one day the following week. He politely declined saying that during his employee orientation, the human resources representative told him he could potentially get in trouble for fraternizing with the customers. I assured Carl that I simply found him interesting and apologized if I had made him feel uncomfortable. His glowing smile told me that he was flattered.

A few weeks later, I ran into Carl at the Twilight Night Club in Columbia. Sasha and I decided to hang out on a Saturday night, as we had no other plans for that particular evening. She had taken a hiatus from her Internet dating swearing for the eighth time she would never meet men like that again. I always tease her about it. I realize it annoys her to no end, but sometimes that's just how I operate.

I noticed Carl on the dance floor dancing as if he could have been on an episode of "Soul Train". He could really move. As he and his dance partner exited the floor heading for the bar, I made up in my mind I would approach him to say hello. He recognized me before I made it there. His attention was no longer on his dance partner and he offered to buy me a drink. She gave me a snide stare, let out a perturbed huff, and walked away. Carl and I shared small talk and decided to exchange phone numbers. I joked with him saying that he already had mine and he should have used it. From there, our romance blossomed. I found Carl to be funny, warm, and caring. It did not matter that he had a blue-collar job and I was a manager at a marketing firm. What mattered most to me was that he had a good heart and no excessive baggage.

I invited Carl to my house for dinner and to my surprise he accepted. I think my cooking was one of the first things that made him interested in me. While we were dating, he often complimented my cooking. He even surprised me and helped in the kitchen. And of course I felt compelled to check out the equipment early in the relationship. I had no complaints in that department. You probably won't believe this, but I once passed out from Carl's expert touch. Immediately after I experienced the best orgasm I ever had, I felt lightheaded and dizzy. I could feel the room spin, my eyes rolled to the back of my head, and pending darkness overcame me. When I opened my eyes, Carl was sitting next to me. I couldn't remember anything from the time he sent my body into a peak of passion until the time I woke up. He told me that I had been unconscious for about a minute. I told him I was fine, but he insisted that he take me to the emergency room at Johns Hopkins.

I embarrassingly explained to the emergency room doctor what I had experienced. He diagnosed me as having experienced a vasovagal syncope. I had actually experienced a vasovagal syncope about five years ago, but under much different circumstances. I was in my office, pulled out one of my desk drawers and hit my knee. The pain sent chills up my spine. When I woke up, I found myself on the floor. The doctor explained that it's a non-life threatening condition in which your blood pressure drops leading to decreased blood flow to the brain resulting in dizziness and fainting. In relation to my latest vasovagal syncope episode and in plain English, Carl had me whipped. He and I often laughed about the experience. It was another reason for Carl to walk around with his chest puffed out. It's not the type of thing you tell your girlfriends for fear that they may see your man in a whole new light and will want a piece of the action.

Carl and I got married two and a half years later after a romance that was like a dream come true. I never thought I could feel love like that. Like almost everything, good things do come to an end. Carl was my every thing until he lost his job and his demeanor changed. It was as if he had become a totally different person. He told me that he had been laid off due to lack of work. I later found out that he had propositioned a customer and she reported him to his corporate security department. Apparently, this was his second incident. The first incident involved him propositioning an undercover cop while on his lunch break at the McDonald's on Hilltop Avenue and Parker Street. The charges were eventually dropped, and the company was forced to give him back pay. But after the second incident, even his union couldn't save his job.

Once Carl lost his job, I was no longer attractive to him. Sure I had put on a little weight, but I felt that it did not make me unattractive. In Carl's eyes, I could not do anything right. I couldn't cook. I had nothing interesting to say. He even told me he no longer enjoyed making love. Based on his comments and actions, I knew he would seek satisfaction outside of our marriage. I began finding phone numbers in his pants pockets and every little thing seemed to heat his temper. When he would go out, he said he was going out with the boys. He would often come back home smelling of sex and cheap discount store perfume. It's really ironic, but when men cheat, they cheat down. They will find the biggest, dirtiest skank in town to have an affair. When women cheat, we have the wherewithal and brains to cheat up. If I were going to cheat on Carl, I would have cheated with somebody like Donald Trump, not Trump Donald.

What gets me is that Carl wasn't even smart with his cheating. He could have at least taken a shower before he came back home to cover some of the evidence. Having sex with him was absolutely out of the question. He refused to use condoms and I was not taking any chances in light of my trust issues with him. No matter how womanly I would get sometimes, it just was not happening. I swear if he had given me a disease, I would have killed him and been a willing permanent guest or even a death row inmate at the Maryland Penitentiary.

Sasha had turned me on to a website which provided public information about arrests and convictions in Maryland. I inputted Carl's full name and soon discovered that his misbehaving included various speeding tickets, possession of a controlled dangerous substance, an open alcoholic container violation, and two solicitations of prostitutes. In a way I wished she had not told me that such information was available with the click of a mouse and a few key strokes. My discovery made me absolutely sick to my stomach. My unconditional love for Carl continued to turn into unconditional hate.

Regina said I was crazy for putting up with Carl's abuse for so long. However, I had it all figured out. I was not about to pay Carl any alimony so I built my case to prove that he was cheating. This lasted for six months. I made sure that any opportunity for intimacy between Carl and I did not exist. The thought of him giving me a sexually transmitted disease totally scared me. It was purely a marriage of convenience until I built my case. The love I once had for him and held so dear dissipated like dried crushed leaves rustling in a strong wind. It's hard to accept the fact that my love for him turned into pure hate, but my brain finally caught up with my pent up emotions. I had no choice but to finally face the fact that my marriage was over.

Before I had a chance to divorce him, Carl put me out of my misery. He died in a car accident caused by his own drunk driving. Thank God he didn't kill anyone else. Ironically, his Mazda RX7 was found wrapped around a telephone pole. Against his parents' wishes, I had him cremated and used the insurance proceeds to open The Bookworm. Many would say I was cruel for doing that. I know for a fact that his parents totally despised me for it. That's their problem. They had to have known well before I married him that he would treat me badly. Carl's mother called my house everyday for a month cursing me out for what I had done to her son. When I threatened to report her for harassment, she came to her senses and the harassment suddenly came to a hard stop. To me, cremation was the only way I knew for sure that bastard was really dead. Besides, I saved over $8,000 by not having him buried. It was the least Carl could do for me after what he put me through. I've never been a vengeful person in the past, but I do have to admit it was the sweetest revenge. Fortunately, it just happened to work out that way and in my favor.

I am looking forward to a new life and a new start. After what that man put me through, don't you think I deserve it? Whoever said good things come to those who wait knew what they were talking about. I can't wait to get together with Sasha and Regina tonight to tell them of The Bookworm's success at our annual holiday outing at Harrison's. For once, maybe I will be the envy in their eyes. I have waited a long time for this. Now it's my turn to shine.

Chapter 2

God is my source and my supply, not my husband.
-Bridgette Rouson

If I thought a Calgon bath could take me away, I would be the first to confess it. This wife and mother thing sometimes has me wanting to pack my bags, run away from home, and not come back anytime soon. Don't get me wrong, I love Keith and my babies with all of my heart, but there are just some days I wish I could just walk out of the door, do a mad dash through the airport and take an island vacation all by myself to get some rest and relaxation. Stella wasn't the only one who needed to get her groove back. I am here to tell you that Regina Webster needs to get her groove back too. I know that I can't possibly be the only married woman with children who feels this way sometimes. Oh to be free and single again!

Being a full-time mother, wife and employee can be oh so draining. At any given time, somebody wants or needs something. I long for the days of not a care in the world except for my own. A peanut butter and jelly sandwich for dinner with a tall glass of milk, sleeping as long as I want on the weekend, with no one yelling, "Mommy, Mommy" are long gone sweet memories of the past.

Despite all of the hustle and bustle of my life, I believe I still look great especially after having a set of twins. Tiffani and Tyrique certainly keep me active. It certainly helps to have a husband that still tells me that I'm beautiful. When his compliments stop, that's my signal to get it back in gear. My naturally curly short hairdo keeps my salon visits to a minimum and I have managed to get my beauty regime down to five minutes. So far, I've been able to stay close to my pre-marriage weight of 135 pounds.

I really think I could deal better with taking care of the kids and the house if Keith would do more on his part. I work just like he does. Of course my secretarial job is not as exciting or as lucrative as his job as an attorney, but I always vowed that I would never be totally dependent on a man for income. Besides, I never really wanted to enter the ranks of management anyway. The office politics alone are difficult to deal with. As an administrative assistant, my exposure to the games can be limited. I have no problem with that. Mama gets on me every now and then by saying I wasted my time getting a bachelor's degree in business. I disagree. I use the education from my degree in my job. Besides, I am always learning.

Keith often tells me I should quit my job and stay home to take care of the kids. My response is that I don't like him making decisions for me. He just doesn't understand that I still want to be independent within our marriage. Mama says there is no such thing. I beg to differ.

I can't tell you how many arguments Keith and I have had over my job. For one, I don't like our children being exposed to our occasional disagreements and secondly, I don't think it's healthy for them to see their parents arguing over nonsense such as that. I decided that I would try to limit how much I tell Keith about the happenings at work or the dealings I have had with my manager Michelle. The very mention of her name makes his blood pressure rise. He even went as far as asking me if I had lost my mind by staying after Michelle's latest episode of manipulating data and blaming me.

Michelle, or Mimi as I had nicknamed her after the Mimi on the *Drew Carey Show* because they could pass for sisters, had some serious issues that went far beyond the workplace. In the first month I had worked for Mimi as her assistant, I knew I had a challenge on my hands. I debated with myself whether or not I should have quit. I decided to stay simply because I did not want to have to face Keith to hear his "I told you so, babe" closing argument.

During my second week of employment, I found Mimi to be arrogant, self-centered, and a liar. I mean she would lie about the simplest of things that mattered to no one. At one point, she made up an imaginary boyfriend named Kirk. According to Mimi, she and Kirk went away just about every weekend. Every Monday like clockwork, she went into a dissertation about what she and Kirk did for the weekend. If they weren't in the Poconos, they were in Key West, attending a Broadway show in New York or trying their luck in Atlantic City. According to Mimi, her parents and friends loved Kirk. Kirk was her everything.

I finally asked Mimi if she had a picture of Kirk. I just had to see a picture of the man who had her stumbling all over herself and had been the cause of the majority of her embellishments. It is now six months later. To date, I have not seen this picture of Kirk. At least it temporarily stopped the Kirk stories and my co-workers and I are enjoying not having to hear about the escapades of Mimi and Kirk first thing on Monday mornings.

Mimi also has the distinction of being the first manager I ever worked for that I don't trust. She questions everything I say or do. If you've ever been micro-managed, you know exactly what I mean. Every little step must be checked before you go to the next step. She'll ask me to call someone for information. When I call them, they tell me that Mimi already called. It's so frustrating. It's literally her way or the highway on pure minutia. How can anyone possibly work for someone like that? I keep telling myself, *this too will pass* and *trials and tribulations will only make one stronger*.

The straw that broke the camel's back happened three days ago. Mimi asked me to prepare a sales report for a meeting. I ran the numbers twice and verified my totals. I transmitted the report to her via email. She told me she wanted to add additional data to the report before emailing the figures to the Vice President of Sales and Marketing, Bob Graves. I knew it was important that the figures be correct.

Apparently, Mimi did some manipulation to the data that caused the file to exaggerate the actual sales figures. Unfortunately, the wrong data made it to Bob and of course he went off. Mimi had the audacity to tell Bob that I gave her wrong data. I debated myself whether or not to tell Bob when I discovered what I had given to Mimi as compared to what she sent did not match. She assured me she had taken the blame for the errors in the figures. I don't believe her. Every time Bob passes my desk, I get the look. You know, the blame it on the dumb secretary look. Keith says I should have walked out at that moment. I don't give up quite that easily. My mama didn't raise a quitter.

Enterprise Marketing Group is an up and coming company and appears to have a bright future. Being a housewife is not necessarily my idea of a bright future. Besides, I want the twins to learn to be independent. My friend Sasha keeps telling me she would kill to be in my shoes. She longs to be in a committed relationship. I always tell her not to always believe the hype. At times, I wish I could be in her shoes. I could come and go as I please. If I want to eat a peanut butter and jelly sandwich and drink a tall glass of milk for dinner, so be it. Every night I literally go kicking and screaming into the kitchen to fix a full course meal. I want my family to eat healthy foods so I make the sacrifice. Tyrique is getting a little chubby because Keith lets him eat far too many sweets when I'm not around and doesn't help him to be active. The Xbox 360 he bought him a few months ago doesn't help either. If he is not watching TV, he's playing with that thing. That's another thing I need to work on. Luckily, Tiffani prefers eating fruit and does a lot of bouncing around the house.

I just wish Keith would share some of the household responsibilities. He believes his domain is the up keep of the house. If something breaks, he's the man. I just wish the man would help out by spending a little more time with me and the kids and a little less time at the office.

Although Keith is a good father, that doesn't always make him a good husband. If his parenting skills with Tiffani and Tyrique were as consistent as his romance skills, perhaps I would have no problem with being a housewife. Hell, when he came home, I would be his dinner. I must admit that Keith's romance skills can get tired at times. Sometimes, he doesn't totally get me in the mood before we make love. I know that his work schedule can get out of hand at times. I need to think of ways to bring back the magic. I want to keep the harmony in our marriage without becoming too much of a freak.

Keith was the ultimate Casanova. Before we were married, he brought me flowers, made dinner, served it by candle light, and surprised me every now and then with little things to show his thoughtfulness. We first met at a cookout at Sasha's house. I lived in Baltimore and Keith lived in Atlanta. He and Sasha's first cousin, Tony, were old college buddies at Clark Atlanta University. Keith just happened to be in Baltimore on business. When I first laid eyes on him, I became mesmerized. His five foot ten inch chocolate covered frame, muscular build, freshly cut hair, and perfectly shaped goatee had me from the very beginning. When he smiled at me for the first time, I felt like I was transformed back to being a teenager with my first high school crush. At that moment, I just wanted to melt.

Keith and I hit it off so well. We had some of the same interests including sightseeing, bowling, professional football, and NASCAR. How many brothers do you know who are into NASCAR? We exchanged numbers and our monthly calls to each other turned into weekly calls. During one of our conversations, I mentioned that my feet were cold. Three days later, I got a package in the mail from him. It was a pair of wool socks with a card thanking me for warming his heart. He said the socks were to warm my Popsicle toes. He made me feel special. This may seem like a simple gesture, but to me that signified he was a caring man.

Later, we began visiting each other's hometowns on a regular basis. He frequently sent me plane tickets for Atlanta. I often thought with all of the available women in Atlanta (I heard the ratio of women to men was ten to one) I wondered why he would spend time and money to have a long distance relationship with me—I finally asked him. His response was that he loved me and that there was no woman to replace me. After eighteen months of getting to know each other better and 45,000 frequent flier miles later, Keith's job relocated him to the Baltimore office. I was absolutely elated. Our relationship blossomed even more. We spent our time together touring museums, going to art shows, watching sports, and enjoying each other's company on weekend getaways. I even learned to enjoy cooking because Keith always commented on what a great cook I was. Sasha and Beverly often teased me that I must have been in love since they hardly ever heard from me. Most of my free time was spent with him. I'm sure if they had been in the same situation, they would have done the same.

Keith asked me to marry him eight months later. I think Mama enjoyed planning the wedding more than I did. Our wedding party consisted of seven bridesmaids, seven groomsmen, a ring bearer, and two flower girls. My sister Betty was my matron of honor; Keith's brother, Joseph was the best man. We invited over 300 guests and had a beautiful church ceremony at Second Avenue Baptist Church followed by a lavish reception at Martin's West in Woodlawn. Our wedding was even featured in *Ebony* magazine in an article entitled, "Wedding Masterpieces: Special Ways to Say I Do".

Keith and I have now been married for eight years. The years have been good to us, but there have been some bumps along the road. I do everything in my power to keep our marriage happy. I love Keith very much and he never fails to tell me how much he loves me. I didn't have the luxury of having two loving parents in my home. I want our marriage to be an example of what marriage is supposed to be for Tiffani and Tyrique.

Sasha thinks romance is the best thing since sliced bread. I often tell her that having a man doesn't make you whole. She believes that once you find *the one* everything just magically falls into place. I can't tell you how many conversations I have had with her regarding these guys she meets. She calls it her adventuresome side. I call it the "you need to wake up and smell the coffee" side.

Sasha is a very intelligent woman. She has a successful career but feels at times that life is not worth living because she doesn't have a man at the moment. She's like a sister to me. I have no problem telling her when she is dead wrong especially when it comes to dating. This last "I am going to date every freak from the Internet" stage was the worst. She insisted on actually meeting men she had chatted with in these so-called chat rooms. What ever happened to the old fashioned way of meeting someone? She claimed that she had talked to these men extensively on line and over the telephone and felt that they were safe. Each time she planned to go on a date, I demanded that she give me all of their vital information including their screen names. This way I could track these devils down especially if she turned up missing. I also demanded that she call me upon meeting these men. She did comply and I followed up later to make sure she was okay and got home safely. Thank God she never had any serious problems, other than a few of them having mental issues. For the life of me, I don't understand why she has to go that route to meet somebody. I guess some of my old fashioned ways will never depart from me. I believe people should meet by doing it the old fashioned way--face-to-face.

For a smart woman, Sasha can be a little too adventuresome with her Internet escapades. One day she will learn. When she least expects·it, the man for her will find her. Perhaps then she will find what she has been searching for and live happily ever after. I know that only happens in fairy tales. In the mean time, I need to concentrate on my marriage and family. I don't want my marriage to end up in a bitter divorce like my parents. Nobody wins in that situation. Not the husband, not the wife and especially not the kids. As a child of divorce, I can attest to that.

I need to seriously think about whether I am going to stay or leave my job. Between Keith's complaining and the headaches from

Mimi, I've hit a crossroad. Beverly offered me a job at her bookstore, but I am reluctant to even consider it. I'd be taking a serious pay cut and more importantly, I don't think I could work for a friend. Beverly can be a bit bossy and at times just says anything out of her mouth. She doesn't care how the person on the other end feels. Her tongue can turn into a razor with mercy for no person, place, or thing. I'd hate to lose a friend over something that's not that important.

In the meantime, I'll continue to handle Mimi in my own way. I just hope it doesn't come down to me killing her and trying to cover it up.

Chapter 3

If you can find someone you can really talk to,
it can help you grow in so many ways.
-Stephanie Mills

This morning I woke up not with a smile on my face for another glorious day granted by the Lord, but with heartache. God, I can't stand it when I feel like this. I just can't seem to stop crying. Every time I think about how I fall into a trap, let a man play with my feelings, and allow myself to get this way, I become angrier and angrier. I keep asking myself, why does this keep happening? What is it about me that makes me appear to be a target? No matter how many times I go through dealing with the rejection and heartache from being in a so-called relationship, the pain always feels like it has hit me for the very first time. There is nothing in this world like having blues like mine. I call it the *Sasha Grant Blues*.

I am so tired of the games and deception. Is there at least one man in Baltimore who has goals and ambition and wants someone who can be supportive? It's Christmas time again and of course once again, I'm alone. One would think I would be used to this by now because I have spent more time alone than with someone special during this time of year. It happens like clockwork. Time goes back so it gets darker earlier. That alone can cause depression. Then here comes Thanksgiving, Christmas and New Year's all of which remind me of all the times I spent alone. And then Valentine's Day arrives with a vengeance. I cringe each time I hear or see an advertisement for chocolates, flowers and jewelry—the things that lovers enjoy giving and receiving on February 14. I end up wallowing in my personal misery for four long months. It's a vicious cycle. The one thing I want for this year for Christmas no amount of money can buy—I want love.

I want the kind of love that transcends all time and space. You know--the unconditional type. A man who loves you no matter what. And of course you love him. There's nothing he won't do for you. Your best interest is always at heart. The two of you do whatever it takes to make the relationship work. You take the bitter with the sweet. I'm probably in *Lalaland* with my thoughts about love and relationships, but I know what I want. I want that unconditional love that typically only comes from your mama and Jesus.

Yesterday I thought about Jordan, my ex. My head tells me that it's over, but my heart doesn't want to believe it and for the life of me, I don't want to let go. No matter how I try to look at it for what it was or even try to justify what happened, the only choice I have is to face reality.

When I returned home from shopping and saw the red blinking light on the answering machine, I haphazardly hit the button to retrieve the message. To my surprise, it was Jordan. His call was date stamped for Sunday at 2:19 p.m. For a brief moment, I could not believe it was him. After seven months (yes, I was counting) he called just to say hello. I willed myself not to call him back after our last conversation. That's when he decided to tell me that he thought it would be best if we were just friends. I swear I put my heart and soul into that relationship, only to be disappointed once again. In a moment of weakness, I listened to the message two additional times because it felt good to hear his rich, baritone voice. He mentioned he would be home from work around 5:00 p.m. I immediately began debating with myself whether or not to call him back or wait until later. I decided to play the waiting game since it had been seven months. A few more hours weren't going to make a difference.

At 10:30 p.m., I picked up the phone to call Jordan, but my fear got the best of me. I hurriedly threw the phone back into the cradle before completing the call. I was so nervous. I literally had to talk myself into redialing. I finally redialed. The phone rang three times; he picked up on the fourth ring.

Words could not express how hurt I was when he retorted in response to my cheery hello, "Can I call you back tomorrow?" and I simultaneously heard a female laugh in the background. I was stunned as I said, "Okay". I didn't bother to ask for an explanation since we were no longer dating. As I sat on the edge of the bed, I haphazardly hung up the phone. At that moment, I wanted to scream to the very top of my lungs. Instead, I decided just to have a good cry—I did not want my neighbors to hear my agony and think that I had lost my mind.

It hit home that he was too busy to talk and had someone new. The pain cut like a newly sharpened knife. Unfortunately, my waiting game backfired even before it materialized. For a brief moment, I just wanted to lie down and die. How could he do this to me especially after I had told him of my past? How could he do the very things to me I told him other men had done which had caused me so much heartache?

I spent the next day feeling more than sorry for myself and wondered about my purpose in life. Sure I enjoyed my job ninety five percent of the time. Being a human resources manager is a tough job. Everyone I interview and their mother think that they are qualified for the job. When I inform them that they were not selected, they always disagree. If they only knew how bad they were during the interview, they would go to the library, no, run to the library to learn how to interview and get some coaching from a professional. I have often thought I could make a killing by teaching people how to prepare résumés and be successful in an interview. They should start by getting some skills.

I try to keep my mind busy and off of the fact that I do not have a man, but I don't believe anything will take away that void. I don't know how some women live without having the love of a good man in their lives. Being a part of the other team is out of the question. I am alone not by choice.

Sometimes, I just sit and think that I would be so much happier if I had someone to go home to. My friend Regina always tells me that having a man doesn't make you whole--another one of her mother's sayings. That Miss Sara could have written a book on relationships from the old school. Miss Sara may be right, but it would be nice to have someone who asks me about my day every now and then. My friend Beverly tells me to be patient. Regina and Beverly are the sisters I never had. For some reason, they seem to think that I know nothing about relationships. The way I look at it, for every failed relationship, it's a lesson learned. I guess that's easy for me to say in my current predicament.

If I had a man, I think I would enjoy life a little bit better. Over the past few years, I have learned to enjoy my own company. At times I think I enjoy my own company a little too much. For instance, my preference is to go to the movies alone. That way, I don't have anybody to talk to while I am trying to enjoy the movie. I just can't stand it when people talk during the movie. When I go to the movies by myself, I am guaranteed not to have to talk to anyone else.

Last night, my co-worker Theresa and I went to Cruisers, a local pub, for dinner. Earlier that day, I really didn't feel like being social, but since we had made plans some time ago to get together, I felt obligated. Besides, I was really looking forward to having a strawberry daiquiri. As the daiquiri did its magic, I was glad I had not cancelled. It was good therapy to talk to someone else about the dates that I had from the "Internet Error" as I had called it.

Over dinner, I began telling Theresa about my many dates I had met via the Internet. I first told her about Don. He was actually the first guy I ever met from a singles chat room. Don and I talked using instant messaging on our home computers and then by phone for four months before deciding to meet in person. The first time we spoke, we exchanged pictures. Although he didn't send a full-body shot, I thought he was quite a handsome man. He had close cut jet black textured hair and a professionally shaped full beard. His warm cocoa skin accentuated his fine facial features.

During our chats, Don often talked about his hardware business and church. He was divorced, lived in Cleveland, and had a five-year-old daughter named Gabrielle. He had owned his own business for seven years and had been a member of the Board of Trustees at his church. Gabrielle was the result of a relationship he had with a member of his congregation. Six months after Gabrielle's birth, her mother decided she wanted no parts of him or motherhood. Without delay, she handed Gabrielle over to Don. He also spoke about the challenges of being a single parent. I could only empathize. My only contact with children was through friends and family. After spending time with some of the children, I was more than happy to get back to my serene environment at home.

During one evening of intense chatting, Don wanted to know when he could meet me in person. A part of me was interested. Another part of me questioned my sanity and the survivability of a long distance relationship. Baltimore is not exactly a hop, skip and a jump from Cleveland. After much contemplation, I decided to take the plunge to meet him.

Days before our meeting, I got cold feet. I questioned myself as to why I had planned to meet someone from the Net. I personally did not know anyone who had met someone via an Internet provider. All I could think about were news reports of Internet dates gone wrong. You hardly ever hear of any successes. In fact, during the evening news, the channel 12 anchorman reported the murder of a young college student in College Park who had been raped and strangled by a man she had met through the Internet. I wondered out loud if I was potentially putting myself in a similar situation. Don could have been an escaped convict or serial rapist for all I knew. Was it possible that I wanted to be in a relationship so bad that I was willing to risk my safety? I kept telling myself that this was really no different than meeting someone in the supermarket or at the Home Depot. I figured if anything, Don at least was technology minded and he had at least one good asset—a computer. My ability to rationalize almost anything at that time simply amazed me.

I was running late to meet Don's flight at the airport. Once I found an open parking space on the short-term parking lot, I made a mad dash to the baggage claim area. I feverishly searched for him without any luck. I tried several times to reach him on his cell phone, but failed. There was nothing left for me to do but go home. He finally called me from his hotel room at the Woodlawn Towne Suites and wanted to know what had happened to me. I explained to him in explicit details what happened. However, he stated that I didn't look hard enough. That should have been my first clue that I was dealing with a real nut case. He definitely had a problem with being patient and it appeared he enjoyed playing the blame game.

I suggested that we go to City Sights, a local restaurant for dinner. City Sights was just a mere few feet away from Don's hotel room. I had enjoyed dining there in the past as they had a delectable seafood menu and it was reasonably priced. The smiling hostess greeted us and then announced there would be a twenty minute wait. Don went ballistic saying that twenty minutes was way too much time to wait for a table. I asked him to calm down and told him that for a Friday evening, a twenty minute wait was quite reasonable for a popular restaurant in the area. His outburst made me cringe as we all of a sudden had become the center of attention for the restaurant's patrons. He stared down at me with a look of disgust and announced he was leaving to go get *himself* something to eat from the Wendy's across the street. I watched him as he exited City Sights heading for Wendy's. I couldn't believe he was acting like an eight-year old child. Needless to say, I never talked to him again. Thank God for favors— both big and small.

My experience with Don didn't deter me from my so-called unconventional dating explorations. Anthony was the second guy I had met by means of the Net. He was a twenty-five year old on-air promotions editor for a local television station, single, never been married, and had no children. In other words, in my eyes, he was a great catch. My only real hesitation was his age. When I met Anthony, I was thirty-one. It wasn't a huge difference, but I just could not get my mind beyond Anthony being six years younger than me. Every time I brought up the differences in our ages, he would comment, "Age is nothing but a number." Over a twelve-week period, our instant message conversations eventually led to telephone conversations. Once again, I was reluctant to give my telephone number to someone I had met on the Net. However, Anthony seemed different. I figured he was somewhat stable since he had never "said" anything that was vulgar up to that point. Besides, it was a nice change of pace to hear a male voice on the other end of the line after a several week hiatus. As we spoke more often over the telephone, I was mesmerized by Anthony's intellect and charm. As the weeks went by, he put the pressure on to meet in person.

After becoming more and more intrigued with Anthony, I finally gave in and we decided to meet in person at Union Station in Washington, DC which was a few subway stops from my company's Farragut North location. Union Station was a convenient spot to meet since I regularly took Amtrak to DC whenever I had a staff meeting at the DC location. Union Station offered a variety of upscale shops and restaurants for every style and palate. The train station was also very busy. I surmised the chance of being harmed should have been slim to none as security was always at high alert due to its proximity to government buildings and the White House.

Anthony described himself as having a Hershey's chocolate complexion, six feet tall, and a football player's physique. I had imagined someone like Donovan McNabb of the Philadelphia Eagles or Ray Lewis of the Baltimore Ravens. In my attention-starved mind and body, I saw nothing but a "tight end". I had described myself to Anthony as five feet, five inches tall with a caramel complexion, shoulder length black hair, and seductive brown eyes. I also told him that if he saw me on the street, he'd definitely look twice. There really was no need for him to know about my extra ten to fifteen pounds covering my frame. Besides, I had gotten pretty good at camouflaging my figure to my advantage. Whenever I complained about the extra weight, Regina always reminded me that Miss Sara always says the only thing that wants a bone is a dog. I again vowed to make real use of my sporadically used gym membership.

A part of me wanted to meet the man with the smooth baritone voice who seemed almost too good to be true, and the other part of me questioned my sanity and motive. I was reluctant to tell anyone I was planning to meet someone else from the Net, but I felt compelled to at least tell Regina, just in case something went awry and Anthony turned out to be an escaped convict. Just before we were scheduled to meet, I hurriedly dashed off to the ladies room to check my hair, make up, clothes and smile one last time. Each time I gazed at my perfectly straight teeth, I thanked God for allowing me to cross paths with Dr. Barron. That man did wonders with dental instruments. I swore by him. I had worn a Jones of New York navy blue suit to work that day with similarly shaded five-inch blue spiked-heels. I decided to wear my hair down. I quickly powdered my nose and refreshed my hot buttered rum lipstick and added a little gloss. I took a deep breath, brushed the front of my jacket and then proceeded to head to the Amtrak/commuter train passenger waiting area.

As I was waiting, I noticed a big, dark, coffee complexioned, burly, man walk past me several times in a short khaki jacket. In actuality, his walk resembled a waddle. The man stopped and stared for three seconds each time. As my meeting time with Anthony approached, I systematically gazed at my watch and continued to look for a fine chocolate complexioned man with a football player's build. It finally dawned on me that the burly gentleman could be no one other than Anthony. My mouth flew open. Anthony appeared larger than life as he hovered around 350 pounds. I could not see myself in a romantic relationship with Anthony even though he had been very charming in our previous conversations. I hate to admit it, but sometimes I can be very shallow. In this world, looks and perceptions can sometimes either make you or break you. Image is everything. If your image isn't together, people simply just don't take you seriously.

In the beginning, I was determined not to allow Anthony's larger than life size to interfere with my getting to know him. Anthony and I found a somewhat secluded spot at the station. It was important for me to still be in view of the public—just in case he tried anything. I politely engaged in conversation with him. He told me I was pretty. His voice was still inviting. His size was not. I cut our encounter short when I told him that I needed to get on the next train back to Baltimore because of a previous commitment that had slipped my mind. I wasn't sure if he believed me or not. At that particular moment, all I thought about was getting out of an uncomfortable situation before my facial expressions disclosed how I was really feeling.

Anthony and I had several dates after we met that evening. I tried to be an adult and not allow my shallowness to potentially hinder a friendship. The more time I spent with him, I began to loosen up to a certain extent. I began to enjoy the time we spent together. He was a very sweet, kind man who offered intelligent conversation and discerning thoughts. He took me to interesting places and we dined at exclusive restaurants. He was genuinely interested in what I had to say. Also, he had no problem picking up the tab which was not always the case with some of my other dates. The most awkward time during our dates was when the evening was coming to a close. My mind fluttered to come up with a plan to let him know I was not romantically interested in him. As far as I was concerned, a friendship was just fine by me.

On several occasions, Anthony's body language indicated that he wanted to kiss me goodnight. My brain just was not going to allow that to happen. A handshake was as far as I had planned to let it go. Each time he motioned for a kiss, I in turn told him that I was not feeling well to discourage him from even trying. I figured he would eventually get the hint and realize that we would be no more than friends. I guess the last straw was when I unintentionally stood Anthony up for a Saturday afternoon date. We simply got our wires crossed. He took it as me playing games based on my previous behavior of not appearing to be interested in him.

I tried to speak with Anthony on several occasions, but he never bothered to return any of my phone calls. I imagine he got tired of my drama and decided to move on. To be honest, I really don't blame him. Some of us say we really want to be in a relationship with a good man, yet we don't always act like it when the opportunity presents itself and is literally staring us right in the face. Sometimes, I could kick myself in the behind. Anthony was proof that there were still some good men out there. Who knows what could have been? That's one puzzle I'll never figure out.

Needless to say, Regina and Beverly had given me the "I told you so" attitude about Don, Anthony and all the other men I had met unconventionally. I know that they care about my well being. I made a habit of giving them all of my dates' vital information. When I first met Don, I asked to see his driver's license. That way I was assured that it was really him. It really would not have mattered if he had tried anything—I only would have known it was truly him.

Theresa in turn had told me about her one Internet encounter, which really was not an encounter in my book. After several hours of instant messaging a guy, he insisted that she come over to his place so they could get to know each other even better. Theresa's response to him was an emphatic, "No, you must be insane. I don't know you from Adam." She blocked him from sending her instant messages and email. He was never heard from again. What happened to

Theresa is probably experienced more often than not. It is those true horror stories that give the Internet and chat rooms a bad name.

Our evening ended on a light note. Theresa and I promised to get together more often. I must say I did have a good time and avoided the monotony of directly going home to an empty house.

I guess the disappointment of dating is that it can be tough to face the reality. The reality is that no matter where you meet a man, they always have some kind of issue. They're either still in a relationship, just got out of one, or are so scarred by a relationship gone bad they don't know how to act.

When I first met Don, I really enjoyed our interaction on the computer. He seemed so kind. I often ask myself how I could have possibly determined if someone was kind simply based on what they typed. What was I thinking? I guess the camouflage of the computer gives you a certain level of comfort with a person you really don't know. Initially, I was hesitant to meet him because of his situation with Gabrielle. I didn't want to put myself in the position of having to deal with any baby mama drama. I've been down that road before. That's a road I'd rather not take again.

My dilemma did cause me to do some serious thinking. I thought about the number of men I personally knew who were single, had a good job, and no children. I counted three and unfortunately none were available. I have three dating rules. One, I don't date people on the job. I learned that tidbit of information from other people's experiences at work. Once the relationship goes awry, it is hard as hell to have to look at that person on a daily basis. And if they start dating someone else on the job, the exchanges between the former lovers typically become even more vicious. Jeff and Marcia were two clerical employees I had to fire. After dating each other for three months, the relationship soured. Jeff's next conquest was for Janice in Accounting. Once Marcia found out, it was on. She confronted Jeff in the company cafeteria which resulted in a fist fight between the two.

Dating rule number two: Never date a married man. This rule seems simple enough. If he's married, that means he is not available. He's not available for impromptu dates, he can't come over for the holidays, and you can't call him at home. It's just not worth it. And besides, do unto others as you would like them to do unto you. Just for the record, a man who says he's separated is still married. I found this one out on my own the hard way.

Dating rule number three: Don't date a man with bad teeth. That's just not attractive. One of the first things I notice about a man is his teeth. Missing, cracked, and discolored teeth just don't pass the hygiene test for me. If his teeth aren't together, chances are he's not together either. Oh, and one more thing. This isn't a rule—it's a given. The man must be gainfully employed, have decent credit, and not live at home with his mama. My former co-worker, Natalie, dated Gerald for nine months. During their relationship, Gerald couldn't keep a decent job if his life depended on it. His mother always came to the rescue. For some reason, this didn't phase Natalie one bit. The final straw for her was when she called Gerald at home and his mother answered and told her that it was after 9 p.m. and she didn't allow calls after that time unless it was an emergency.

Honestly speaking, I'm not a jealous person, but I am getting so tired of hearing about my girlfriends' happy lives. Some of my friends seem to have it all. Regina is married to a successful attorney and has a great family life. Beverly owns a bookstore and is living large not answering to anyone. I often think of what it would be like to be in their shoes and have it all so to speak.

I am determined now more than ever to focus more on my career and less on getting and keeping a man. My search for a low maintenance, high performance man has been futile. I think that if I channel my energies to alternative outlets, I will eventually get over Jordan and conquer my fear of relationships. My question is--how long must things be this way? When am I going to finally discover and maintain a little happiness with a love of my own?

Chapter 4

Your attitude about who you are and what you have is a very little thing that makes a very big difference.
-Theodore Roosevelt

Things were hopping at Harrison's. The restaurant was festively decorated for the holidays. A vast array of poinsettias abundantly hung from the ceiling, Nat King Cole's classic, *The Christmas Song*, could be heard playing over the stereo system, and the patrons were genuinely happy. Twinkling Christmas trees were placed strategically around the restaurant, so that no matter where you looked—to the right or to the left or to the front or the back—you saw a brightly decorated tree. There was an abundance of Victorian trees, traditional trees with multi-colored glass ornaments, Santa trees with a multitude of images of Santa Claus, and even a Disney tree. This tree featured colorful ornamental images of Mickey, Minnie,

Pluto, and Daffy Duck. The servers were crowned with Santa hats with their first names emblazoned in silver glitter. The beauty and spirit of the holidays were in the air.

Beverly was the first to arrive, followed by Sasha and Regina who had carpooled together.

Beverly was the first to speak. "Hey, girlfriends!" she exclaimed as they took each other into a group hug.

Beverly as usual was dressed to the tee. Her black suede suit fit her perfectly and managed to camouflage the few pounds she had gained in the last six months.

"Girl, you look great," said Sasha. Regina nodded in agreement.

"It must be my new lease on life," Beverly lightheartedly boasted.

At that moment, the hostess politely interrupted and asked if they had a reservation. Regina told her the reservation was under her name. The trio was escorted to their table, promptly took off their coats, and were handed menus.

As they perused the menus, Regina asked, "So, Bev, what's this new lease on life? How is business going at The Bookworm?"

"Things are great and they couldn't be better. Just today, I pulled in over $4,000 in book sales. I never dreamed this business would be this successful. I may have to add an additional person in the near future. I realize it is the holidays and generally people spend more money during this time of year, but I just feel that The Bookworm is my niche!"

Sasha emphatically said, "I am so proud of you! You go girl!"

The three women high-fived each other which immediately brought back memories of old. They had lots in common, yet each had very different lives. Somehow there was a common denominator that made their bond of friendship strong.

The server introduced herself and then took their drink orders. They each ordered their favorite drinks. Sasha ordered a strawberry daiquiri, Regina ordered a piña colada, and Beverly ordered a mudslide topped with whip cream and a cherry. The server returned with their drinks then took their meal requests. While they waited for their meals, they sipped their drinks allowing the alcohol to soothe their senses.

"Alright, Gina, you are the designated driver tonight," winked Sasha as she took a long sip of her daiquiri. "This drink is out of this world and I will be having another."

"Who says I'm the designated driver? You know after one drink Sash, you will be no good to anyone," laughed Regina. "And besides, I'm the one who always plans our get togethers. I deserve to go home drunk for once in my life."

Beverly chimed, "Now you know Keith and the twins will think you have lost your mind if you go home drunk. That is just so out of character for you anyway, Suzy Homemaker."

"Excuse me, that's Mrs. Suzy Homemaker to you," Regina shot back. The three women briefly shared a chuckle.

"So, Sash, what's going on with the men in your life? You know we live vicariously through you. Have you heard from the infamous Jordan?"

Beverly's pointed question caused a brief rumbling in Sasha's stomach. She looked at the stark white linen table cloth and took a deep cleansing breath before speaking.

"Well, I have just come to the realization that he is out of my life. I just have to get over it. I refuse to dwell on it by trying to figure out why he all of a sudden thinks it's better for us to just be friends. I don't want to be friends with him. Men get me with that line especially after they get the goodies. I had kind of accepted the fact that he was devastated that his ex was relocating and taking Dawn with her to Delaware to be closer to her parents. But in the back of my mind, I know he has met somebody else. The last time I called him, I heard a woman laugh in the background. He just won't be a man about it and just tell me what's really going on."

Beverly added, "I was watching an old episode of Hollywood Squares last week. One of the questions was 'How does a man end a relationship?' The answer is he just stops calling." She nonchalantly took a long sip of her drink.

The sting of Beverly's response really hit home with Sasha. It had been more than a while since her and Jordan's relationship had been on track when they had been dating. The miles between them made matters worse. One time she called, he groggily answered the telephone and hung up. She assumed she had the wrong number and never bothered to call back. In reviewing her telephone bill, she did have the right number. Another time she called, he said he was busy and would call her back. That call never came.

"I guess game shows can provide you with some valuable information after all," Sasha sighed. "I just want to get on with my life and not dwell on Jordan. As hard as it seems, I will survive."

"Sash," interjected Regina. "You know, Keith and I had a long distance relationship for nearly two years. Even with all those ready, willing, able, and eligible women in Atlanta, we survived. Of course I had my suspicions every now and then, but my point is this—Keith made the effort to keep the relationship alive."

"By the way, have you heard from Richard lately?" inquired Beverly.

It seemed that Beverly and Regina were aware of all of Sasha's men stories. It made her realize that she had dated more men that the two of them put together and then some. Sasha and Richard had dated on and off over the years. They insisted that he was married because Richard never gave Sasha his home telephone number, she never saw him on any holidays or weekends, and they had never met him personally. He appeared to be one with something to hide.

"He came over last night to install a motion detector light on my front porch," said Sasha.

"So, did he do a good job?" asked Regina.

"To be honest he didn't do the job. Apparently he thought that we were getting together for him to look at what I needed and then purchase the light fixture. After I got the light fixture from Home Depot, we returned back to my place, we ate some leftovers I had in the fridge and watched a little TV."

"Hmmm, I bet he got a good look at what he needed," grimaced Regina as she winked at Beverly. Beverly and Regina both bit their bottom lip to keep from bursting into laughter.

"Alright, you guys. I will admit it. I did get a Scooby snack," confessed Sasha. A 'Scooby snack' was their phrase for having sex. When Regina and Sasha had adult conversations at Regina's house, they never knew when one of the twins would be listening. Sasha came up with the phrase Scooby snack to avoid giving the twins any ammunition to tell all of her business to anyone else. Regina was particularly careful around Tyrique. He had a knack for striking up a conversation with anyone who would listen. He was particularly good at telling Keith and Regina's business and would often add additional untruths.

Beverly beamed, "Well--was it good?"

"It was alright. Not as good as Jordan, though. I guess I got used to his passion."

"Sweetie, somebody else will find you", added Regina. "You are too nice and too wonderful of a person to settle just for anyone. Just wait and see. As Sara would say, it's the man who chooses the woman, not the woman who chooses the man."

Beverly turned to Regina. "Why is it that your mother always, and I mean always, has something to say about relationships? You would think she wrote a book or something."

"No, Mama didn't write a book, but I have found her advice to be true. It is my duty as your friend, old buddy, and pal to pass along some good 411 to the both of you. Naturally, I want to see the two of you totally happy. You may have great jobs and careers, but those great jobs and careers won't caress you at night, ask you how your day was, nor will they love you back. And as Mama says, when you're right, you're right."

Sasha and Beverly realized that there was some truth to what Regina was saying. She was the only 'stable' one in the trio. To them, Regina did not let the hustle and bustle of office politics get to her. Even though Regina was an attentive listener, she felt obligated to pass on her mother's advice. It appeared to help her get through the trying times of her own relationships. For every heartache and disappointment Sasha and Beverly had experienced, Regina had one of Miss Sara's sayings to put things back into perspective. At times they became annoyed at 'Miss Sara's Words of Wisdom', as they had called them, but deep down inside, they knew that Miss Sara was probably right.

A different server approached their table with their meals. "Okay, who had the shrimp and pasta primavera?" inquired the server. That was Beverly's dish.

"Buffalo chicken fingers and fries?" Sasha signaled it was hers.

"And last but not least, the Steak and Shrimp Platter." It was handed to Regina. The server asked if they needed anything else and they all responded 'no'. The server quickly departed to take orders from the newly arrived guests at the next table.

The three held hands as Regina said the blessing.

"Most Precious and Holy Father, we thank you for this food we are about to receive to nourish our bodies and strengthen our souls. Please bless the hands that have prepared it. Lord, we also want to thank you for bringing us through another year as close friends. Yes we have been through some things that have been tough over the past year, but Holy Father you brought us through and made a way out of no way. Remind us Lord that no matter what may come our way, our lives are in your Holy Hands. I ask that you bless each of us and guide us to your marvelous throne in glory in all that we do. Bless our families and friends both near and far. May they be kept safe and close to You especially during this time of year. These things we pray in your Precious Holy Name. Amen."

The three women had slight tears in their eyes. They had always admired Regina's ability to pray. They were sure Miss Sara's upbringing had something to do with that as well. After hugging and drying their tears, they enjoyed their meals. Most times, they each ordered something different so that each could taste each other's meals. It really didn't matter because each of them had their favorite dishes either way.

As usual, Regina discussed the latest antics of the twins. It never ceased to amaze Sasha and Beverly how they could get into so much mischief. Regina told them of Tiffani and Tyrique's scheme to get Keith to take them to the movies to see the latest Muppets movie. Tyrique in his infinite wisdom tried to pass off his own handwriting as Regina's. Tiffani helped him write what to say.

Keith decided to go along with their scheme for a few minutes by inquiring as to why Regina would write such a note. Then he questioned why Regina's handwriting looked so much like Tyrique's. Tiffani insisted that Regina had written the note and their mother would be upset if they did not get to see the Muppets movie that afternoon.

After Keith had revealed that he knew the two were not telling the truth, they were both scolded and sent to their respective rooms. No TV, no toys, and no talking to each other for the rest of the evening. The two were inseparable. That was punishment enough.

The three had a good time rehashing the past of how they all met and became friends and what they had initially thought of each other. The trio used to work together at a downtown Baltimore insurance company and coincidentally happened to live in the same area. As new employees, they attended the same new employee orientation session. They hit it off naturally. Regina and Beverly were a couple of years older than Sasha.

Regina suggested that they meet after work for drinks at the Penny Lion Bar and Grill, a local tavern frequented by several business people in the area. From there, they made it a ritual of meeting there at least once a month to catch up on each other's lives. Over the years, the threesome became close. They went through heartaches, trials, tribulations and job changes together.

"Bev, I'd like to bring the twins down to The Bookworm so they can get some books while they're on their school break. Do you have any interactive books for them?" asked Regina.

"I overloaded on children's books for the holidays. I have books that moo, coo, and stew, " laughed Beverly.

"Okay, we'll be down on the Tuesday after Christmas. I'll be on vacation that week and need to keep their little minds active and out of mischief while they're out of school. Keith is taking them to the Baltimore Aquarium on Wednesday and to the Maryland Science Center on Thursday. That will give me some time to myself. Perhaps the three of us can spend a day at the day spa on one of those days?" Regina beamed.

"Sounds like a plan to me!" exclaimed Sasha.

Beverly said, "Count me in, too!"

The three women discussed their respective plans for the holidays. Beverly was planning to fly south to her parent's house in Florida. Regina planned a lavish, festive dinner for her family that included Miss Sara, her sisters, aunt, uncle and cousins as well as some of Keith's relatives. Sasha shared that she planned to be alone because her parents would be on a seven day Royal Caribbean Cruise to the southern Caribbean. The Grants began taking cruises for the holidays a few years ago. Sasha insisted that it really did not bother her that she wouldn't be with her family during Christmas. Deep down inside, there were times she really wished she had a brother or a sister growing up to keep her company. Almost every one she knew had at least one sibling and could not relate to her plight of having her own everything growing up and not having to share anything with anybody.

Regina retorted, "Sasha, please. Who do you think you're fooling? Please don't make me come to your house and embarrass you in front of your neighbors. You know I'll have my cousin Winston stop by your house with his police cruiser and lights flashing if you don't show up for dinner on Christmas day at 5:00 p.m. And that's Eastern Standard Time not Sasha time. I don't want you to be alone for the holidays. Besides, you know the twins always look forward to seeing you. Please do not disappoint my babies," Regina pleaded. "I can hear them complaining to each other that you didn't come see them on Christmas day. You know how much they love you." Regina smiled and gently massaged Sasha's shoulder with one hand.

"Well, alright. If you insist, I'll be there," Sasha jokingly sighed. "I certainly don't want to disappoint the dynamic duo."

Regina confidently responded, "Well, alrighty then. We've got ourselves a plan."

Beverly announced that she would pick up the check to Sasha and Regina's delight. They figured The Bookworm must have been doing really well. They grabbed their coats and hugged each other while saying goodbye. It was the end of a delightful evening. They each knew that good friends were hard to come by these days. The Cinnamon Girls, as they had nicknamed themselves, had toasted the evening to good things happening in the New Year. Perhaps each of them would finally get what they were looking for.

◎◎◎

During the ride back to Sasha's house, Regina and Sasha talked more in depth about Sasha's recent heartache involving Jordan.

"Sash, I am worried about you. You just have not been yourself lately. Is there anything else bothering you?" Regina asked.

Sasha took in a deep breath and paused. She said tearfully, "Gina, you know this time of year has traditionally been hard for me. This time of year just reminds me of how very pathetic my life is right now. You're right. My good job won't ever love me back. I stopped going to church for no reason at all. It used to be that a sermon from Reverend Isaacs could get me through the week until the next Sunday. I stay at work late just to delay the fact that I go home to an empty house. I wake up alone, I go to bed alone, and most times I eat alone. I don't know how much of this solitary confinement I can take. Gina, I am so tired of being alone."

Gina pulled her white Grand Jeep Cherokee over to the right into the parking lot of the Seven-Eleven, put the vehicle in park and turned off the radio.

Gina did her best to console, Sasha. "Look sweetie, I know how hard this time of the year is for you. You have lots of people who love you and care about you and your well being. You've got to stop feeling so sorry for yourself. How many times have I told you that having a man won't make you a better person? Trust me, I know." Regina handed her some Kleenex from the glove compartment to wipe her tear-streaked face.

"Sure, Keith gets on my nerves at times. Sometimes I just want to sell him to the highest bidder." Regina's comment brought a brief smile to Sasha's face. "My suggestion is to work on you. How about going to the gym, doing some community work, or volunteering at a hospital? Just don't overwork yourself at work. You need some balance in your life. If something happened to you, they would express their condolences to your parents and then next day they'd be looking for your replacement."

"You're right, Gina. I know I should be doing these things, but it is easier said than done. I know I need to focus." Sasha's sobs became a little less noticeable.

"I'll even go to the gym with you. That will give Keith more time to spend with the twins and I can keep my girlish figure," Regina laughed. "Who knows, I might get flexible enough to show him some new tricks."

"Gina, I understand what you are saying. Trust me, I do, but you have no idea how hard it is out here."

"Yes, I do. I used to be single, too. All I am saying is to be patient. When you least expect it, expect it. Sometimes you have to go with the flow. Don't look at this time in your life as a valley. Look at it as a time when you can be good to yourself as well as others. Take the energy from dwelling on your loneliness and place it on something where you can perhaps make a difference. I'm sure there are some young girls who would love to have you as a mentor. And weren't you going to do some redecorating? Sasha, stop feeling so sorry for yourself. Do you know how many women would love to be in your shoes? In fact, you are looking at one. Sometimes I long for the days when I was single and free and didn't have a care in the world. After spending eight hours in that crazy office, I have another job waiting for me at home. Sometimes I just want to tell Keith and the kids to stop calling my name," Regina laughed.

"I find that hard to believe," said Sasha.

"Believe it, it's true. I get tired of stepping over toys, telling people what to do more than three times, and negotiating for the simplest of decisions. Do you know what it's like to try to reason with children?"

Regina and Sasha shared another brief chuckle. Sasha was able to see a hint of the downside of the other side of life she longed for—to be a wife and mother.

"You've provided some insight on how the other half lives. In a way, I wish I were in your shoes."

"I guess I should be thankful for that," replied Sasha.

After Regina felt she had sufficiently calmed Sasha, she backed out of the parking space and headed for the parking lot's exit to take Sasha home. She suggested that Sasha come to her house to stay overnight then go home in the morning. Sasha politely declined because she did not want to intrude on her friend. Secondly, she preferred the comfort of her own home.

After seeing that Sasha had made it into her house safely, she sped off to head home. After stopping at the traffic light, she grabbed her cellular phone from her purse and hit the speed dial button for home.

"Hello, Mrs. Webster," Keith answered.

"Hey, baby," Regina swooned. "I'm on my way home. Are the kids asleep?"

"Finally. They were not too happy about going to bed without kissing their Mommy goodnight. I finally had to threaten to punish them. I was in no mood to negotiate tonight."

Regina sighed, "I'll make it up to them in the morning."

"Well, what about me? Are you going to make things up to me tonight?"

"Hmmm. I don't see why not, baby. I know you have been pulling double duty these days. It's the least I can do for you," Regina grinned.

"Okay, babe. Drive safely. I don't want you driving too fast, but I got some good loving waiting just for you."

As Regina disconnected the cellular phone, she smiled and thought to herself, *I really am blessed.*

Chapter 5

One love. One heart. Let's get together and feel all right.
-Bob Marley

Christmas dinner at the Webster's was quite lavish. Regina was extremely meticulous when it came to planning any type of party—especially a dinner party. Every detail was taken care of from the color scheme and decorations to the appetizers, the main course, and desserts. Her talents in arts and crafts really shined during the festive seasons.

The dining room table was decorated in holiday accent colors. The crimson red linen tablecloth complimented the ivory placemats woven with gold trim. The carefully crafted centerpiece was a floral arrangement consisting of blossoming red and white roses with hints of greenery, touches of baby's breath, and miniature pinecones perched upon a clear crystal base. The slender red tapered candles placed in solid brass candleholders were arranged to the right and left of the centerpiece. Each place setting consisted of Mikasa dinnerware, a red linen napkin, appropriately placed silverware, a crystal goblet with 'Noel' etched in gold, and a white name card with the individual's name in script.

The white pine Christmas tree was placed in front of the huge picture window in the living room. Miniature white lights brought out the decorated tree's warmth by gently stroking a multitude of gold metallic bows and white frosted gold bulbs. The tree was topped with a beautiful African-American angel dressed in a gold gown complete with a halo and wings.

Scents of cinnamon and pine permeated the air along with the smells of some good down home Southern cooking. Regina had spent the last two days cleaning the house and preparing a feast fit for a king and queen. The holiday menu consisted of the family's traditional feast of turkey, ham, lasagna, fried chicken, baked chicken, corn bread stuffing, string beans, collard greens, macaroni and cheese, homemade applesauce, mashed potatoes and gravy, candied sweet potatoes, fresh rolls, lima beans, potato salad, sauerkraut, and of course Sara's peach cobbler, pineapple upside down cake, sweet potato pies and corn pudding. Over the years, Regina had learned to perfect many of her mother's recipes, but the desserts she left to Sara. Her cousin Winston always exclaimed that unless a woman was at least sixty years old, she could not have possibly perfected the art of making a good sweet potato pie. In his humble opinion, the perfection came with trial, error, and age. He always made a habit of asking who made the sweet potato pie and their age.

Regina swore that neither Martha Stewart nor B. Smith could have done a better job of preparing the Webster's home for receiving family and friends. The home could have easily been featured in an issue of "Better Homes and Gardens".

"Here comes one of my other favorite daughters," said Miss Sara as she greeted Sasha with a warm embrace and kiss on the cheek. She wore her green, red, and white Christmas dress as she had called it. Regina said that her mother's wearing of her Christmas dress had been a tradition for the last six years, but noted that as her mother put on a few pounds each year, the Christmas dress got a little less comfortable and steadily rose above her knees. Her silver gray hair was perfectly coiffed.

"You are certainly looking good, girl. What have you been doing with yourself since the last time I saw you?" asked Miss Sara.

"You know the story of my life, Miss Sara. Nothing much has changed," Sasha smiled. She prepared herself as she had an inkling of Miss Sara's next question.

Miss Sara asked as if on cue, "So, are you seeing anybody you may be marrying anytime soon?" The woman always had a look of concern when it came to Sasha's well being. On a few occasions, Regina had mentioned Sasha's encounters to her mother much to Sasha's admonishment. Miss Sara was well aware that times had changed since she was Regina and Sasha's age and often wondered what the world was coming to. The more times changed, the more Miss Sara stayed the same. She had no intentions of changing. As far as Miss Sara was concerned, that was fine with her.

Sasha laughed, "There are no good eligible men left, Miss Sara. They are either married, gay, or in jail. If they aren't one of the above, then they are crazy or unemployed. I have come to the conclusion that there is no such thing as a low maintenance, high performance man."

"Well, baby, you need to ask God to send you what your heart desires. Trust me, He will give it to you. And if you're looking, stop. That's what's wrong with you modern women. Ya'll go out looking for men. The man is supposed to find you, not the other way around.

And what's this about a low maintenance, high performance man, Sasha? In all my years of livin' I ain't never run into any of them. There's no such thing. You have to take things with a grain of salt, baby."

Sasha thought of how many times she had received that advice from Miss Sara. She never really paid it much attention as Miss Sara was one to talk. According to Regina, her father preferred the bachelor's lifestyle and made no bones about it. Although, Regina loved her father, she realized that her parents were from two different sides of the track. Miss Sara primarily lived without a man of her own. Sasha believed that Miss Sara's experiences with men were somewhat limited for the most part, yet she spoke of wisdom and had a way of looking at things through another perspective.

"Perhaps you're right, Miss Sara, but the reality is that men have so many choices. They have no problem with having three or four women at once. They don't care who gets hurt. They just want somebody to take care of their every need. The sad thing is that some of these women put up with that kind of nonsense. I don't want to deal with any man who feels that he needs to have a different flavor every week. It's just not worth it. I will just have to be an old maid. I don't want to be one, but I'll be a happy and healthy one."

Miss Sara and Sasha's conversation was interrupted as Tiffani ran into her grandmother's arms and made herself comfortable on Miss Sara's lap.

"How's Grandma's pudding pop?" asked Sara.

"Pudding pop, Grandma? You know my name is Tiffani!" Tiffani exclaimed.

"Yes, Grandma knows your name is Tiffani. Pudding pop is my special nickname just for you because you are so sweet." Miss Sara slightly pinched Tiffani's right cheek and kissed her left cheek.

The little girl squealed with childish joy and excitement as her pig tails twirled in the air. She enjoyed having her Grandma all to herself.

"Well, I'll leave you two ladies to yourselves to enjoy each other's company," said Sasha as she used the opportunity to exit to the kitchen to see if Regina needed any help and more importantly to tame the conversation about her lack of a love life with Miss Sara.

Regina and her sisters Betty and Carolyn were busily doing the final preparations for dinner. As Sasha entered the kitchen, the three were just about to exit to the dining room with the turkey, ham and some of the side dishes.

"Sash, grab a couple of those side dishes on the kitchen table," requested Regina. Sasha could not help but notice how good the food looked and smelled. It reminded her of the family get togethers with her own family. The family tradition of holiday get togethers disappeared at the Grant household over the years as some of her immediate family members began having families of their own. She often missed those happier festive times.

After all the prepared dishes were placed on the festively decorated dining room table, Keith blessed the food. Regina made sure the children's table was taken care of first. The twins and their cousins Kwame and Jessica eagerly awaited their plates.

Everyone exclaimed about the good food. Several of the adults had unhooked and unbuttoned their clothing to accommodate their expanded waistlines. A true sign that they ate too much was when a few decided to discard their shoes under the dining room table. Cousin Winston exclaimed he had eaten so much he was ready for an old fashioned porch and a swing. Aunt Freda exclaimed she was glad she had worn her eating pants. As usual, many of the family members did more than their fair share of good eating and made no apologies about it.

After dinner, the table was cleared, the dishes were washed, and the leftovers were put away. The extra plastic ware came in handy for those who wanted to take food home before Regina did her tradition of officially "closing the kitchen". This meant that if anyone wanted anything else to eat, they would have to use a paper plate and a plastic fork. Many of the family members retired to the living room to exchange gifts and talk about old times and new happenings. It really made Sasha miss those times growing up. Regina noticed a strange look in Sasha's eyes. She nudged Sasha. "Are you okay?"

Sasha beamed, "Of course, I am. I was just reminiscing about my growing up and having great family get togethers. It brings back a lot of happy memories."

"I know what you mean. I love my family to death, but it is almost eleven o'clock. They don't have to go home, but they have got to get the you know what up outta here," admonished Regina. "Besides Keith and I have to go to work tomorrow. He can be some kind of grouchy when he doesn't get enough sleep. Thank God Christmas is on a Friday next year.

Cousin Winston and his wife Mary were the first to say goodbye to the family. He offered to drive Miss Sara home. Soon thereafter, other family members followed suit and left. Sasha stayed to help Regina and Keith do a final clean up.

"Thank you so much you guys," said Sasha. "I really appreciate you inviting me to dinner."

"You know you're always welcomed to come here anytime. Besides, you always earn your keep by staying to help clean up," joked Keith. Regina nudged him in his side.

"You know he is just being silly, Sash. Pay him no mind," said Regina.

Keith grabbed Regina from behind and hugged her. Sasha could clearly see the love Keith had for Regina. He was definitely one of a kind. She couldn't help but wonder when if ever she was going to find someone who was compatible. She quickly stopped her thought process as jealously crept inside of her heart.

Regina retrieved Sasha's coat from the hall closet and walked her to her car. "You know the routine. Call me when you get in the house," said Regina. She waved as Sasha drove away in her black Lexus RX350.

◎◎◎

Sasha was determined to make it through the Christmas and New Year's holidays despite her negative thoughts surrounding her being alone without a significant other to share special times of the year. Regina was right. She needed to stop feeling so sorry for herself and get even more active. She had made up her mind that she would get over Jordan and take the energy she used to beat herself up about the relationship or lack there of towards getting into other activities. She planned to peruse the public library and The Bookworm for some ideas.

Her lack of a boyfriend also gave her the opportunity to catch up on her housekeeping as well as some reading for pleasure. She wanted to learn how to make candles, brush up on her Spanish just in case she decided to take a dream vacation to Spain this coming summer, and pick up a few romance novels. At times, reading such novels momentarily took her away from the hustle and bustle of life as she read stories in which the "knight in shining armor" took the main character away and they lived happily ever after. She often wondered why life couldn't be like that and then she quickly reminded herself that they were only books and were far from life's realities. But there was no real harm in letting her mind and heart wander, if only for a few moments to take her mind into another realm for a little pleasure.

Chapter 6

I was born to be happy.
-Christin Knight.

After the holidays, Sasha took a short hiatus from work. She and Beverly decided to have lunch downtown not far from The Bookworm. Their relationship was slightly different than hers and Regina's. Sasha admired Beverly for her strong will and her ability to simultaneously cope with various issues without skipping a beat. She often wondered how she did it.

The two women had decided to meet at Vellegia's in the Little Italy section of downtown Baltimore. The restaurant's ambiance coupled with its traditional Italian menu was a favorite in the area. Sasha especially enjoyed the seafood lasagna—it was one of her absolute favorites. She ordered it almost every time she dined there. Beverly traditionally ordered the spaghetti and Italian sausage with a side Caesar salad.

"This seafood lasagna is the bomb," said Sasha as she allowed a forkful of the dish to tantalize her taste buds. "Do you want some, Bev?"

"No, thanks. Have some spaghetti?"

"No, I'm fine. I will be totally content after I finish. How were the holidays in Florida?"

"Not bad, the folks were cool. It was really good to get some rest and relaxation. I was a little nervous about leaving the store, but James really did a good job of holding down the fort."

"I have got to give you credit, Bev. I don't know if I would have left my store in the hands of a new employee. I know you checked his references, but I don't think I would have felt so comfortable that soon."

Beverly held her tongue for a moment and took a deep cleansing breath. She knew if she used a certain tone with Sasha, she would have taken offense. She quickly softened her speech. "Sasha, I personally checked James' references. They were very favorable."

"What about a criminal background check?" inquired Sasha.

"Well, I checked his employment references for the past ten years. All were good. One place actually wanted to hire him back. I even checked that website you told me about a while back. Just because you, my dear, have hired a criminal or two over the years, doesn't mean that I will." Beverly's tone had changed noticeably.

"Bev, I am just trying to look out for you." Sasha's concern shifted. Beverly somehow had her way of throwing things that had gone wrong unknowingly back into Sasha's face. "We use a vendor that's very thorough in their background checks. If the person did it, they find it. I am just asking that you run a criminal background check on your employees for your benefit and safety. You'll be better off if you just take the time to check. What's the harm in checking, Bev?" Sasha asked blatantly.

"What about that guy you hired who raped one of your company's customers? I'm sure she got some type of compensation for having to go through that ordeal. I know you ran the background check on him and it came back clear," Beverly shot back.

"Yeah, but you know I had very serious reservations about hiring him in the first place. Initially the vendor told me he had been charged with assault and battery. When I actually received the report, it was clear. I fought tooth and nail to have his employment offer rescinded. Our Legal department advised me that I had no reason not to hire him because he hadn't been convicted of anything. If I had rescinded his offer, he would have had legal recourse to sue the company. Now we are facing a situation where he allegedly sexually assaulted one of our customers and the customer is suing the company for negligent hiring."

"Well, I don't have a gut feeling that James committed some crime. Besides, he works well with customers. Hell, half of the female customers try to flirt with him. As long as they keep buying, I don't care. He's polite and he's great at getting customers to buy more than they intended to buy. I don't know about your company, but cash is still king around here. On top of that, he has proven to me that he is responsible. That's more than I can say for the men in general in my life."

Sasha took a slight breath and had settled in her mind that she was fighting a losing battle with Beverly. Once her mind had been made up, that was it and there was no turning back.

"Bev, how are you really doing? Have you settled everything with Carl's affairs?

"Things are coming along. I have my attorney trying to settle everything. I'll be so glad when everything is finalized. I want to just move on with my life and put my energy into making The Bookworm even more profitable. I have a couple of popular authors coming in for book signings. And I find that if you give folks a little food, they will come."

"You would be surprised at all of the fine men that come into the bookstore, Sash. You ought to visit more often. I know you can take some time to break away from your busy schedule."

"Bev, if there are so many fine men that visit The Bookworm, why aren't you making a move?" asked Sasha jokingly.

"Getting a man is not my top priority right now, unlike some of you hussies," smirked Beverly. "I have bigger fish to fry. I need to grab a bigger piece of the pie from my competitors."

Sasha could not help but smile at Beverly. She was a jewel indeed. Even though she and Beverly had their spats over the years, they both realized that each had valid points on either side of the argument. Beverly knew she could be hard headed at times and always wanted her way, but she could always count on Sasha as well as Regina for a reality check. It was totally her choice whether or not she would heed their advice.

"Well girl, I gotta get back to the fort. I certainly don't want all hell to break loose at the store while I am out being a lady of leisure," chuckled Beverly. They settled the check, promised to have lunch again soon, and reminded each other that they needed to call Regina for a "spring fling" to Atlantic City. They hugged each other as they said their good-byes. Sasha told Beverly she would visit The Bookworm sometime during the next few days.

"Bev, remember what I told you—it's better to be safe than sorry. It won't hurt to check. What have you got to lose?"

"Yeah, yeah. Yadda, yadda, yadda. Whatev, Sasha."

Somehow, Sasha expected that type of response from Beverly.

Chapter 7

Life has to be lived, that's all there is to it.
-Eleanor Roosevelt

It felt so good to be in his big strong Hershey covered arms. She could see herself in living color sitting next to him at a white linen covered table adorned with a lovely crystal vase of a dozen red roses at an exclusive restaurant. She nudged her back to his massive chest. The warmth from his body next to hers was quite soothing. The caress of his long, thick fingers on her delicate hands sent her mind into a whirlwind. He gently began planting soft kisses behind her ear and continued a slow descent to her awaiting neck...

Nooooooo, it can't be a 5 a.m., Sasha thought as she wiped the sleep from her eyes, sat up, and stretched to turn off the obnoxious buzz of the alarm clock. She became startled for a moment as she quickly remembered her dream. Her dream about Shaquille O'Neal had taken her aback. *Why would I be dreaming about him*, she thought.

In any event, the dream did bring a smile to her face. The weird thing was she felt the warmth of somebody. She didn't know if it was the warmth of the cotton blanket or her heated hormones.

It seemed it was only seconds ago since she had dragged herself into bed and closed her tired eyes for a deep deserving sleep. A few hours before, she had spent most of the evening and wee hours of the morning putting the final touches on a PowerPoint presentation for a mentoring project called TOPS (Talent Organized for Progressive Spotlighting). The program was designed to help mentor employees and help them prepare them for upper level management positions. It was important that the information was presented well in order to get buy in from the Galaxy Consulting Group's executive team. The organization had been cited more than a few times by the Equal Employment Opportunity Commission because of the organization's lack of minorities and women in its upper ranks. When she was hired, she was charged with increasing diversity within the organization.

In the two years she had been with Galaxy, she had to investigate discrimination claims, scandals involving employees, office romances gone wrong, and several thefts. At times she felt she could write a best seller based on some of the things that had occurred at Galaxy. As the human resources manager, she was privy to tremendous amounts of confidential information. At times, some of the confidential information warranted the company to relieve more than a few employees of their duties. Sasha was called upon each time to facilitate the terminations. She was responsible for doing the time-consuming, behind-the-scene activities required to ensure the employees were treated fairly and the company did not violate any human resources related laws or company policies. This meant communicating with the Legal department, the Vice President of Human Resources, the Chief Executive Officer, and the department of the terminating employee for full concurrence.

The first time Sasha had to terminate an employee, it was for falsification of his employment application. He did not disclose a theft conviction on his application that had occurred three years prior to his date of hire. After the employee was terminated, his spouse begged and pleaded with Sasha to rehire her husband. On several occasions, she left messages accusing Sasha of taking food out of her babies' mouths and being a home wrecker. The telephone calls continued for two weeks. She assumed the employee had found other employment. It was often difficult for her to comprehend why there was so much drama at the organization. She felt it was proof that far too many people's lives revolved around the workplace.

After turning off the snooze alarm for the second time in ten minutes, Sasha eventually talked herself out of bed, brushed her teeth, showered and dressed. As she began putting on her makeup, she thought about the full day ahead of her. She had scheduled a meeting with one of her clients to discuss a revised recruiting strategy for Information Technology staff members and had several interviews for open positions, two of which were for her administrative assistant opening which had been vacant far too long. It seemed that she was too busy helping her clients with their staffing needs and ignoring her own.

Her administrative assistant opening had been vacant for over a month. Her former assistant decided that Sasha was far too demanding because she always wanted perfection in her assignments. Typos definitely were not acceptable. Sasha documented several occasions of Kelly's unexcused absences and times she was late for work as well as grave errors that made the department look less than favorable. Her meticulous documentation would eventually support Kelly's termination.

The last straw for Sasha was when Kelly mistakenly sent a personal email message to everyone in the company detailing her after work sexual escapade with one of the building's security guards on top of the conference table in the executive boardroom. To make matters even worse and in their infinite wisdom, they decided to videotape the act for viewing at a later date and for a permanent keepsake. The email was the talk of the company. The company's telephone lines lit up like a Christmas tree as employees candidly gossiped and productivity came to a complete halt. The email was meant for one of Kelly's girlfriends at another company. Once the email reached Georgia Collins, the President of Galaxy, Sasha was immediately summoned to her office to explain.

Georgia had printed out the email and abruptly handed the paper to Sasha. Georgia's petite frame and fiery auburn hair stood before her.

Georgia sternly said, "I know a human resources employee can't possibly be that stupid to send an email like this to the entire company. Where did you get her from? How long has she been working here? Humor me. This is a joke, right?"

In a serious tone, Sasha said, "Unfortunately, it's not a joke. Apparently, Kelly used the company's email system to send what she thought was a personal email to everyone at Galaxy. Once I get back to my office, she will no longer be an employee here."

Georgia remarked sarcastically, "Where on earth did you find her, Sasha? I thought you were a better judge of character than that. I trust that a hiring error such as this will not occur again. Terminate her immediately. Don't bother calling Legal on this one. I want her out of this building now. Be more careful about who you hire to replace her. I would hate for such an incident such as this ruin your very promising career here at Galaxy."

Sasha could feel her blood pressure rise. "Georgia, I had no idea that Kelly would do something like that. She's probably not the first person to ever send such an email, and she probably won't be the last. It's unfortunate that she did what she did. I'll make sure that today is her last day with us."

"Sasha, just handle it," huffed Georgia. "And another thing, make sure you call the vendor and get rid of that security guard, too." Georgia abruptly picked up her telephone, began dialing while Sasha was sitting in the guest chair. That was her way of signaling to Sasha that the conversation was over and she was moving on to the next item on her agenda.

Once Sasha returned to her office, she walked in on Kelly in her cubicle as she was in the midst of packing her personal effects. Apparently the buzz in the organization got back to her. The two women met briefly in Sasha's office. Sasha offered Kelly the choice of either being terminated for misuse of company resources or resign. Kelly decided to take the latter choice.

"Well, I guess I really hung myself this time," Kelly weakly smiled. "What ever happened to progressive discipline? I hear you talking to some of the managers about a verbal warning followed by a written warning. Why are you treating me differently, Sasha?" Kelly started to pout.

"Kelly, you're an at will employee—Galaxy doesn't have to go through progressive discipline with you. Besides, what you did was very serious. You treated the boardroom as if it were your own bedroom. What on earth were you thinking? Kelly, I know you are smarter than that." Sasha's tone was harsh.

Sasha tried to read Kelly's somber eyes. "Kelly, the best thing I can tell you is to look at this as a lesson. Keep your work life separate from your personal life and don't use the company's resources as your own."

"I guess I wasn't really thinking about work during that time. I was going through a tough time at home, so I used work as an outlet. John and I had been talking for a while and even went out on dates a few times. The opportunity presented itself and it seemed like an okay thing to do at the time," Kelly explained. "I realize now that it wasn't the right thing to do, especially in the office. I feel so embarrassed."

"Take this as a lesson learned, Kelly. You have a whole lot of work years ahead of you. It's not a requirement, but keep your work and home lives separate. I've been around a little longer than you. When things work out romantically with someone at work, that's great, but when they don't work out, it's like a living hell. You have to look that person in the face everyday. God forbid they start dating someone else at work. I didn't have to have experienced that to tell you that it's true. I've witnessed it more times than I care to admit. Never mix your money and your honey."

"Well, I guess asking for a reference is out of the question", seriously said Kelly.

"Kelly, you know that company policy dictates that we only verify dates of employment, job title, and reason for leaving. I'm sure you'll find something. You need to focus and tap into your potential."

"Gee, thanks," said Kelly dryly. She gave Sasha one last look as if she was about to burst into singing the first line of "And I Am Telling You". She stood up, walked out of Sasha's office, picked up her box of personal effects from her former desk, and swiftly headed for the elevator hoping not to run into anyone she knew.

◎◎◎

In Sasha's search for a replacement for Kelly, she became overly cautious which made it even more difficult for her to find a replacement. The two interviews she had scheduled didn't pan out well. One candidate did horribly on the typing test and the other candidate lied about her experience on her résumé. Sasha continued to spend hours combing over résumés for suitable candidates. When Georgia noticed that Sasha was working excessive hours and had not found a replacement for Kelly, she questioned why it was taking her so long to find a replacement. At that moment, Sasha made her search for an assistant a priority. She definitely did not want to be a staple on Georgia's hit list.

As Sasha took a bite into her cream cheese coated cinnamon raisin bagel, the telephone rang. She wondered aloud who would be calling her so early in the morning.

"Sasha Marie Grant, it's your mother. Why haven't we heard from you, lately?" Marian Grant quizzically asked her only child. Her mother's unique greeting made Sasha smile every time.

"Hi, Ma. Sorry, but I have been a bit busy. How are you doing?"

"Just fine, baby girl. I just called to check on you. Your daddy and I don't hear from you as often as we'd like. What have you been up to? How's work? Did you meet anybody yet?"

Marian's barrage of questions often started her conversations with Sasha. Her dad was always the quiet one. It was a wonder that he ever got in a word edgewise with Marian as a wife.

"Ma, I'm fine." Sasha hesitated briefly; she thought about telling Marian about Jordan and then immediately squashed the thought. She was not in the mood for a "when are you getting married and giving me some grandchildren" speech. She honestly believed that her mother was living for the day she would plan Sasha's wedding. Marian had been a wedding coordinator for several of her friends' daughters over the years. Sasha had attended a few. She was extremely impressed with her mother's take charge attitude to ensure everything went smoothly and without a hitch.

"I'm going up to New York this spring for a wedding." Sasha teased, "Maybe I'll find your son-in-law up there."

"Just as long as he's got a good job and no excess baggage. You know your Daddy and I aren't getting any younger." Marian sighed. "We'll be so old by the time you get hitched, we won't be any good to our grandchildren. We were hoping that you would be married and settled down by now." Marian's southern drawl became more apparent.

"Mama, why must we have this conversation?" Sasha pleaded. She began feeling the tinge of a headache rising to the occasion.

"Baby girl, I'm just a concerned mother. Daddy and I want the best for you. A good job just isn't good enough. Church is important and so is spirituality. When was the last time you went to church? Knowing yourself is also important. I hope you are not still devastated because of that Derrick fella. I wouldn't have liked him anyway. And you know that I can read people a mile away."

"Darren, Mama," Sasha corrected. "His name was Darren." Darren was a guy Sasha met while on vacation with Beverly in the Virgin Islands. Darren's suaveness allowed him to gain Sasha's trust. Darren was able to "borrow" $1,000 in traveler's checks from Sasha without her knowledge. She didn't notice the travelers checks were missing until four days into her vacation.

"Well, whoever he was--but baby, life goes on."

Marian's obvious disgust with Darren managed to linger. She was never really fond of any other guys Sasha managed to date. A nice doctor would have been great. Her dad, a military man, was especially critical, but whatever his baby girl wanted he tried to understand. He just wanted her to be happy.

Sasha quickly changed the subject. "Where's my Daddy?"

"Hold on, sweetie. George! Sasha's on the phone. George! He must be reading the paper."

Sounding slightly annoyed, George answered, "What is it, Marian?! I'm trying to read the paper. He readjusted his body in his lazy boy lounger. "Can't a man read his newspaper in peace?!"

"It's your daughter, George."

"Alright, Marian, I'm coming. George rose from his reclining position to get to the telephone. Over the years, the aging process had slowed his body, but not his spirit. He fondly tapped Marian on the behind as she handed the telephone over to him. Since George's retirement from the military, he had mellowed to the point that his old army buddies nick named him Captain Softie.

"Hey, sweetheart. Is your mother up to her usual?" George grimaced.

"How did you know Daddy?" Sasha pouted.

"I know your mother. We've been married only forty years," George laughed. "Listen, we're both concerned about you. It shouldn't hurt to pick up the phone every now and then or stop over for dinner every once in a while. Now should it?"

"No Daddy, it shouldn't," Sasha breathed a slightly noticeable sigh.

"So we'll see you next Sunday after church for dinner?"

"Yes, Daddy, you will. I'll even bake you your favorite double chocolate cake."

"That's my girl! We can watch the football game after dinner like we did in the old days. We'll I'll let you go. Here's Mama." Sasha used to think that her Dad always wanted a son. They had what she labeled as boy outings such as fishing, hunting, and attending live sporting events.

"Ma, I'll see you on Sunday."

"Okay, we love you." Marian said.

"Love you, too. Bye."

During the evening drive back home, Sasha listened to her favorite radio station, 95.7 featuring Rodney Charles of his self-titled afternoon show. As Tony Terry's, *When I'm With You*, played from the speakers, she thought of her dilemma—trying to balance her work and home life. Her dateless weekends were taken by her increased interest in trying to forget how she longed for some male company. With all the drama at Galaxy and trying to keep up with the two graduate classes she was taking at Loyola College, she had not talked with either Regina or Beverly for any length of time. Their recent interactions included a brief 'Hey, how have you been?' with Beverly or an occasional workout session with Regina. Between work and school, and no real personal life, in her mind she was convinced that her life was becoming out of control. It was not a good feeling.

Chapter 8

If you love 'em in the morning with their eyes full of crust; if you love 'em at night with their hair full of rollers, chances are, you're in love.
-Miles Davis

"Mommy, I'm thirsty," yawned Tiffani, as she climbed into bed next to Regina. Keith felt Tiffani's hand brush across his strategically placed hand encircling Regina's waist. Tiffani's small whining voice woke him from a restful sleep. Half asleep, Regina turned on the crystal table lamp and groggily said, "What's wrong, sweetie?"

"I want something to drink, please. I'm thirsty."

Regina took a deep breath and silently cursed Keith for not locking their bedroom door. She and Tiffani got out of bed. Regina grabbed her silk burgundy, black and green floral robe and black furry slippers and hurriedly put them on. She then made Tiffani go get her slippers before the pair headed to the kitchen for Tiffani's drink. She had reminded Keith on more than a few occasions to lock the bedroom door to keep the twins from entering at any whim. Out of habit, Keith often slept in the nude. He and Regina agreed that they were not ready for questions regarding male/female sex organs from the children. After Tyrique had come running through their bedroom door while they were in heated passion, Regina insisted that Keith go to the hardware store the next day to get a lock for their bedroom door.

Upon Tyrique's unexpected visit, it appeared that his father was hurting his mother based on Regina's moans and Keith's motions. He began sobbing uncontrollably as he jumped on Keith's back and began pounding it to protect his mother. Tyrique appeared traumatized from what he had witnessed. Both Regina and Keith talked to Tyrique trying to explain to him that Mommy and Daddy were showing how much they loved each other and not that Keith was hurting Regina. As imagined, Tyrique did not quite understand and refused to go near Keith for a couple of weeks.

Keith had to make the extra effort to get the father and son relationship with Tyrique back on track. He spent as much time as possible with Tyrique to regain his trust. They went to movies and sports events around town, McDonald's more times than Keith wanted to remember, and spent time reading together. Keith and Regina made sure they greeted each other with hugs and kisses in front of Tiffani and Tyrique so they could see the love they shared. At first, Regina felt that Tyrique had been psychologically damaged. She called the Employee Assistance Program counselor assigned to her company and told him of the situation. The counselor explained that he did not see any long-term effects of Tyrique witnessing his parents having sex. To them, it was a relief.

After giving Tiffani a half a glass of water, Regina put her back to bed and reminded her that she had better not pee in the bed. She tucked her in again, kissed her on the forehead and closed the door to her bedroom. Tiffani yelled, "Thank you, Mommy!" Regina briefly opened the door and said, "You're welcome, baby," then quickly shut the door and headed back down the hall to bed.

Once inside the bedroom, Regina closed and locked the door. She glanced at the digital alarm clock on the walnut nightstand. It read 12:03 a.m. As she was getting back into bed, she then noticed that Keith was fully awake. "Baby, how many times must I remind you to lock the door," Regina admonished. "I don't want another incident with one the kids walking in on us again."

"Babe, I am sorry, but I had sleep on my mind. Blame it on my twelve-hour day. I'll try to remember that tidbit of information in the future," Keith said as he snuggled his lean body along Regina's backside. "Hmmm, babe, you feel so good." He gave her a slight squeeze as his right hand massaged her abdomen under her pink silk nightgown.

"I see you two have other things in mind other than sleep right now," joked Regina. She could feel the mold of Keith's growing manhood against her buttocks. She felt so safe and secure in Keith's strong arms.

Keith began gently kissing the nape of Regina's neck. He enjoyed the smoothness of her skin. She always bathed using scented bath gels and lotions. He especially loved the Victoria's Secret Pear Glace' scented shower gel and lotion she had been using lately. That particular scent on her drove him absolutely wild.

Regina nudged her body to turn to face Keith and said, "I love you, baby". She could feel the core of her desire increase its nectar. She began gently stroking his right cheek. He had recently begun to grow a beard. His five o'clock shadow was turning into midnight. She then began nibbling on his ear lobe. He felt as if he had been touched by an angel.

Keith delicately touched her cheek and looked deeply into her eyes. He took in her beauty for a few moments and smiled. He loved her more than she could ever imagine. He would definitely marry her all over again.

"I love you more, darling," Keith responded. He wanted to embrace her forever. He could not imagine living life without her. To him, she was the epitome of a woman.

When they decided to pursue a long distance relationship, his buddies advised him to maintain a relationship with Regina as well as pursue relationships with other women in Atlanta. His conscious and Keith, Jr. often had knock down drag out fights over who would win when it came to pursuing intimate pleasures with other women. Keith, Jr. did come close to winning a few times. Keith had made up his mind to actively pursue Regina. He knew she was special and was definitely marriage material. The other women he had been dating prior to Regina pursued Keith based on his looks and potential income. His dilemma was trying to decide how he was going to see Regina on a regular basis without going broke.

Keith still had thousands of dollars in student loans to pay from law school. His buddies said he was crazy for doing it, but he took on a part-time job in addition to his full-time job at Brug, Williams and Alade to help him keep up with his expenses and to maintain his long distance relationship with Regina. The company paid transfer to the Baltimore office was a blessing and a dream come true. The disappearance of the hundred of miles between them made him realize how very much he wanted her to be a part of his life for an eternity.

Keith continued to cradle Regina in his arms and placed slow, deliberate and gentle kisses on her face. Regina could feel the increased moistness of her desire. He then masterfully guided his skillful tongue into her awaiting mouth and teased her passion. Her femininity more than came as alive as he played a soothing melody on her full voluptuous lips.

He knew it was time. Keith's powerful hands circled her inner thighs. She made it easy for him by not wearing any barrier to her moistness. He lightly and circularly massaged her essence. His touch caused her to moan and rotate her eager lower torso. Keith's hardness had become ripe to perfection.

"Aren't you forgetting something?" Regina said breathlessly, as she pointed to the top drawer of the nightstand. She reminded him that she had stopped taking the pill. Keith pleaded, "Baby, I need to feel you," as he continued providing passionate kisses over her enlarged nipples. Regina gave into her passion.

Keith began his quest. He delicately tilted Regina's hips as his maleness took over. She knew that her mind, body and soul were in for an impassioned treat. Keith navigated his manhood into her overly moist canal. Her walls closed in on him as he created a passion she had experienced with him several times before. Each time they made love, it was always different from the last time. After forty-five minutes of his persistent commotion plummeting into the very core of her soul, Regina began moaning uncontrollably and tightened her grip on Keith's physique. She suddenly felt as if she had been on a roller coaster that had descended 1,000 feet at 500 miles per hour. He had hit the peak of her passion.

A few moments later, he offered a moan of completion and oneness. At his peak, he bellowed Regina's name and continued to hold her tightly. He didn't want their embrace to end. He released her slightly and ended their union by brushing his lips upon hers. Regina felt safer with Keith than any other time in her life.

When she gazed at the digital clock again, it read 12:48 a.m. She realized that she was not going to get as much sleep she would have liked as the time for her to start her day was only four hours and twelve minutes away. However, she had no doubt in her mind--Keith was definitely worth it.

Life can't possibly get any better than this, she thought, as she drifted off to sleep in Keith's arms.

Chapter 9

You get what you expect.
-Alvin Alley

It's going to be a good day, Beverly thought as she arrived at The Bookworm at 8:30 a.m. Her decision to locate the store in the Gallery Mall in downtown Baltimore turned out to be a wise one. The proximity to Baltimore's Inner Harbor and other tourist attractions transpired into increased exposure to potential customers. Business was still good, but not as good as it had been for the past few months.

The poetry readings and soothing atmosphere brought varied readers looking for the right book to hold their interest to either take them temporarily away from whatever personal issues they were experiencing at the moment or to increase their knowledge in a particular subject. The number of women who were attracted to romance novels never ceased to amaze her. She often wondered why these books were so popular since most of them ended the same—the hero and the heroine fall in love and live happily ever after. However, business was business to her. Never mind how the books were sold as long as they were sold.

After entering the store, Beverly closed and locked the gate. Her two salespeople James Smith and Sharon Scott, who had been with her since the beginning, would be arriving about fifteen minutes later. So far, her selection of the two had been good. After hearing many of Sasha's horror stories involving employees over the years, it made her a bit cautious of the interview and hiring process. Sasha helped her develop an employment application along with interview questions and explained the various employment laws. As usual, Sasha was quite thorough. She even taught Beverly how to probe for answers as well as how to read a candidate's body language. She wanted to tell Sasha that if she had been that particular and thorough when it came to dating, she could have avoided a lot of the heartache over the years, but she held back because she knew she would have been offended by her openness and honesty.

Sasha volunteered to help interview candidates with Beverly. When it came to selecting the final two candidates, she and Sasha did not agree on the hiring of James. Sasha felt that his frequent job changes were a sign of instability. For the past five years, 35 year old James had worked at twelve different companies. Beverly wanted to give him the opportunity to start over. During his interview, he admitted that he had changed jobs because he was not sure which direction his life was going. He had a background in retail sales and proved to be a smooth talker during the interview. In addition, he indicated that he attended the University of Maryland. Although Beverly was impressed with him, Sasha expressed that James was nothing more than a talker. She wasn't impressed with his charm nor charisma. She also noted that James had been attending Maryland for over six years full-time and had yet to obtain his degree. He was definitely easy on the eyes. His likeness was that of a younger Denzel Washington. Sasha believed that James' attractiveness fueled the fact that Beverly wanted to give him a chance.

The other salesperson Beverly hired was Sharon Scott, a recent graduate of Morgan State University. Sharon had obtained her bachelor's degree in business administration and had spent four summers working in retail. Sharon interviewed extremely well. She told them of her future ambitions and plans to attend graduate school. They knew that Sharon would be seeking other employment opportunities with a more lucrative employer sooner rather than later, but they decided to hire her because they believed she would be an asset for the time being.

Beverly unlocked her office door and placed her black Coach purse in her desk drawer and brief case on the side of her cherry wood modular desk. She took a brief moment to get comfortable in her black leather office chair then began reviewing her day planner. She made notations of tasks she needed to complete for the day.

She then went to the checkout area of the store to ready the cash registers, made sure the proper supplies were available, and then began brewing a fresh pot of Colombian blend coffee. A few moments later, James arrived followed by Sharon.

"Good Morning, Bev," greeted James. Sometimes James' overly morning cheerfulness annoyed Beverly because at times it appeared plastic. Beverly noted his expensive taste in clothing. She thought he had probably spent the majority of his paychecks at the Brooks Brothers store located on the lower level of the mall. For the life of her, she could not figure out how he was able to dress so well on the salary she paid him.

"Hi, Bev," said Sharon. Sharon dressed much more comparable to her salary. She often talked of the designer bargains she was able to get from the Value City at the Westview Mall in

Catonsville in Baltimore County. Sharon was a petite size four. Anything and everything appeared to look great on her. Beverly chalked it up to the fact she was twenty-one years old and had tremendous amounts of energy.

"Hey, guys," said Beverly. "I have some items that need to be taken care of today. We got in a new shipment that needs to be unpacked and inventoried. James, you can handle that. When you're done, you can do the new window display. Sharon, you can take care of the customers.

In the few months James and Sharon had worked for Beverly, they knew that she could be stern, but for the most part she was fair. They knew she was a smart businesswoman and she ran a very tight ship. She did not talk much about her personal life with them and they figured that it was how it should be, however, that did not stop them from discussing their personal lives with her or with each other.

Beverly learned that James liked to party at any opportunity he could get. He often went to Northwest Washington, DC to go clubbing. Her concern was that he got to work in good condition and on time. So far, there were no problems. Sharon was far more conservative. The highlight of her weekend was going to church at Calvary African Methodist Episcopal Church and finding good bargains at the Patapsco Flea Market. The flea market had over 200 vendors. The vendors sold items such as discounted Avon, Amway, linen, seafood, fruit, "designer" clothing, hair care products, and jewelry. They even had a food court.

"I'm heading out to run some errands. I should be back in two to three hours. Hit me on the cell if necessary," Beverly said as she exited the store on her way to the bank and to see her accountant.

Over the last few months she had become very comfortable leaving James and Sharon to handle The Bookworm. Both Regina and Sasha advised her not to do that until her employees had been there a while longer. She disagreed stating that she trained them well and trusted the pair.

◎◎◎

On her lunch hour, Sasha decided to visit Beverly at The Bookworm and to finally pick up *Office Politics*. Regina's sister, Betty, mentioned that she had read the book over a two-day period and could not put it down. Her school work and work at Galaxy had been keeping her busy as usual; it was always great to find some time to sit back and relax in her living room, read, and sip on her homemade concoction of iced tea lemonade.

"Good afternoon, Miss Grant," smirked James, as he looked Sasha up and down. At times, he made Sasha slightly nervous with his facial expressions and the tone of his voice. She often thought he stared at her as if she had been the last juicy New York strip steak on the grill and he had not had a meal in days. Beverly told her that she was imagining things and that she was going over board with her suspicions of James.

"Hi, James. Hey, Sharon. Is Bev around?" Sasha inquired.
"She left to run some errands, but she's been gone a while. I imagine she'll be back shortly. Perhaps I can help you with something?" inquired Sharon.

"No, I just thought I would stop by to say hello and to pick up a couple of new books. I guess I can browse a little until she gets back." Sasha went over to the "African-American Studies" section of the store. Beverly had stocked the section well. She read many of the books that had been on the shelves. It made her realize how much she had not read. This piqued her interest to consider buying more books on compact disc. As she perused the bookshelves, a smooth, masculine voice interrupted her concentration.

"Excuse me, but do you read a lot?"

Before looking up, she thought that was a dumb question considering the fact that they were in a bookstore. When she gazed up, she could not help but notice the ebony stranger's handsome face and beautiful pearly smile. His smile alone made her knees weak. In a matter of two seconds flat, she estimated his height to be at six feet. For a brief moment, she did not notice that he was showing her the cover of a Toni Morrison book. She suddenly snapped out of her temporary hypnotic state the stranger had placed upon her.

"Yes, I do," Sasha smiled and confidently responded.

"Have you read this one, yet?" the stranger asked as he tilted the book so that Sasha could get a better view.

"No I haven't, but Toni Morrison is a great writer. I'll have to find time to read that one. Are you looking for a particular book?"

Sasha noticed that his hands and nails were well groomed and a wedding band was not present. She momentarily hesitated as she remembered that the absence of a wedding band did not always signify that a man was single. She unfortunately had to learn that the hard way.

"No, not really. I'll be on vacation next week visiting my brother, his wife, and their children in Connecticut. I just wanted a good book or two to take with me just in case I run out of exciting things to do." Sasha noticed the perfectly shaped dimples in the stranger's cheeks. They accented his sensuous lips and smile. She then noticed how very professionally he was dressed.

"Oh, I see. What type of books interest you?" She suddenly began to feel like she was a salesperson at The Bookworm.

"Well, I enjoy fiction as well as non-fiction. I especially enjoy a good mystery," he smiled.

"Walter Mosley is a pretty good writer. I really enjoyed *Cinnamon Kiss*." Sasha reached for a copy from the upper shelf and handed it to him.

"Thank you. By the way, my name is Darrell. Darrell Payson." Darrell extended his hand to Sasha.

"Nice to meet you, Darrell. I'm Sasha." Sasha melted from the warmth and comfort from Darrell's soft yet strong hands. "I am a friend of the owner of The Bookworm."

"Oh, really," Darrell as a matter of fact commented. "Your friend has a great bookstore. It's been a while since I have read a good book or two. It's also been a while since I have had a vacation."

"It has been a while since I had a nice relaxing vacation, too. If I had one I probably would not know what to do with myself," Sasha remarked. She noticed Darrell's striking muscular build. He looked to be in his mid-thirties. He was definitely no stranger to the gym.

"Sasha, would I be too forward if I ask you to join me for a cup of coffee or better yet lunch? I bet guys try to come on to you all the time. I'm not trying to come on or anything like that. I would just like a little company for lunch. No strings attached. We can get a quick bite to eat from one of the vendors in the food court."

"Sure, Darrell. I'd like that." Sasha was beginning to feel like a giddy schoolgirl. In the few moments she had met Darrell, she mentally had him at the altar. She suddenly caught her runaway mind and told herself it was just lunch—nothing more, nothing less.

Sasha and Darrell approached the counter to pay for their purchases. She noticed that Darrell paid for his purchase with a credit card. She figured if he turned out to be crazy, he could be traced through his credit card purchase.

"Sharon, please tell Bev I stopped by and to call me tonight."

"Will do," said Sharon. "Have a nice day."

"You do the same," said Sasha. Sasha thought, *perhaps it will be a good day.*

◎◎◎

"How much time do you have for lunch, Sasha?" Darrell inquired as they began their descent on the escalator to the food court.

"I work only a few blocks away. We should be okay on time."

"Do you mind if we do lunch at Harbor Place?"

"No, not at all." Sasha and Darrell crossed Light Street and headed to Phillips Express.

The duo ordered the Maryland crab cake sandwich platter. Over lunch, Sasha found herself becoming intrigued with Darrell. She learned he was a financial planner with Pride Financial and had been divorced for three years. He and his ex-wife, Cheryl, did not have any children. According to Darrell, they split after he caught her cheating red handed.

He had come home early from work because he felt like he was coming down with the flu. Upon his arrival, he noticed an unfamiliar car parked in the front of his house. Naturally, he was concerned. As he entered the house, he heard two voices radiating from the master bedroom, one of which was Cheryl's. He opened the master bedroom door and discovered Cheryl and her personal trainer, William, in a body lock. Darrell and William confronted each other which led to a physical showdown. Cheryl called the police once the confrontation ensued. To top it all off, she decided to leave with William. Sasha could not help but feel compassion for Darrell. With her experiences with men, it was difficult for her to fathom that men could actually get emotional about relationships gone awry. It was bad enough that Darrell caught his ex with another man. It was truly insult to injury when he discovered them in their marital bed.

"Darrell, I'm so sorry about what happened," Sasha sympathized. "That must have been a very difficult time for you." Her naivety spoke for her. She never new anyone personally who had experienced that type of situation. It was something that hadn't really crossed her mind.

"Couple's get togethers took on a whole new meaning for me. It was one of the most difficult things that ever happened to me, but life goes on. I have not dated much since my divorce. I do miss being in a relationship and it's been a while since a woman has intrigued me. However, I'm in no rush. I've learned to be content."

Sasha made a mental note of Darrell's statement. She knew very well he was out making a booty call or two to somebody. She could not imagine any man as good looking as Darrell having any lonely, dateless, weekends. Her intuition radar she nicknamed *sashadar* kicked in at full speed. She was somewhat surprised at his openness which unrelentingly intrigued her even more.

They continued their conversation of getting to know each other until Sasha looked at her watch and noticed that it was almost 1:30 p.m.

"Darrell, I have got to get back to the office. My manager is expecting to meet with me at 2 o'clock to discuss a proposal," said Sasha.

"It has been indeed a pleasure. Perhaps we can go to the movies and have dinner or visit some local museums when I return from Connecticut?"

Sasha's heart did a little leap for joy. She enjoyed Darrell's company and was hoping they could meet again. Her initial apprehensiveness had disappeared. The calm of the healing process had begun.

"I would like that, Darrell," Sasha said as she extended her hand to shake his. "Thank you for lunch and the great company. Have a great trip"

"No, thank you, Sasha," smiled Darrell. "Again, it was my pleasure. I hope to speak with you when I get back in town."

Sasha wrote her home telephone number on her business card and handed it to Darrell. Darrell handed her his card from his wallet. His card included his home, work, and cellular numbers.

Sasha and Darrell went their separate ways. For the first time in a long time, Sasha went back to work with a smile and a glow on her face.

Chapter 10

When one door closes, another one opens.
-African-American folklore

One of the things Regina was proud of was that she could separate her family life from her work life. Whatever issues she had been dealing with which were external to the workplace, were dropped once she went to work. Once she left work, she left the issues of work there. She found that she had more harmony in her home and was able to keep the peace with Keith when she did not mention work issues. Mimi was still up to her antics, but Regina decided not to sweat the small stuff before not sweating the small stuff became a popular phrase courtesy of Miss Sara. Besides, there was a rumor floating around the office that Mimi had been looking for an employment opportunity outside of the company.

Regina was very organized. Every piece of paper had its place. She kept the neatest desk anyone had ever seen. Everything was labeled. She had taken a one-day class from "The Clutter Lady" and it really paid off. Her files were organized, pens, pencils, paperclips, and other office supplies were placed into containers, and she used stackable tray bins to organize her workflow. She could put her hands on what she needed at any given time. Her excellent organizational skills helped make her job that much easier.

Using her day planner, Regina used a "To Do List" and arranged the list of things she needed to do for the day based on priority. Today's list included paying the office bills, ordering supplies, reporting the monthly sales in an Excel spreadsheet, and preparing a PowerPoint presentation for Mimi. She hoped that the number of incoming telephone calls would be low in order to complete her tasks for the day.

"Regina, can you come to my office for a minute," yelled Mimi as she interrupted Regina's concentration on the computer. Regina often wondered why Mimi refused to use the intercom button on her telephone whenever she needed to have a face-to-face conversation with her. Regina grabbed her note pad and pen and headed for Mimi's office. She immediately sat down in Mimi's guest chair.

"Yes, Mi…Michelle," hesitated Regina. On many occasions she caught herself almost calling Michelle Mimi to her face. That type of faux pas would result in some type of awkward explanation. She wanted to avoid any confrontation with Mimi at all costs.

"I just wanted to let you know that I'll be leaving the company effective February 1. I have decided to pursue other interests with the U.S. government," said Mimi.

For a brief moment, Regina's mouth immediately flew open. Once she felt a smile coming across her face, she quickly halted it. It was the news she had been waiting to hear which seemed like a lifetime. She felt herself wanting to do cartwheels, a dance, and say a hallelujah or two. Mimi's leaving was like a dream come true. A huge sigh of relief came over her. All of Mimi games and antics were coming to an end in two weeks. She thought, *God, thank you for answering my prayer!*

"Congratulations, Michelle!" gleamed Regina. "I'm so happy for you! What will you do with the government?" Regina faked appearing to be genuinely interested in Michelle's new endeavor.

"I'll be an internal consultant for various programs. The job will involve a lot of travel throughout the country. My new director estimates that I'll be traveling about fifty percent of the time. I'm really excited about it. I will even get to travel to Hawaii."

"Oh, that sounds so exciting!" Regina exclaimed. She made a mental note of the people she wanted to call to tell them of Mimi's departure. That was the best news she had heard in a while.

"Well, it was a very tough decision for me. I thought about it and weighed my options. I looked at the pros and cons and even talked with my parents. I think this will be a great move."

"If you're happy, then I am happy for you. How did Bob take the news?"

"As expected, he tried to talk me out of it by saying that he believed I would be making a bad move. That just made me want to leave even more. This is an opportunity I just can't afford to miss. After all, this is my life."

"Well, I am going to miss you, Michelle," lied Regina. Let's do lunch before you leave to celebrate your new job." Regina immediately began thinking of ideas for an appropriate departing gift.

"Sounds good," responded Michelle. "I guess our human resources representative will be advertising my job soon. You'll have a new manager before you know it. I think the job will be filled internally."

"Who do you think will get it?"

"If I had to pick, I'd say Ken Cunningham. Bob really likes the work he has done over the past year."

Ken Cunningham had been a marketing consultant with the company for two years. Regina liked him because he was very down to earth and was one of the few managers in the office who spoke to her on a regular basis. He was white, in his late-forties, had salt and pepper thinning hair, wore silver wire rimmed glasses, and sported a slight beer belly. Ken had been married for fifteen years and had three children ranging in ages from seven to thirteen. Ken and Regina on occasion would swap *you won't believe this* stories about their children. Regina believed that Ken would be a great manager. Anybody other than Mimi would have been an improvement.

"Well, I guess I'll have to wait and see," responded Regina. "Is there anything I can help you with to make your transition easier?"

"I'm going to start cleaning out my desk and making a list of pending items for Bob and whoever is selected for the position. I'll need your assistance on a list of action items."

Michelle dictated a "To Do List" to Regina. Together they set deadlines. The conversation was especially pleasant. Regina believed that Michelle's personality issues were caused by situations outside of the company. She was aware that she did not always get along with her parents and had only a few friends. In a sense, Regina felt sorry for her.

Upon returning to her desk, Regina marked Mimi's last day in her planner by drawing a smiley face on the date. Her days of dealing with the boss from hell soon would be over. When she noticed that Mimi was on the telephone, she decided to give Keith a quick call at work.

"This is Keith Webster."

"Hi, Sweetheart...I got some good news..."

Chapter 11

Heaven is where you will be when
you are okay right where you are.
-Sun Ra

Upon returning home from work after a ten hour day, Sasha immediately flung her purse and portfolio on the sofa, took off her coat, hung it in the hall closet, flipped her shoes off in the middle of the living room floor, and sighed a "Thank You, Jesus." It felt good to be in the comfort of her home. Her meeting with Georgia lasted longer than she had expected. For every answer she had given Georgia in response to her concerns about the proposal to reorganize one of the company's departments, Georgia had three additional questions. It became a tug of war. Sasha kept wondering throughout the meeting when Georgia would retire so that she could put her and everyone else in the company out of their misery.

Although Georgia was an excellent manager, she often pushed her employees to the limit. She had been with the organization for over thirty years and had seen lots of changes—some good and some bad. She was a great negotiator and had a knack for motivating employees to meet goals far beyond their imagination and expectations. Georgia often boasted of her superior delegation skills. It was her delegation skills that kept the company running at its peak efficiency.

Sasha noticed that her answering machine indicated that she had several messages. She hit the message indicator button to retrieve the messages.

"Hey, it's Regina. That boss witch of mine has decided to resign! I am soooooo glad she decided to resign before I had to kill her. She'll be riding away on her broomstick in two weeks. Call me!"

Beep

"Sash, this is Bev. Sharon told me you stopped by the store today. I went to see my accountant. He believes I have a theft problem at the store. Call me when you get a chance. Talk to you later."

Beep

"This is your Mother just calling to check on you. Call us."

Beep

"Hello, Miss Grant. This is Richard. What are you doing tonight? Give me a call on my cell phone. Bye."

Sasha mumbled, "Give me a break. I know what you want, but you ain't getting it."

The answering machine automatically rewound itself after Richard's message. Even though the antiquated machine had done its job for several years, Sasha planned to replace it with voice mail very shortly. She figured as long as it did what it was supposed to do, it worked for her.

She decided to microwave some of her mother's leftover meatloaf accompanied with a garden salad and a tall glass of lemonade iced tea. It was a quick meal and hit the spot. She grabbed the mail, quickly reviewed it and threw out the abundance of junk mail. She thought there should have been some law on the books to prevent the wasting of trees on such nonsense.

The first call she returned was her mother's. Marian was just checking in and wanted to know how the job was coming along in addition to everything else that was going on with her. Marian told her of the recent death of one of her long time neighbors, Miss Ethel. Sasha always knew when Marian started off a question with "Do you remember...?" *it* was often followed up with her telling Sasha about somebody's death. Half of the people she really didn't remember. She would tell Marian that she remembered them in order to limit the number of facts Marian just had to tell in order to get her to remember the person. Most recently, the number of questions beginning with, "Do you remember" from Marian had increased. Sasha figured that a lot of her parents' friends and acquaintances were getting up in age and the inevitable had to happen.

She then called Regina. Regina gave her the news about Mimi. And of course she had to throw in a Tiffani and Tyrique story. The latest was that the twins decided to redecorate their rooms. They drew pictures on their bedroom walls using permanent magic markers. Nothing removed their little Picasso masterpieces. She knew what Keith and Regina would be doing over the weekend.

She called Beverly next. "Hi, Bev. It's Sasha."

"Hey, Sash. I heard you stopped by today."

"I decided to stop by to pick up a couple of novels. You won't believe what I also picked up," Sasha swooned.

"Hmmm. Let me guess," joked Beverly.

"I met a guy. His name is Darrell and he works at the Pride Financial office down the street from The Bookworm. Hopefully he and I can get together when he returns from vacation in Connecticut."

"Oh. So what did you guys talk about?" asked Beverly.

"We talked about him. We talked about me. He's divorced and doesn't have any children. He likes all kinds of sports, graduated from the University of Pennsylvania, lives in Towson, is a Big Brother volunteer, and is a member of Omega Psi Phi fraternity." Sasha conveniently left out the part about Darrell's philandering ex-wife and her lover.

"Hmmm. He sounds most interesting. Now, Sash...you know what they say about those Que dogs and their reputations," laughed Beverly.

"Yeah, yeah, I've heard it," smiled Sasha. "Well, I guess I'll just have to find out for myself. Hopefully he will call me. If not, that's ok too."

"Here we go again. Why are you setting yourself up to be a victim? Sometimes girl, I swear you ask for it. I bet when you met him, you had visions of you and him as the bride and groom at your extravagant wedding--didn't you?" Beverly paused. "Please don't start that thinking ahead of yourself stuff. Just try to take it one day at a time. Men come a dime a dozen."

Sometimes, Beverly could make Sasha so angry. Beverly could not possibly understand how her brassy words hurt Sasha's feelings. It was a wonder that they had remained friends for so long. Sasha let the sting of Beverly's comments linger for a moment.

"Bev, trust me. I'll take it one day at a time. Any thoughts of Darrell and I going down the aisle have been squashed. He just happens to be—no let me correct myself—he appears to be a nice guy.

If he never calls again, I will not get down on myself because life goes on." Sasha decided to quickly change the subject.

"So, what's your accountant saying about some theft?"

"He's been reviewing the books and for some reason things just don't add up. He wants to take some more time before he comes to a conclusion, but he thinks someone is either stealing books or money."

"How could that possibly happen?

"At this point, your guess is just as good as mine."

"I bet it's that James character you hired. You know how he gives me the creeps."

"I beg to differ. I don't think he would do anything like that. I just think that there are customer's walking out with the books. I plan to meet with James and Sharon tomorrow. We have got to tighten up our ship."

"Well, I'd still be on the look out for Mr. Wonderful. I think he is the prime suspect. Have you thought about installing a security camera?"

"I have given it some serious thought, but I'm not quite convinced I need to do that just yet. I'm tired of this nonsense. I have much better and more important things to do other than to track down thieves."

"I heard that," responded Sasha.

"I'll keep you posted on what happens. I would hate to have to pull out a can of whoop ass on whoever the thief is," Beverly said lightheartedly.

"I certainly pity the fool who is doing it. You take care. Call me if you need anything, okay?"

"I will. Take care. See ya."

Sasha decided that she would not call Richard. She decided that if he was not willing and able to provide a home telephone number, he was not worth calling. She was tired of his impromptu visits that usually ended with her clothes *accidentally* falling off. Yes, Sasha Grant had finally come to her senses about him.

Before retiring to bed, she decided to take a relaxing bubble bath in her jacuzzi. It had become an evening ritual for her to take a bath by candlelight. She purchased an abundance of scented candles and bath gels. The combination of the aromas from the candles and bath gels transformed her into a state of tranquility. Sleep usually came to her easily after experiencing total relaxation.

After her bath and soothing her body in passion fruit body butter, she knelt down on the side of her queen-sized canopy bed to pray. She felt a burning need to talk to God and to thank him for her blessings. Initially it felt odd to pray because lately she had prayed only when she was feeling depressed or lonely. The other times she prayed was when things were not going right in her life. After her prayer, she cried tears. For the first time in a long time, they were tears of joy.

Chapter 12

You don't own the future and you don't own the past.
Today is all you have.
-Les Brown

It had been three weeks since Sasha had heard from Darrell. During the week he was vacationing in Connecticut, she found her mind wandering to thoughts about him and wondered several times that if by any chance he had been thinking of her too. She kept telling herself to get him out of her mind and turn her attention to the here and now. It was easier said than done.

Although Darrell intrigued her, she believed he was like any other man--they never call when they say they are going to call. She placed his card in the pocket of her planner and debated whether or not to call him. She quickly squashed the thought because she did not want him to think she was being far too forward. At times she wanted to be more forward, but that just was not her. Her friend Lola from Pittsburgh told her to stop being so passive when it came to getting a man. "Girl, you have got to go for it before somebody else goes for it," she remembered Lola saying. Lola's personality was much more flamboyant than anyone Sasha knew. Even more so than Beverly's. Lola had no problem picking up men at local clubs for a one or two night stand. Sasha had warned her about the potential of syphilis, gonorrhea, or even worse, AIDS. Lola's flippant response was that she was careful about these things and that life was for living—not staying home reading a good book.

She quickly diverted her attention back to the report she was typing on the computer. Her Wednesday deadline was quickly approaching.

"Sasha," said Rosa Tyrell as she peeked into Sasha's office. "I'm about to go to lunch. Can I get you anything while I'm out?"

Rosa was Sasha's new assistant. When Sasha interviewed her, she had to hold back from wanting to offer her the job on the spot. Rosa labeled herself as "old school" meaning that she was into doing things right the first time around. Rosa stated that she just did not understand the young people of today because most of them wanted instant gratification without working hard. As Rosa put it, they wanted something for nothing. She was a retiree who had worked part-time as an office assistant at a construction company. At the construction company, she often had to train the new office assistants, many of which had very little office experience. She found that in most instances they would half way complete the assignment she had given to them. She eventually had to clean up what they messed up. This annoyed Rosa to no end.

Sasha's gut told her that Rosa was indeed a good fit for the company. Her maturity alone spoke that she did not have to worry about her potentially embarrassing the department as Kelly had done. Besides, Sasha could not even imagine Rosa on top of a boardroom table doing the unimaginable let alone disgracing herself in any manner. Rosa reminded her of one of her neighbors growing up who often told her parents of her mischief—dependable, all seeing and knowing, and always right on time. Rosa had a robust figure which amply filled the suits she wore to work. The only thing missing was her fancy Sunday church hats which were her crown and glory. Her warm chestnut brown complexion continued to glow even at age sixty-two.

"No thanks, Rosa. I'll probably get something quick out of the vending machine. I need to finish up this report," responded Sasha.

"Now, Sasha," said Rosa sounding like a scolding Marian. "That's not healthy. Let me at least pick you up a sandwich."

"No really, that's okay. Besides, I'm not that hungry anyway."

"Well, I won't argue with you. I'll be back in an hour."

Rosa was a regular churchgoer and more like a mother figure. Every Monday morning like clockwork, Rosa would tell Sasha about what a good time she had in church on Sunday. She had even invited Sasha to a couple of the church services.

At times, Sasha caught herself wanting to scream profanities particularly when her workday was not going well. She knew she had not been brought up that way. Rosa was a constant reminder of that fact. She often bit her tongue whenever she wanted curse out loud as Rosa's desk was just outside of her office and within hearing distance. Rosa's religious demeanor was a constant reminder that profanity was not appropriate. Sasha had to settle for silently cursing folks out under her breath.

The spontaneous ring of the telephone interrupted Sasha's intense concentration on her report.

"Galaxy Human Resources. This is Sasha Grant. May I help you?"

"Hello Sasha," said the vaguely familiar voice. "This is Darrell Payson. Remember me? We met at your friend's bookstore."

Sasha's mouth flew open, and then she grinned. The tenseness which had shrouded her shoulders had become a part of the past. Darrell's call was a pleasant surprise.

"Ah, Darrell, of course I remember you," Sasha replied. "How was your vacation in Connecticut?"

She caught herself wanting to bless him out for not calling as he had promised. She decided it was better to give him the impression that she had not really given him that much thought. The call from him alone quickly changed her attitude and demeanor.

"Before I tell you about my vacation, I must apologize for not calling sooner. I put your card in my suit jacket without realizing it. I had been frantically trying to find your number for two weeks when it dawned on me that I had put it there."

"No problem, Darrell," replied Sasha. She hesitated as whether or not to believe him. His defense sounded like the typical male plea.

"My vacation was good, but not as relaxing as I would have liked. My brother David and I had a good time hanging out. He's a financial planner as well. His wife Pam is an attorney and a great cook. I wanted to stay a few extra days just for her home cooking. I now truly understand why my brother has put on a few extra pounds. To top it off, my nieces have more than enough energy to keep me going. I tell you, energy like that is wasted on the young. My time there was so busy--I didn't even get to read either of those books. Being with Monica and Melanie kept me quite busy."

Sasha concluded that Darrell liked being around children. "How old are your nieces?" she asked.

"Monica is ten and Melanie is eight. Old enough to know what to ask for from their uncle," boasted Darrell.

Sasha and Darrell shared a light laugh.

"My friend Regina has a set of twins who are six years old. They are more than a handful. Sometimes I swear they have been here before because they are wise beyond their years. Some of the stuff they do and say is absolutely unbelievable. I don't remember being quite that rambunctious when I was growing up. On the other hand, perhaps I was, but don't remember," exclaimed Sasha. They shared a second laugh.

"Sasha, I was wondering if you would like to go out to dinner and then see a movie on Friday night," Darrell said in a serious tone.

"Let me check my calendar." Sasha knew she had no plans for Friday night. After allowing Darrell to hear the rustling of several pages in her planner, she told him that her Friday night was free and clear, just as she had expected. They agreed that they would meet at Sasha's house at 7:00 p.m. She gave him her address and the directions to her house and then immediately began thinking about what she would wear and how to find time to clean the house. Lately, she had been neglecting her housekeeping duties. Marian would have been absolutely appalled. Every time she thought about getting a housekeeper, she realized that she would have to do some pre-cleaning—after all she did not want the person to think that her house always looked like a family of ten had lived there. Somehow, the family of ten had managed to set up house at Sasha's for the last couple of months.

"I look forward to Friday night, Miss Grant," said Darrell.

"Me too, Darrell." As they ended the call, Sasha looked forward to Friday night more than Darrell could have ever imagined.

◎◎◎

After finishing her report, Sasha began reviewing things she could pass on to Rosa. Rosa was more than efficient. Sasha's biggest worry with her was that she would run out of things for her to do. Rosa was her own powerhouse when it came to getting things done. Sasha knew that she did not have to check up on her. If she gave her an assignment, she could consider the job done. She wished she could hire more employees like her.

Sasha noted the additional meetings she had for the week in her planner. *If only meetings really solved problems they would be worth the time*, she thought as she made mental notes of where she had to be for the rest of the week. Although her current job did not involve a lot of out-of-state travel, it did involve quite of bit of local travel. She often missed the travel of a previous position at an accounting firm. In her former position, she traveled to San Francisco, Las Vegas, Orlando, Atlanta, Boston, and Dallas. In her job with Galaxy, the extent of her travel was to places such as Marriottsville, Olney, and Middletown. Other than the employees she had made friends with along the way, the travel was the only other thing she missed about her old job.

As the clock on her computer read 6:15 p.m. and Rosa had long left to go home for the evening, Sasha decided to end her work day. She was proud of the fact that she was able to get a lot done despite several interruptions. She planned to stop at the supermarket to pick up a few things and then begin the task of cleaning the house. Even though it was only Tuesday, she figured she needed all the time she could get in order to remove any remnants of the imaginary family of ten who had invaded her house and long overstayed their welcome. She did not want to give Darrell the impression that keeping a clean house was not her forte. Somehow, her best self needed to emerge quick, fast, and in a hurry.

Chapter 13

One's work may be finished someday, but one's education, never.
                    -Alexandre Dumas, the Elder

"Good morning, Regina," Ken Cunningham sang as he unlocked the door to his office.

"Good morning to you too, Ken," responded Regina. "What are you so happy about?"

"Oh, nothing in particular. I am just happy to be alive," grinned Ken. "Besides, I have the dubious distinction of being locked up behind doors in an upcoming meeting with the Vice Presidents. What more can a guy ask for?" Ken's dry sense of humor tickled Regina. She often wondered how a man that silly got as far as he did with the company. She blamed it on his ability to schmooze with the big boys and play a great golf game.

Ken's demeanor was totally different than that of Mimi's. He was definitely a breath of fresh air from what she had experienced in the past. His management style was much more relaxed and straightforward. With Mimi, Regina had the unduly responsibility of always trying to figure out what kind of tricks Mimi had in her bag. Regina quickly learned that she could trust Mimi as far as she could throw her.

"Well, do enjoy," snickered Regina. She promptly turned her attention back to paying the office bills before preparing for her meeting with Ken.

Ken's businessman appearance reminded Regina of a used car salesman. He was always dressed in a stark white, starched shirt and had a multitude of brightly colored ties. He often skipped the suit jacket unless he had a meeting. His twenty years of experience showed prominently on his middle aged face and his graying hair and wire framed glasses gave him a distinguishing look.

Ken and Regina had a daily ritual of meeting 8:30 a.m. every morning. During their meetings, they discussed Ken's agenda for the day as well as his projects. Regina's talents with word processing, spreadsheet, and presentation software came in handy for Ken's meetings which often included presentations to his superiors. He was delighted that he could depend on her to help him look good to his peers and the company's leadership team.

At exactly 8:30 a.m., Regina promptly walked into Ken's office with pen, pencil and pad in hand. They seated themselves in the gray and burgundy tapestry upholstered armed chairs at his cherry wood circular table. Ken's panoramic window view of the city's skyline was breath taking.

"These are the charts I'd like for you to do in PowerPoint for Thursday's meeting," Ken began.

Regina began reviewing the charts and the scribble below each chart. She wanted to make sure she could understand Ken's handwriting. With handwriting like his, he should have been a doctor. She and the other secretaries often found themselves pooling together to figure out each other's boss' handwriting which resembled childlike scribbling.

"What's this, Ken?" Regina asked pointing to the chicken scratch on the paper.

"Let me see," said Ken as he squinted without his glasses. "Looks like it says projected totals."

Regina thought, *you could have fooled me.* As if he were reading Regina's mind, he responded, "Please don't ask me to change my handwriting. I have been writing like this far too long."

Regina laughed to herself. Despite Ken's handwriting, he was by far a better manager than Michelle could ever be. Some of her co-workers claimed that they preferred to work for men as opposed to women because their female bosses were much more temperamental. Their personal experiences with female managers proved that between premenstrual syndrome and menopause, their female bosses took them through unnecessary changes with their mood swings and changes in temperature. They exclaimed that with their male bosses, they knew exactly what mood they would be at the beginning of the day and could most likely predict when his mood would change for the better or worse based on the day's events.

Ken and Regina continued their caucus. Ken graciously decided to provide lunch for Thursday's meeting. He and Regina perused several menus of local caterers. They decided on a variety of sandwiches, a Caesar salad, and a variety of assorted sodas and cookies for dessert. Ken told her to put in an order for herself. Mimi certainly would not have given her that courtesy.

When Regina accidentally knocked her pencil onto the mauve carpet, she reached down to pick it up. Ken's glimpse of her ample cleavage under her ivory blouse gave him a spontaneous erection. He did his best to hide his expression. It had been more than a while since he had made love to Doris. Between taking care of the kids and the house, Doris just had not been in the mood. Her full day literally zapped her energy.

Regina did not notice Ken's reaction to a glimpse of her bosom. She continued to place her attention on the meeting's activities.

"Ken, do you mind if I take a half day off on next Friday? I forgot that the children and I have a dental appointment in the morning."

"Why don't you take the whole day off? I don't believe much will be happening in the office that day. You have really helped me out a lot and have put in extra time to help things run smoothly. Don't worry about recording the time off."

Regina was surprised. Mimi would have never extended that offer. "Thanks, Ken. I really appreciate your thoughtfulness," Regina smiled. "I'll start working on your charts." As Regina extended her body away from the chair and exited Ken's office, he could not help but admire the roundness of her buttocks in her black skirt. *Hmmm, hmmm,* he thought. *What I wouldn't do for one night of that.*

Regina continued to work on the charts for Ken's meeting and answered her incoming calls. She could not help but admire him for his wit and schoolboy charm. The fact that he only used his state of the art, top of the line computer for retrieving and responding to electronic mail did not even bother him. She figured that doing his computer work was the least she could do for him. In the four weeks he had been her manager, her quality of work life had soared.

She and Veronica, another administrative assistant in the department, had planned to have lunch at 12:30. Veronica stopped by

Regina's desk with her coat in hand. Veronica had been with the company for fifteen years as an assistant. It had been her one and only job since graduating from high school. She dressed youthfully and her wardrobe mainly consisted of skirts which were three inches above her knees, fishnet pantyhose, five inch pumps, and fashionable blouses which accentuated her tawny exterior and shoulder length naturally curly dark hair.

"Let's roll, Regina," rushed Veronica. "I need to get outta here before I have to hurt that boss of mine."

"Okay, okay. Let me save my file and I'll be ready to go," responded Regina. Regina grabbed her coat and purse as the pair headed towards the elevator. They did a brisk walk to the Wendy's three blocks away. After ordering and getting their food, they found a table near the window of the restaurant.

"So what's happening? Why are you in such a bunch?" asked Regina.

"Marcia is driving me crazy. She changes her mind every five minutes about how she wants things done. I mean even the simplest of decisions are difficult for her. She asks me for my opinion on everything. She is paid the big bucks to make the decisions. The problem is she doesn't make the decisions without my input."

"Uh, Ronni, she probably got you for a bargain," said Regina light heartedly.

"Check this out. Yesterday she came in the office all upset because her boyfriend called her dumb because she burned dinner the night before. I spent most of the morning with her in her office behind closed doors trying to console her. After I spent half of my morning sympathizing with her, she later got ticked because I hadn't finished half of what she had given me to do. Has she lost her mind or what?!"

"You have got to be kidding me. She's crazy. I think it's time for you to move on to greener pastures. Life is far too short to be miserable."

"You got that right. How are things working out with Ken?"

"So far, great. He has his little quirks here and there, but they are manageable. I have learned that you have got to manage your boss. Think about it, Ronni. Where would they be without us?"

"Up a creek without a paddle, no doubt. Marcia wouldn't know her head from a hole in the ground. Speaking of whacked out bosses, have you heard the latest on Michelle?"

"See, I was enjoying my lunch as well as your company until you mentioned that evil woman to me," admonished Regina. "What havoc is she up to now? Just don't tell me she's coming back to the company."

"No, no, nothing like that. You know she and Marcia were supposedly good friends. I overheard her on the phone with Michelle. Marcia made the mistake of putting her on speakerphone. I heard her tell Marcia that she is pregnant by Kirk and they are getting married next month."

Regina let out a huge gasped followed by hysterical laughter. "You have got to be kidding me! That is a lie if I ever heard one! She is too much. She obviously needs some help. Can you imagine? She needs to see a psychologist, psychiatrist, or somebody. That woman has some very serious issues. I just don't understand how she keeps up with her constant lying."

"I guess desperate times call for desperate measures."

"Desperate is right. Despite the fact she was a horrible manager, I still felt sorry for her. Whenever she closed her office door for extended periods of time, I knew she sat in that office crying like a baby. Like clockwork, I would go in to talk with her and give her the same speech. Two weeks later I was giving the same speech. It was like it was a vicious cycle."

"Can you imagine Michelle pregnant?"

"Hell, no," stated Regina. "If it's true, I feel so very sorry for the child she's bringing into the world. You know what? I ought to call her out of the blue and just ask her about how things going. I wonder if she will even mention her pending nuptials and upcoming little bundle of joy. I'd bet my next paycheck that she'll say nothing of the sort."

"Gina, I have got to hand it to you. You had to put up with a lot with that demented woman. She lies like a rug."

Regina and Veronica's conversation diverted to Veronica's latest hobby—running trips to Atlantic City. Veronica had made more that her share of "donations" to Donald Trump and Merv Griffin's casinos. Veronica looked at gambling as a sport and took calculated risks to get more than she had bargained for. She had even budgeted money each month to lose in hopes that her "investment" would pay off. On several occasions, she tried to talk Regina into joining her on one of her trips. Regina explained that she was not willing to make that kind of investment. Besides, that was time she could be doing other things.

"Regina, you need to learn to live a little yourself. You and Keith should consider coming on one of my trips. My daughter Valerie can watch the kids. She doesn't charge very much. If she can keep her younger brother and sister in line, she can certainly handle Tiffani and Tyrique."

"Yeah, you don't know about the antics of the dynamic duo. They will have Valerie along with Angela and Christopher tied up, bound, and locked into your kitchen cabinets," said Regina. "I can see their little legs running around your house like they own the place."

"They can't be that bad. Nobody is that bad."

"Well, you don't know Tiffani and Tyrique. For the most part, they are good children. When they get bored or don't have enough activity, their minds start scheming."

Veronica laughed, "I'll take your word for it." She noticed it was 1:20 p.m. "Gina, I know I don't need to remind you that I work for a psychopath. She expects my butt to be back in my chair three minutes before my lunch hour is up. I guess we ought to get back to the dungeon."

Regina grinned. "You're right. Let's get back. I need to finish Ken's slides so that he has ample time to make changes."

The two women headed back to work to finish what was to be another busy day of taking orders from their bosses. The five o'clock hour was their release to freedom until the next business day.

Chapter 14

Where's my check?

-Andre Pritchett

Beverly sat across the desk from her certified public accountant, Craig Abbott. She had known him since her freshman year at Loyola College. They met during an Accounting 101 class. After working at a big five accounting firm for seven years, Craig started his own certified public accounting firm which eventually became a thriving business venture. His clients primarily consisted of established small and medium sized businesses in the Baltimore metropolitan area.

"Bev, somebody is stealing. Your numbers just don't add up. It appears that you are loosing at least $500 a week in either merchandise or in cash sales." Craig's studious facial features sternly peered over his black rimmed glasses at Beverly.

"Craig, I think you're overreacting," responded Beverly. "That can't possibly be true."

"What about your employees? Do you think any of them could be the culprit?" Craig asked. His overly grown, dark, bushy eyebrows continued to rise.

"No. They have worked out great so far. They're on time and don't have any performance problems. Besides, I can't imagine any of them doing such a thing."

"Bev, don't take this the wrong way, but you are so cautious when it comes to other people and other things. It appears that you are having a difficult time believing me."

"No, Craig. It's not that. I've worked so hard to make The Bookworm successful. You know I have faith in the work you have done for me. However, it could be the way the computer system is programmed."

"But, Bev, you're using a standardized program. There is nothing wrong with the tracking of your inventory. I am telling you that either a customer or customers are walking out with your merchandise and aren't paying anything. I would go as far as saying it could be one of your employees. What you need to do is to install a security camera and not tell anyone. That's the only way you are going to find out who it is."

"Craig, I run an extremely tight ship. I know where every dollar goes and where it comes from. Nothing much gets by me."

"I thought that was my job," said Craig, pointedly. "Your employees have keys to the store, right?" asked Craig.

Beverly responded, "Yes."

"Your employees have a security code for the alarm system, right?"

Beverly nodded her head yes.

"Bev, why don't you just leave the door open at night and just let everybody have a free for all? I don't get it. Why are you having such a difficult time believing me? If you don't want me as your accountant, just say so. I can refer you to someone else. Perhaps you will believe them."

Beverly finally gave in to Craig. The thought of somebody stealing under her nose finally sank in and was enough to make her cringe. She did the legwork on the installation of security cameras by getting bids from various companies. She decided to go with Security First Security Systems and was able to arrange an after hours installation with the sales representative. The camera was installed in the ceiling above the cash register and was able to videotape from any angle throughout the store. Upon the completion of the installation, hesitation came over Beverly; she still had not decided whether or not she would tell James and Sharon of the newly added security measures. She felt that she was not being honest with them. Craig made a follow up telephone call again advising her not to tell them. She decided to heed his advice—at least for now.

For the first few nights, Beverly took the videotapes home to review them. Each time she saw nothing out of the ordinary. She cursed Craig for making her feel guilty about not trusting her employees. Upon her fourth night of reviewing the extremely boring tapes, she decided to take a hiatus from viewing them until she believed that a theft had occurred. As she rewound the last tape, the telephone rang.

"Hello," said Beverly.

"Hi Bev. It's Sasha. I haven't talked to you in a few weeks. I just called to chat for a bit. Is this a bad time?"

"No, not at all. I just finished looking at some tapes from the store. My accountant still insists that somebody is stealing. I think he has lost his mind. Sharon and James have been great employees.

They come to work on time and I don't have to follow up on everything I tell them to do. Besides, thieves don't steal books. They steal electronics and jewelry."

"Well, he must have a good reason to think that, Bev. If you catch someone on tape, at least you have evidence that can get them prosecuted.

"I realize that," snapped Beverly. "I think I'll take the other piece of advice he gave me and get a new accountant."

"Bev, you can be so stubborn sometimes. I swear. The man is just trying to do what you hired him to do."

"Next," Beverly exclaimed. That was her way of abruptly letting anyone know she did not want to continue the conversation.

"Okay, okay. I get your message loud and clear. Sasha transitioned to the next topic. "Have you heard from Gina?"

"No, I haven't. I haven't talked to her in two weeks. At that time, I think things were going well with her new boss. Perhaps I can get her in on a three-way call. Hold on a sec."

Sasha cradled the telephone receiver on her neck and began painting her nails cranberry red while she waited patiently for Beverly to return.

"Sash, you there?"

"Yes, Bev," said Sasha.

"Gina, you there?"

"Yes, Bev, I'm here."

"Technology is just grand, isn't it?" commented Beverly.

"I was just thinking about ya'll. We haven't had a Cinnamon Girls reunion in a while," said Regina. "You know I need to have a reunion on a regular basis. Keith and the kids need to give me a little vacation. Hold on a sec. I gotta do a little motherly discipline."

Sasha and Beverly could overhear Regina scolding Tyrique. She threatened to give him a time out until time next week. Whatever

Tyrique was doing, he continued to do as he pleased. The next thing they heard was Tyrique's loud sobs. Apparently, he finally got the message.

"Girls, I tell you. Don't have any kids. You'll be in your grave quicker than you can say your ABC's."

Sasha and Beverly often wondered where Regina got her dry sense of humor. No doubt it was probably another one of Miss Sara's influences.

"So what's up with you two?" asked Regina.

"Darrell finally called me," said Sasha. "We have a date on Friday. You know I started cleaning the house like my life depended on it."

Beverly added, "I don't know why you don't go on and get a housekeeper. I know you can afford it. But wait—it's only you. Your house should stay spotless." Without hesitation, Beverly transitioned to another question without waiting for Sasha's response. "Where are you going on this date?"

"We plan to go out to dinner and then to a movie."

"Nice," chimed Regina. "You know the rules. You need to give me his information."

"Gina, I did not meet him on the Internet. Request denied."

"Excuse me, but you don't know him that well. Between you and Bev, I don't know who is more stubborn. Just give me the information before you get me all worked up over you."

Sasha decided to give Regina and Beverly all the information she had on Darrell. It was the least she could do to shut them up and escape a pending barrage of questioning.

"I expect a call from you the moment you hit the door on Friday night," said Beverly.

"Hey, I may not be back until Saturday afternoon," smiled Sasha.

"Look, I don't want to have to pull out the Marian card out on you, but I will if I have to," laughed Regina. "Darrell better not turn out to be a nut case. Tyrique can pull a mean upper cut."

"Don't worry. I'll be careful." I don't think he has any skeletons in his closet," said Sasha.

"Bev, how many times have we heard that bogus statement?" asked Regina. "Let's just start naming them—there was Anthony, Richard, David, Dwayne, Paul, oh, and we can't forget Jordan. And then there was…"

"Okay, stop it," Sasha interrupted. "You've made your point." Quickly changing the subject, Sasha asked, "Gina, how are things at work?"

"Actually, things couldn't be better. But wait, you have not heard the latest. My co-worker Ronni told me that she overheard her manager and Mimi talking on the phone. Apparently Mimi has made up some lie that she's pregnant and Kirk is the father. On top of that, they're getting married next month."

Beverly and Sasha hooted like they were silly junior high school girls.

"Tell me it isn't so," laughed Beverly. "She is one sick puppy."

The threesome ended their conversation on a light note and promised to have a Cinnamon Girls reunion in the next few weeks. As usual, Regina was designated to make the arrangements. She really didn't mind. She felt that true friendship was a gift from God. She treasured every moment she spent with her dear close friends.

◎◎◎

"Hurry up you idiot! Punch in the code so we can get in and get outta here," shouted the male voice.

"I'm coming! I hate it when you talk to me that way! I'm not stupid!" retorted the high pitched female voice.

"Look girl, just bring your slow ass on. We got a job to do," responded the male voice.

The two entered The Bookworm in dark clothing with flashlights and huge duffle bags in hand along with an oversized mailroom cart. They began strategically taking books from the bookshelves and stuffing them into the bags.

"Hey, check in the back to see if any new shipments have come in," yelled the male voice to the female. He demanded, "And check her office. She may have something in there. I bet she still don't know we got her social security and credit card numbers."

The female did what she was told. She managed to push two huge cardboard boxes to the checkout counter. The muscular male lifted the boxes and placed them on the cart. They did a final casing of The Bookworm and carefully traced back their steps to avoid leaving any evidence of their heist.

As quickly as they had entered The Bookworm, they left.

Chapter 15

To understand how any society functions, you must understand the relationship between the men and the women.
-Angela Davis

The exquisite split-level townhouse was an interior decorator's dream. The living room alone provided pristine surroundings that exuded the home owner's taste for some of the finer things in life. The room's plush ivory carpet and contemporary furnishings provided comfort and warmth to the room. The modern elegance of the sofa, loveseat and oversized chair with ottoman were upholstered in mint green, beige, and sunset orange tapestry. The circular glass cocktail and end tables were accented with solid brass trim and a marble base. Austrian crystal lamps with mint green shades crowned each end table on each end of the sofa. The lighting from the lamps and the classic fireplace provided a gateway to the room's ambience. The cocktail table was graced with a fresh floral bouquet of peach and white roses with hints of baby's breath and greenery. The sweet smelling scent from the roses permeated the atmosphere. A white tiled ceiling lingered over the recently semi-gloss painted off-white walls. Contemporary African-American artwork from several prominent artists was hung on each wall and offered a small sampling of the black experience. Draperies matching the seating adorned the huge picture window and custom-made, eggshell white, fabric covered mini-blinds controlled the internal and external view of the world. Smooth and cozy jazz melodies played softly from the room's speakers. The room definitely had a charm all its own and was a preview to the rest of the beautifully decorated home.

If only it would stay this spotless forever, Sasha thought as she gave the room a final walk-through. She left work early on Friday to get ready for her date with Darrell. She wanted everything to be perfect from the spotless house to looking as good as possible. As she was getting ready for the date, an air of skepticism suddenly hit her as she took a leisurely bath. Her thoughts went back to some of her first meetings with the men she had dated over the years. Quite a few of the dates had given her the pre-date jitters and made her ask herself what she was doing. She finally calmed herself and figured that Friday's date would be better than spending another evening alone. She decided to wear a newly purchased pair of black jeans, a pale pink cotton sweater, and three inch mules. She placed hints of Escape on her wrists and behind her ears.

It was 6:55 p.m. Darrell would be arriving shortly. As she instinctively peered out of the blinds at the picture window, she noticed a black BMW M5 sedan had pulled into her driveway. The moment the driver stepped out of the car, her heart skipped a beat. It was Darrell and he was on time.

She quickly left her post at the window, and ran to the powder room's full-length mirror to do one final check. She had to admit the workouts with Regina had helped. The black jeans and sweater she wore spoke volumes.

Sasha immediately went to the door when she heard the doorbell ring. She stopped in mid-stream and took a deep breath while trying to coach herself into being up beat and not overly excited since it had been a while since a man had walked through her door. Out of habit, she peered through the door's peephole then unlocked the door for Darrell to enter.

"Hello. Don't you look great," greeted Darrell.

"Thank you, Darrell. Welcome. Did you have any problems finding my place?"

"No, not at all." Darrell eyed his immediate surroundings. "Sasha, you have a beautiful home. I ought to hire you to help me out. My place could use a little bit of a woman's touch. I still want it to be masculine, but contemporary."

"Thanks for the compliment," blushed Sasha. "I read interior decorating magazines and visit furniture stores and model houses to get some ideas. Let me take your coat. Can I get you something to drink?"

"Do you have any orange juice?" asked Darrell as he handed Sasha his black leather jacket. He was wearing stone washed blue jeans and a long sleeved white cotton Ralph Lauren shirt. The aroma of the Armani Code for Men he wore pleased her senses. He looked particularly handsome.

"Sure do," responded Sasha. She went into the kitchen to get Darrell's juice. She decided she would have a glass of orange juice herself even though her first choice would have been a glass of white Zinfandel to calm her heightened nerves.

She placed the drinks on the hand carved coasters she bought during her trip to Ghana three years ago. She sat down on the loveseat which was to the right of the sofa. Darrell had seated himself on the middle cushion of the sofa.

"Have you decided what you would like to see at the movies?" asked Darrell.

"It has been a while since I have had that pleasure. I hear that Eddie Murphy has a new movie. Perhaps we can see that?"

"Most of the movies at the mall have a 9:00 or 10:00 p.m. showing. We can go get a bite to eat first, and then get to the movies. How does that sound?"

Sasha found the movie listing for the Muvico Theater at Arundel Mills Mall. "The Eddie Murphy movie starts at 9:25. That gives us plenty of time."

Sasha was feeling a burning need to get to know her date. She quizzed, "Darrell, do you have any other brothers or sisters?"

"Well, I told you about my brother David in Connecticut. I have an older sister, Denise, who is married and an obstetrician. She lives in Chicago. Unfortunately, our parents were killed in a car accident ten years ago with my younger sister."

"Oh, Darrell, I am so sorry to hear that." The mood of the room suddenly felt somber.

"What about you? Do you have any brothers or sisters, Sasha?"

"I'm an only child. And yes I did grow up being spoiled," she grimaced. "By the time I was seven, I had really learned the game. My parents had become such pushovers. On top of that, I learned to let my creativity do its own thing. I can't tell you how many imaginary friends I had growing up." The two shared a brief laugh.

"Well, I guess we'd better head out," remarked Darrell. "Do you like Mexican food?"

"I love Mexican."

"We can go to Enrique's on Route 40," said Darrell. Sasha grabbed their coats and they headed out of the door to Darrell's car. Like a gentleman, Darrell opened the passenger's side door for Sasha and saw that she was comfortably seated in the beige leather seat. She thought of how good it felt to be on the passenger's side. Two stars for Darrell. He received star number one when he arrived on time. Darrell then got in on the driver's side, fastened his seatbelt, and started the engine. The engine of the M5 purred like a kitten as they headed to the restaurant. The smell of fresh pine and the melodies compliments of a Miles Davis compact disk made the ride that much more enjoyable.

Once seated at Enrique's, Darrell and Sasha were handed menus and their drink orders were taken. They both ordered a glass of iced tea.

"I think I'll have some enchiladas tonight," said Sasha as she viewed the varied menu items.

"Hmmm. I'm a taco man myself. I think I could eat tacos everyday if I had to."

Darrell could not help but notice Sasha's beautiful twinkling dark eyes. If eyes were the window into the soul, her soul was very deep. He wondered why the attractive woman in his presence was not attached. He wanted to know what made her laugh and what made her cry. At times he could notice that something was missing in her life. He just could not pinpoint it.

"Shall I begin calling you José, Mr. Payson?" smiled Sasha.

"No, that won't be necessary, señorita."

"Se habla Español, Señor Payson?"

"Not hardly. I just happen to remember a little Spanish from my seventh grade Spanish class. That's all I care to reveal regarding my knowledge of the Spanish language," Darrell humbly responded.

"Si, señor. That's about all I know as well. Okay—we're even." They laughed at each other.

"Are we ready to order?" asked the server.

Sasha ordered first followed by Darrell. They continued their general conversation until their food was served. As they enjoyed their meals, a woman in her late twenties approached Sasha. She was dressed in a short, black, low cut spandex dress, exposing her double Ds, complimented with coffee shaded sheer pantyhose and black stiletto heels. Her slightly protruding tummy didn't hinder her confidence. She looked as if she had just left a makeup session at the hands of a new student at Miss Mae's Beauty Academy. The blue and green eye shadow palette just didn't fly with the sheer cotton candy lip gloss she wore.

"Sasha! How are you doing?!"

"Great and you, Erika?" Sasha conjured up memories of when Erika was the department's administrative assistant at the insurance company they worked. Not one pleasant memory came to mind. She remembered Erika for her poor work habits and persistent drama with men. It always appeared that Erika always had something out of the ordinary going on in her life. Her tardiness and poor work habits eventually led to the termination of her employment. Erika had the audacity to be surprised about her ultimate loss of employment with the company.

"I'm doing good. Fancy meeting you here," said Erika as she glanced Darrell's way waiting to be introduced.

"Erika, this is my friend, Darrell." Erika extended her well manicured hand to Darrell. It was evident that she kept regular appointments at the sculptured nail salon.

"Nice to meet you, Darrell," said Erika. Sasha could not help but notice that Erika held onto Darrell's hand a little longer than the normal handshake.

"Erika, are you here with anyone?" inquired Sasha.

"Yeah, I guess you could say that. Let's just say I needed something to do." Erika rolled her eyes signifying that her date was definitely not the one. "I had to run to the ladies room. He's waiting for me in the car. I'd better go so I can get this evening over with. Oh, I need to update you on your old boss. She's at it again."

Erika reached into her Louis Vuitton knockoff purse for a pen and note pad. She wrote down her name and home telephone number on the first sheet, flipped the page, anxiously tore it from the note pad and handed the sheet to Sasha. Erika grinned mischievously and eagerly requested Sasha's number. Sasha felt forced and obligated to give it to her. In the back of her mind, she didn't want to appear rude in front of Darrell. Her sixth sense immediately told her she would probably regret her decision somewhere down the line.

"Oh, I can't wait to hear all about it. I wonder who Irene has her pitch fork stuck into now," she smirked. She was confident she would not hear back from Erika. They really had nothing in common when they worked together back at the insurance company and she figured they definitely did not have anything in common now.

"Okay, I will. It was nice meeting you, Darrell. Take care." As Erika walked away, Sasha noticed she had a bit more switch in her walk. She tried to maintain her composure in front of Darrell. She wanted to shake her head in disgust.

After finishing their meals, Darrell picked up the check. Star number three for Darrell. They headed to the Muvico Movie Theater. The ticket line was so long that it wrapped around the theater. Based on the long line, apparently more than a few folks decided to spend the evening watching the big screen. Since the weather was a little brisk, Darrell asked Sasha to wait on the inside to protect her from the cold. Star number four for Darrell.

After getting the tickets, Darrell purchased popcorn and drinks. Even though they were full from dinner, a movie just didn't feel right without traditional movie snacks. They quickly found good seats in the middle of the theater. Being with someone at a movie theater was unusual for Sasha. While the previews were shown, Darrell turned to Sasha and jokingly said, "I hope you are not one of those women who insist on carrying on a full conversation during the movie."

Sasha laughed. "No. I was hoping you weren't one of those men who insist on talking to the screen and telling the characters what to do."

"You are alright with me Sasha," responded Darrell as he placed his arm around her shoulder. Star number five for Darrell.

◎◎◎

On the drive back to Sasha's, they discussed their opinions of the movie.

"I've seen better," said Darrell.

"Darrell, were you and I watching the same movie? I thought it was great."

"Yeah, I noticed that you were cracking up quite a bit, Miss Grant."

"Well, I needed a good laugh and I got one."

"And you sure did." He enjoyed her laugh. It was hearty, yet dignified. Her smile lit up the atmosphere.

Before they knew it, they were back at Sasha's house. Darrell pulled up in the driveway and put the M5 in park.

"Thank you so much for a great evening, Sasha. I had a great time."

"Would you like to come in for a night cap?" Sasha asked.

"I would love to, but I have to get an early start tomorrow. I need to review some client accounts over the weekend and some of my frat brothers are coming over tomorrow night. Since most of them are married, they don't get released very often."

"Released?" questioned Sasha.

"That's their term, not mine," replied Darrell. "I guess their women have the upper hand."

Sasha decided not to respond to Darrell's comment. She did not want to start a gender debate to end what had been a wonderful evening.

"Well, on that note, I will bid you a good night. I had a wonderful time with you this evening. Perhaps we can do this again real soon."

Darrell smiled and extended his hand for a handshake. Sasha's mouth dropped as she extended her hand and placed it in his. He gave her hand a slight squeeze. She thought that a handshake was an unusual way to end a date.

"I'd like that. I had a great time as well." responded Sasha. She turned to get out of the car and headed for her front door. Once she got in, she signaled to Darrell that all was well and locked the storm door. She peered from the door and watched him as he drove away. She then secured the entrance door.

He didn't even try to kiss me. He must be gay, Sasha thought as she took off her coat and hung it in the living room closet. It was 11:58 p.m. and too late to call Regina. She decided she would call her on Saturday morning.

As she began undressing to get a quick shower before retiring to bed, the telephone rang. Without bothering to look at the caller ID, she picked up the telephone figuring it had to be important.

"Hi Sasha! It's Erika. It was great seeing you tonight." Sasha was surprised to hear from her so soon especially at nearly midnight. She had hoped that after their brief contact at the restaurant their personal contact would immediately revert back to its original nonexistent state. Erika quickly began making her point.

"I see you have a new friend."

"Yes," responded Sasha. "You are probably referring to Darrell. He's a financial planner," Sasha slightly bragged. As soon as she said it, she wanted to kick herself. It dawned on her that Erika wasn't calling just to catch up on old times.

"Wow. I'm glad I called. I have been looking for a financial planner," Erika lied again. "My cousin recently passed away and left me some cash I'd like to invest. Do you have his work number?"

Sasha was becoming angry and impatient. She didn't know whether or not to believe Erika's story. She reluctantly gave her Darrell's full name and office telephone number. Erika then had the audacity to ask for his home number.

"Thanks, girl," a grateful Erika said. "I heard a few weeks ago that Irene fired Vanessa Porter. You remember her, right?"

"I remember her. When she came on board, the office took bets on how long it would be before Irene got to her. I'm surprised she lasted as long as she did. She's stronger than I thought. She may not think it was for the best, but she'll eventually move on to something better. She's just another one of Irene's victims."

"Yeah," replied Erika. "We all were victims of Irene at one time or another."

Sasha didn't want to go there with Erika. "On that note, I gotta go," abruptly said Sasha. "Nice catching up with you," she lied. "Take care."

"You take care, too." Immediately after hanging up, Erika began contemplating her next step. Once she got settled at home, she planned to Google Darrell's full name on her computer. In the interim, she'd call him.

Erika said out loud, "This is just enough to get me started."

◎◎◎

Sasha's telephone rang again one minute later. This time she made the effort to view the caller ID display before answering.

"Sash, how is your date going? Is he still there?" whispered Regina.

"Why are you whispering?" asked Sasha.

"Keith is asleep and I don't want to wake him up," replied Regina.

"I really had a good time, but he didn't even try to kiss me good night."

"What? Let's just call the police on him. He must be the last of the respectable men left on the planet. He deserves to die by lethal injection."

"Obviously he's gay. I mean he shook my hand to end the date."

"Oh, I see. If he had tried to attack you, you would have considered him to be a great date, huh?"

"No...I guess I was just expecting the date to end a little differently."

"Oh, now I see. So you wanted to entertain him in your bedroom. Tell me this--what would George and Marian have to say about that? I bet they still think you are a virgin," Regina laughed.

"Oh, I'm really scared now," Sasha teased. "Okay--you are being silly now. You know me better than that."

"What I'm trying to get you to understand is that there are some decent men left despite what the statistics say. All men aren't dogs, Sasha. Just like all women aren't the 'b' and 'h' words." Regina was habitually meticulous about not using profanity or slang. She never knew when one of the twins would be within earshot and the last thing she needed was one of them to start using curse words and street language.

"Point well taken, Gina. You won't believe who I ran into while I was with Darrell. Since you'll never guess, I'm just going to tell you—Erika Bellamy."

"What? That girl used to put the 't' in trouble. I hear they are still finding mistakes in the office she made three years ago. What does she want from you?"

"She commented on Darrell and I mentioned that he was a financial planner. She mentioned that she needed one. She also gave me the latest on Irene."

"Please tell me that you didn't give that woman his information."

"Then I guess I shouldn't tell you," said Sasha bluntly. She could feel her body stiffen as she awaited Regina's pending response.

Regina needed a brief moment of silence. She couldn't believe what she had just heard.

Regina replied, "I need to put this conversation on hold for now. Girl, I don't believe you sometimes. Let's chat over the weekend. Keith just turned over and stopped snoring. I don't want to wake him up."

"Okay, thanks for checking in on me. Good night."

"Oh, one more thing. When are you coming over to take the children to the zoo? Tiffani said you promised them."

"That little stinker. I did not make that promise."

"Girl, see what I go through? Now I've got to give her a time out for lying."

"Gina, please don't do that. I'll take them this weekend."

"Oh, no. She has to learn that lying is not acceptable in this house. I'll take care of Miss Tiffani first thing in the morning. Girl, just wait until you have kids. You'll truly understand my kiddie drama."

"Oh, Gina please just talk to her. I don't think she needs to be punished," Sasha pleaded.

"Sasha, I know you mean well, however, Tiffani needs to learn."

Sasha decided it was better that she not argue her point. After all, she was nobody's mother. "Alright, you are the parent. I'll call you tomorrow. Bye."

"See ya girl. Bye."

Feeling sorry for Tiffani and her pending fate, Sasha hung up the telephone, got a quick shower, caressed her limber body with raspberry vanilla lotion, put on a fresh pale blue satin sleep shirt, and easily under slid under the comforting Egyptian cotton sheets into her queen sized canopy bed. As she lay, staring at the ceiling, her thoughts quickly drifted to Darrell. She reflected on the five stars he had earned during the evening. His mannerisms and charm were sweet. The scent from his cologne was a unique combination of manly yet woodsy. The scent dazzled her senses. He was like no other man she had met. Her curiosity concerning him was getting the best of her. His mystery intrigued her mind, body, and spirit. She began slowly drifting off to sleep with thoughts of him. When she caught herself smiling, she reminded herself of all the pain and heartache of the past. Her dreamy eyes began to swell with hurts of the past. She haphazardly recalled all the times she was made to feel special by a man, only to learn that she was nothing more than a pawn in the game of love. Her tears slowly soaked her freshly cleansed face and rolled down her satin covered pillow as she drifted off into a deep, disheartening slumber.

Darrell's drive back to his house in Towson took a mere twenty minutes. It allowed him to ponder the evening's events. His charming schoolboy grin started from the time he left Sasha's and continued until he drove into the garage of his three story town house. Sasha Grant had definitely tickled his fancy. He spent a great evening with a beautiful woman who was quite charming and most importantly, had a great sense of humor. He hoped he had impressed her just the same.

For the life of him, he could not put his finger on what was different about Sasha. He simply enjoyed talking to her. Every time she spoke, he noticed the sparkle in her eyes along with a distant gaze as if she were looking through him. At times he could swear that her mind was elsewhere. On top of that, he could not possibly imagine why she was still single. A woman like her was quite unique. He had often read article after article from his subscription to Essence magazine about single women who were successful with their careers, but had no one to share their successes. His fraternity brothers often teased him about his subscription. He simply explained that Essence was his window to learn more about women and their point of view. The subscription had certainly more than paid for itself over the years.

As Darrell grabbed the mail from his black metal mailbox, he inserted the key into the front door and stepped onto the plush tan carpet. He placed his keys on its usual hook in the kitchen then placed the mail on the butcher's block. He opened the refrigerator and grabbed a bottle of spring water, twisted off the top, pressed the opening to his mouth, and allowed the cold pristine liquid to saturate his dry throat. He gathered the mail from the butcher's block and made his way upstairs to the master bedroom. There he placed the mail on the nightstand and began undressing. His thoughts drifted back to Sasha and their evening. He smiled as he remembered that his manhood had been feeling a little happy as well. If women had ever figured out that men thought about sex practically everyday for no reason at all most times, many of them would be busted on a regular basis.

Darrell jumped into the shower to discard the slight evening sweat he had worked up. Upon his return to the master bedroom, he picked up the telephone to check for voicemail. Upon hearing the stutter tone, he dialed the number for voice mail and input his password.

"You have one new message, received on Saturday at 12:05 a.m." the soothing automated female voice breathed.

An unfamiliar voice began speaking. "Hi Darrell. This is Erika Bellamy. Hopefully, you remember me. I met you tonight at Enrique's on Route 40."

Darrell scratched his head as he feverishly tried to remember the name and the voice. This further made him try to remember how the woman got his number.

"My former co-worker Sasha said you could possibly help me. I understand that you're a financial planner. I'd like to learn how to better manage my money and retire one of these days because I don't want to have to work forever. Can I make an appointment with you as soon as possible? Please call me at 410-555-1080. That's my home number. My work number is 410-555-1000, extension 254. I look forward to hearing from you."

Darrell suddenly remembered Erika. He could not help but recall her valiant stride as she exited Enrique's. He thought that she was loose and had quite a nerve to flirt with him in front of Sasha. Some women never ceased to amaze him with their blatant flirting. His dad would surely say that times have changed. Darrell began wondering why Erika would call him at such a late hour. The only women who would call him so late were interested in spending the night. Since the bitter episode with Cheryl and William, he had become defensive about the intentions of women in general. He swore that he would never be that gullible again. He wrote Erika's numbers down on a note pad with a notation of the reason for her call. He decided he would follow up with her sometime next week. It bothered him a bit that Sasha had given out his home telephone number to one of her girlfriends. He began thinking that she probably was trying to be helpful to a friend.

In the interim, he smiled as he savored the crown of a wonderful evening with Sasha. He was smitten with her childlike innocence and charm. As the steaming hot water from the showerhead pounded his muscular body, he closed his eyes and his thoughts unmistakably gravitated to her. He wondered aloud how long could he wait for her to realize that he wanted her to be an important part of his life. He made up his mind she was worth the wait.

Chapter 16

The sun also shines on the wicked.
-Seneca

The smile on Erika's face said it all. She could not have planned it better if she tried. Running into Sasha rekindled the hate she had harbored for her for years. It was the spark she needed to commence her mission—destroy Sasha Grant by any means necessary. Making immediate contact with Darrell was only the beginning.

As she inserted the key into the lock, turned the cylinder, and opened the door to her personal world away from the hustle and bustle of city life and behind her private, closed doors, she was happy to be at home and out of the company of Tony Solomon. He fulfilled his purpose for the evening. She simply wanted a decent meal without having to pay for it out of her pocket. She didn't worry about the puzzled look on his face when she requested that he stop on the way home at the twenty-four hour Walgreen's for a half gallon of two percent milk. She used the opportunity to secretly call Sasha, then Darrell from her cellular phone without Tony's knowledge.

Erika's quaint, one-bedroom apartment located on East 25th Street also served its purpose. It had wall-to-wall carpet, freshly painted egg shell walls, and working appliances and plumbing. It was not located in the best neighborhood, nor was it located in the worst. She felt safe enough to go out on occasion to get a late night snack or a pack of Newports without fearing for her life. That wasn't true of all the neighborhoods in the city.

For two seconds, she eyed the blinking red light on the base of the cordless telephone stand placed on the glass end table in the living room. The sparsely furnished room had a winter green cloth sleeper sofa and a twin glass table on the opposite end. The room's lighting illuminated from a single white laminated halogen floor lamp. She surmised it was her mother or another bill collector calling to harass her for money. Each time a bill collector called, she answered, *Baltimore City Morgue. May I help you?* Knowing that the caller would be thrown off and startled by her greeting, she silently laughed when the caller apologetically stuttered, *Oh, I'm sorry. I must have the wrong number.* Other times she pretended she couldn't speak English or made death threats. Still they called with their rehearsed pitches to get paid what was owed to them.

Curiosity got the best of her. She walked towards the red blinking light, picked up the cordless telephone, pressed the caller ID button to identify the reason for the call waiting notification. She identified a call from her mother, one from an unknown name and unknown number, and Greg Richmond, a former male companion. She wondered aloud how on earth he got her number. She surmised it was once again her meddling mother. She shook her head in disgust and tucked the dangling strands of synthetic highlighted blond hair back in place behind her right double pierced ear. She had no intention of calling anyone back tonight.

Martha Bellamy raised her only child to get what she wanted through other people. Erika's childhood memories primarily consisted of she and Martha begging for handouts in front of the world famous Lexington Market, the home of some of the finest baked goods, fresh meats, poultry and seafood, and delectable chocolate confections. Her earliest memory was when she was five years old. Martha knew that most people would give in to a poor, homeless looking child. She purposely dressed Erika to play on their sympathy. When they went on their fall/winter begging sprees, Martha dressed Erika in dusty brown corduroy pants, dirty and tattered white tennis shoes, a torn puffy white coat and a black knit cap which was littered with hundreds of ivory lint balls. For the spring/summer begging sprees, her *costume* consisted of a blue and white dingy seersucker dress and scuffed black patent leather shoes with no socks. Erika hung close to her mother who wasn't dressed much better. Martha's 1960's wardrobe had somehow stood the test of time despite its outdated appearance. Together, the two of them were a true, pitiful sight. As tourists and shoppers passed by, their worn faces tugged on the hearts of the strangers. Scrooge himself had to finally give in. On one of their best days, they cleared over three hundred dollars. Some of the money would be used for food and shelter. Martha's alcohol addiction would also see its share of the take.

Although Martha had made strides over the years and was able to recover from her addiction, Erika's harsh childhood realities remained forever on her mind. She never forgave Martha and reminded her of it every chance she could get. Despite Martha's miraculous transformation and multiple requests for forgiveness from her daughter, the venom in Erika's heart prevailed. Martha continued to believe in the power of prayer and that one day Erika would find it in her heart to forgive her for the sins she committed against her. She often told Erika that she would have to be on her death bed when the chains of hate for her would finally be broken. Only then it would be too late. She sincerely hoped that Erika would come around while she was amongst those in the land of the living.

Erika was determined to stand her ground no matter what. She was not at all impressed that Martha had found the Lord. As far as she was concerned, it was because of Martha, her life was a total mess. She could only imagine what her life would have been like if her father had been around.

Jimmy Bellamy had issues of his own. For most of his adult life, he had been arrested several times and had been in out of the penal system for loitering, possession of marijuana, petty theft and trespassing. He finally reached the cross roads when he botched an armed robbery at a Catonsville convenience store with one of his neighborhood buddies which ended in the taking of a life. Jimmy was identified as the shooter who fatally wounded the store's owner who happened to be a happily married father of two young girls. Jimmy's selfish and heinous act resulted in him being confined to the Jessup Correctional Institution in Maryland for the rest of his life with no chance of parole.

The last time Erika saw Jimmy, she was twenty years old. She hated the dank, musty smell of the facility and what it stood for. The heavy atmosphere, the careless attitudes, and the hopelessness invaded her mind every time she visited him. A hard life at the facility had taken its toll on Jimmy's appearance. At forty-five years old, he had the appearance of a man in his sixties. He often apologized to her for the mistakes he had made and his lack of parenting skills. He admitted that he had mistreated Martha and could have been a much better husband and father. Erika grew tired of the excuses of both of her parents. After her last visit nine years ago, she vowed never to return to Jessup. She cut him completely and fully out of her life. She changed her telephone number to an unpublished and unlisted one. She disbanded her relationship with him by writing a letter simply stating that she was too busy to visit or write to him anymore. For the first time in his life, Jimmy cried. Truth be told, Erika did not want any reminders that he had ever been a parent to her. She wanted to shun her past with the quickness of the pierce of a rattlesnake bite without looking back and with no regrets.

Erika's failed relationships frequently clouded her mind. Each time she thought she found what she had labeled as true love, she eventually discovered that it was not at all the case. It was only after giving her time, money and body, the truth became apparent. The men she allowed in her life used and abused her only for the moment and at their pleasure. She often found herself begging for completeness. In her eyes, completeness meant a husband and children of her own. To prove her love, she made it a habit to demonstrate what she could do for them early in the relationship. This typically included paying their bills and allowing them to use her credit cards. Her early out of the gate attitude often turned the tables on her resulting in thousands of dollars in debt with nothing to show for it. Soon thereafter when the relationships were over and all the dust had settled, depression hit and it hit hard.

Regular refills of Zyprexa to treat her schizophrenia had helped her to feel better, but she forcefully depended less and less on its assistance in helping her feel more like a normal person. Nevertheless, the drug's side effects had taken its toll—she frequently experienced sleepiness, an upset stomach, and dizziness. To avoid the unwanted effects of the medication, she often missed the once per day dosage figuring she could do without it. She felt she could have more control over her life based on her own free will and the prescribed medication was no longer needed.

Erika never had any real friends growing up in Baltimore. The neighborhood children were often her worst enemies. They persistently taunted her about her ragged and outdated clothes, unkempt hair and large teeth. When she did meet people who honestly wanted to get to get to know her better, she was too embarrassed and ashamed of her family and background to open up to them. She especially made it a point to avoid any close personal relationships with females. Martha taught her at a young age that females just couldn't be trusted. Martha had experienced more than a few episodes with competitive females when she had tried to befriend women in the community who could watch Erika when she was unable to adequately care for her on her own, they turned out to be the same women who seduced Jimmy with no regard for Martha or Erika. They used him and he in turn used them for personal satisfaction.

As Erika walked to the kitchen, she grabbed a cigarette from her purse and lit it with the assistance of a transparent green plastic Bic lighter. The menthol from the cigarette temporarily calmed her senses and relaxed her mind. She thought about Sasha more intensely as she poured herself a double shot of Hennessey and added a few ounces of a store brand cherry flavored cola over five large ice cubes in a twenty-four ounce jar which formerly contained kosher dill pickles. Although their conversation was brief, Erika brought herself back to the moment at the restaurant. She felt the bile from her stomach churn as she recounted the many times Sasha made her feel less than a person. She even surprised herself that she was able to keep a straight face and act as if she enjoyed talking to her. It was because of Sasha, she lost the first good paying job she had in a long time. Sasha's no nonsense approach hit Erika where it hurt her the most—her pocket. She simply concluded that Sasha was out to get her because she was jealous of the relationship she had at the time. Every time she heard Sasha laugh, she gathered that she was laughing at her simply because she was there. It wasn't her fault that Sasha couldn't find and keep a man. Erika's relationship with Larry eventually turned out to be another dead end, loveless encounter.

The wheels of motion churned in Erika's head. Her lips alternated between puffs from her cigarette and slow sips of her drink. As she breathed in the last bit of smoke, she allowed the sting of the tobacco to swirl around her spiral curls. She vowed that running into Sasha was a new beginning for her and the end of Sasha.

"You still think you are a prize, Miss Grant, don't you?" Erika yelled out loud. She pictured Sasha's face and imagined standing toe to toe and shoulder to shoulder with her.

She stared at Sasha's image in her head with her eyes intently focused and hissed, "Mark my words, Sasha Grant. As sure as you walk this earth, you're gonna wish you never did what you did to me. It's officially on."

Chapter 17

You've been tricked! You've been had! Hoodwinked! Bamboozled!
-El-Hajj Malik El Shabazz (Malcolm X)

Ken Cunningham was a man on a mission. He completed his research on the latest trends in the industry. Regina was quite instrumental in assisting him and her research skills proved to be invaluable. They spent the last few evenings reviewing his presentation and double checking the PowerPoint slide show and related handouts. Both had stayed late in order to meet the project deadline for a sales meeting with a client.

The pair had mapped out Ken's plan and took advantage of the serene surroundings of the executive boardroom to help them spread things out a bit. The room's large polished mahogany table surrounded by high back black leather chairs gave the room the appearance that many top decisions had been made there by the company's executive team. While they focused their attention on the very important project that would be a make or break for him, Ken tried to forget his not so happy home life. He and Doris' lack of intimacy had been clouding his mind more frequently. At times he couldn't believe that she was the same woman he had fallen in love with several years ago. When they dated and one year into their marriage, their love life was like a fairy tale where everything was perfect and everyone lived happily ever after. The income from his job allowed them to have luxuries usually reserved for a high two-person income household. With Ken's income, Doris had the option of being a stay at home mother. She played house as if her life depended on it. The house was always impeccably spotless and there was always a gourmet dinner waiting for him when he returned from a hard day's work. He looked forward to going home to his beautiful wife. However, after their first child was born, she let herself as well as the fairy tale go.

After Megan was born, the forty pounds Doris had gained stayed with her along with the addition of another forty caused by depression and stress of her drastically changed lifestyle. The candlelight dinners were a thing of the past. When Ken arrived home after a long day in the office, he quickly discovered that the house was a wreck and dinner was no where to be found. When Christopher was born followed by Jennifer, their relationship had become even more strained. Their constant fights over the household became a regular family event.

At times, Ken could not stand to look at Doris and had resorted to calling her names. Too often the children had become witnesses to their heated arguments and the effects had become evident in their attitudes and persistently failing school grades. The three had been disciplined by their teachers and sent to the principal's office for disrupting class and causing uproars with their classmates. They were subsequently referred to school counselors. Letters were sent to Ken and Doris reminding them of the schools' policies on unruly students. Ken's memories of playing with them on a daily basis, visits to the Maryland Zoo in Baltimore, and movie theater outings were as distant as clouds in the sunset. His absenteeism as a father took its toll on the children as well as Doris.

As Ken's home life became more and more out of control, he often turned to the bottle for comfort and he became a regular at several bars in Fells Point. On more than a few occasions, he turned his attention to prostitutes in Baltimore's red light district nicknamed the "Block" in place of what he was not getting from Doris at home. He prided himself on being careful as to not allowing his secret life to become exposed. He drank just enough to help him temporarily forget his troubles. When he went to the Block to fulfill his manly needs, he limited his escapades to prostitutes who would satisfy him in ways that were not considered sexual intercourse by some standards. Since he and Doris no longer shared a bedroom, he had an easier time covering his tracks. Each time he came home from being out late, an argument ensued as soon as he hit the door. He often found himself wanting to physically assault Doris in order to avoid hearing her nagging about their situation. Although the bills were paid, they were far from being a happy and cohesive family unit. He figured the cost of staying in the situation was far less expensive than trying to leave. The potential cost of alimony and child support alone was enough to make him grin and bear it for the long haul.

Ken found solace at work. Work gave him the outlet he needed during the day. His work environment at the company allowed him to be a key stakeholder in the organization and his creative talents were appreciated by his superiors as evident by the commendations he had received in the form of performance bonuses and awards. He enjoyed meeting with clients and using his power influences to close deals. He clung to the business like an addict to their drug of choice as if his life depended on it. His high was driven by his successes.

The longer he worked with Regina, he found himself becoming even more and more attracted to her. Not only was she a great administrative assistant, she had become a sensual woman who constantly invaded his daily fantasies about her seducing him first thing upon his arrival to the office. When his mind was not totally on his work, it meandered to her. His mind caused him to think of her in inappropriate ways. At first, he admonished himself for doing so. When things became worse at home, the fantasies were his way of helping him forget what he had waiting for him at home. Regina's smooth mocha complexion, sensuous smile, and shapely physique drove him into a tailspin. He had to catch himself from exposing his true feelings to her several times. If he had taken a chance by letting her know the true reflections of his feelings for her, he would surely face sexual harassment charges. Workplace rules had surely changed over the years. The company's sexual harassment policy clearly indicated that sexual harassment would not be tolerated under any circumstances. The company even required all employees to attend a training program which outlined the company's policy and included a video and an interactive segment to help employees become aware of how serious the company was about protecting its interests and its employees.

Ken enjoyed his encounters with Regina at work. He found her smart and resourceful. He was surprised that she did not do more with her business degree. Although she appeared ambitious, she gave the air that she was content with her current job and that her home life was far more important. Their discussions of family life gave him further insight into her being. She appeared to have her priorities together. He on the other hand, found himself limiting his discussions concerning his home life with her. He saw no need in getting too personal with his assistant. One slip of his tongue could damage the larger than life image he had painted of himself for her and put an untimely conclusion to his stellar career.

"Gina, these slides look great. I've got to hand it to you. I don't know what I would do without you," said Ken as he admired the work Regina had done with the PowerPoint slides.

Regina was a true whiz when it came to the computer. With advances in technology, she was able to turn the transparencies he formerly used for his sales presentations into interactive presentations that highlighted the company's offerings with various sound effects designed to draw in the audience. The hardest part for Ken was learning how to operate the laptop and the LCD projector for the eye catching presentation. He learned to operate both for the purposes of getting through the presentation. Regina's tutelage helped him with ease through the transition.

"Thanks, Ken," Regina smiled. "I must say they do look great. I knew you were good with those old transparencies, but now I know you will knock them dead now that you are armed with your high tech weapons."

"You have no idea how pleased I am with your work, Gina. This really livens up the presentation. Now they will really think I know what I am talking about." Ken's eyes sparked with merriment.

Ken was genuinely impressed. His eyes dazzled as the presentation slides appeared on the screen in a continuous mode. In his excitement, he unconsciously walked over to Regina and placed his hands on her shoulders. His thumbs grazed the exposed skin just below the nape of her neck. He began massaging her shoulders. "Oh, Gina, you are a powerhouse," he commented. His voice sounded strong and virile as he began fantasizing about her being submissive to him at his pleasure.

Regina hesitated, stiffened, and then stopped dead in her tracks. His touch made her normally relaxed body rigid and taut. His cold, clammy fingers against her skin made her shudder. She began feeling uncomfortable and awkward. She knew in her mind that he was not coming on to her and convinced herself that Ken very well knew that inappropriate and unwanted touching was not acceptable in the workplace. After all, they had attended the same sexual harassment workshop together and even sat next to each other. She began thinking of the best way to handle Ken's offensive behavior. Her heart began to beat faster as the continuous motion of his touching became even more uncomfortable.

"Ah, Ken," Regina said as she turned and stood up to face him from her sitting position. It's getting late and I need to head for home. My family has probably sent out a search party for me." Regina tried to grin as she glanced at her watch. It was later than she had originally thought. She had told Keith that she would be home by 7.p.m. It was already 7:20 p.m. "Perhaps we could finish up tomorrow? I don't mind coming in a little early."

Ken finally caught himself invading her personal space. "Sure. I didn't realize that is was so late. I don't want to be the cause of any family friction," he apologized. He hoped that his obvious indiscretion was not as blatant as it had appeared. He could feel the redness of his face rise to the occasion. "I'll see you tomorrow. No need to come in any earlier than your normal start time. Job well done," he commented as he nervously cleared his throat.

Regina began shutting down the computer and the LCD projector then gathered the papers from the boardroom. Once at her desk, she grabbed her purse from her desk drawer. She could see Ken out of the corner of her eye preparing to leave as well. The awkward moments between the two had become evident through the silence associated with their encounter in the boardroom. Hesitantly, Regina finally broke the silence.

"Ken, I'll see you in the morning. Have a good evening," said Regina sighing from weariness.

"You do the same. Thanks again for all of your help," Ken said as he exited and closed the door to his office. His mind escaped to getting a drink and physical relief from his repressed sexual frustration. He did not know how much longer he could pretend that Regina was merely his administrative assistant. The incident in the boardroom could come back to haunt him. He decided to put it out of his mind for now. He could fulfill his fantasy later on that evening with Cindy. Cindy sure knew how to make him feel good and help him forget about his troubles at home.

As Regina walked to the parking lot adjacent to the office building, she once again tried to shake off the incident in the boardroom with Ken. *Perhaps his touching was innocent*, she thought. She could not imagine where his inappropriate behavior came from. He seemed to be a happily married man. She thought about mentioning the incident to Keith when she got home, but soon squashed the thought. She just wasn't in the mood to hear him barrage her about her job. He'd really go off if she told him about Ken's behavior. It was a conversation reserved for Sasha to get advice on how to handle Ken. Keith no doubt would be ticked enough that she was getting home much later than she had originally stated. Her late nights in the office had become more frequent and had begun to cause tensions in the household. Whenever they had an argument about one of them not spending enough time at home, he always brought up the fact that she was beginning to pay more attention to her job than Tiffani and Tyrique. She in turn brought up the fact that they both were responsible for the children's well being.

Lately, Regina had difficulty trying to keep the peace at the Webster residence. She was the primary caregiver of the children. When she returned home from a long day at work, she resumed her second full-time job as a mother. She was the one who prepared dinner, helped them with their homework and gave them their baths in the evening. Keith made contributions to raising the children on a regular basis, but his contribution was not as significant as Regina's. Regina's late evenings put him in a position of having to pick up the ball.

Keith very seldom talked about work issues at home other than briefly mentioning some of his high profile cases. He and Regina had set aside some space in their home for his home office. The twins knew that Daddy was off limits when he went into the "computer room" as they had named it. Regina often told them Keith was working on some "very important stuff" and he could not be disturbed. Even though she really knew they did not understand exactly why their Daddy was off limits, they were overjoyed when he took breaks every now and then to play with them.

It had been a while since Keith and Regina had made love. In the past, their sharing of each other had been a constant staple. No matter what went on in the workplace, they knew that they could count on each other for comfort and support. They greeted each other with a kiss without fail once they arrived at home. Keith enjoyed Regina's full lips. She in turn was delighted by his caring touch. Many romantic nights were started from the longing they had for each other's caress.

Once the children came along their lives had changed; however, they vowed to keep the passion in their marriage. Once the children had been tucked in for the evening, they spent time talking about their relationship and each other. Conversations about their hopes and dreams remained the topic of many discussions. Keith admired Regina for her zest for life. To him, she was his dream come true and the center of his universe. His buddies often teased him and labeled him as "whipped".

When Regina got into the vehicle, she rested her purse on the front passenger seat. She took a deep breath, as she pulled the cellular phone from her purse. She shook her head as she contemplated Keith's forthcoming response to her long overdue arrival. She had a career just like he did. He would just have to learn to be flexible just as she had to be flexible with the changes in his work life. She thought of her mother's words of wisdom. None seem to fit the situation at hand. All she knew was that frustration had overtaken her. Not only did she feel violated by Ken, she felt like a neglectful parent and an uncompromising spouse. She reminisced about Tiffani's comment last week that she never played with her. The comment had brought tears to her eyes as her daughter gave her a dose of reality. She cradled Tiffani in her arms and silently cried as the sharpness of her baby's tone crushed her heart. Tiffani was right. She had not spent any quality time with the children in a while and it was obvious.

Regina's thoughts quickly shifted back to the incident with Ken. The thought of him touching her in a sexual way brought on a sudden headache and an uneasy feeling in her stomach.

She remembered the time Sasha told her about an employee who had made suggestive comments and continued to ask her out after she told him she was not interested in dating him. She finally reported him to her manager after he cornered her in the elevator and grabbed her breast. Regina remembered how upset Sasha was when the employee received no more than a slap on the wrist. He was counseled by his supervisor and required to attend a sexual harassment class. Sasha even called the Equal Employment Opportunity Commission, but the counselor stated that since there were no witnesses to the events and the company had taken the appropriate steps to correct the employee's behavior, no action probably would be taken. She hated seeing Sasha so hurt and humiliated. They spent time talking about the incident. Sasha felt powerless and angry because she felt more admonished than the accused. She now knew how Sasha really felt. Sasha eventually left that company because of the incident. Regina felt it was definitely their loss. She decided she would make some time to call Sasha for some advice on what to do about Ken. The uncomfortable feelings she was beginning experience made her doubt herself and her well being.

Regina snapped out of her temporary trance, started the engine, plugged her cellular phone into the adapter, and then called home. She took another deep breath as she dialed home and contemplated an explanation for Keith. The phone rang four times before it went to voice mail. She hesitated before hanging up without leaving a message and figured Keith had taken the children to McDonald's or Wendy's for yet another fast food dinner. She was sure Tiffani and Tyrique didn't mind. She decided at that moment things would begin to change starting with her by explaining to Ken first thing tomorrow that her heavy workload was seriously affecting her home life. The late nights would have to stop. She did not mind taking some work home on occasion to help out, but she physically needed to be home with her family. She prayed that Ken would understand as he was a family man with responsibilities of his own.

Satisfied with her decision, she exited the parking lot and headed for home. Again, she contemplated what she would say to Keith as far as an explanation for her lateness, hoping he would understand with minimal argument. In any event, she vowed to make things better. She refused to risk losing what she and Keith had built together. She sighed as she tried to think of how to straighten out her priorities to get her life back in some type of order.

Chapter 18

Your wealth can be stolen, but the precious
riches buried deep in your soul cannot.
-Minnie Ripperton

"James, we got a big shipment in late yesterday. I need for you to unpack the shipment and get it inventoried," said Beverly as she checked off her list of things to do. "Sharon, I need for you to make some calls and do some follow up with a few vendors."

She did not wait for them to answer. She knew that once she spoke a directive, it was expected that the orders would be followed. Beverly continued to do a walk through of the store. The small bookstore had become quite prosperous. She was quite proud and pleased with its progress and very thankful for the many referrals she had received from her regular customers. Also, she often had book sales and signings for prominent as well as up and coming authors. She paid careful attention to just about every little detail in the store from the storefront displays to how the featured books were arranged on the shelves.   She carefully trained her staff to be customer focused—it was the only way to truly beat the competition.

In a few short hours she would be on her way to Aruba. She closed her eyes for a brief moment and pictured herself relaxing on the glorious beach basking in the sun and enjoying the calling and serenade of the sea. It had been a long awaited vacation. She tried to get someone to accompany her on the trip. Sasha felt that she could not take a vacation with her current schedule, Regina had far too many family obligations, and her sister Brenda had no money due to loans she had made to her last boyfriend which still remained unpaid after more than a year. That left no one but her. As far as Beverly was concerned, she figured she'd see Brenda and Marc on an episode of Judge Judy sometime in the near future. Sasha, Regina and Brenda were the three people she could possibly tolerate on an extended vacation.   At first she was hesitant about vacationing alone.   She began thinking of the last time she took a nice relaxing vacation that was longer than a weekend. It was with Carl. *So much for that*, she thought.

Beverly preferred to vacation without having a set schedule. The last time she, Sasha and Regina vacationed together, she wanted to literally kill Sasha. Sasha preferred to have detailed, set plans each day from sun up to sundown. It was her way of making the best of the vacation. Beverly preferred to do things impromptu and at the spur of the moment. The two constantly bumped heads on sights to see, places to eat, and after hours activities. Regina's job was to keep the peace amongst them. Regina finally called a truce when she thought Beverly was about to smack Sasha across the table at the

Captain's Ball during their Royal Caribbean cruise to the Bahamas six years ago.

As Sharon and James busied themselves with their duties before the store officially opened, Beverly continued reviewing her checklist. She had gotten to the point where she felt comfortable leaving them in charge of The Bookworm without having to check in on a regular basis. She was sure that her family and friends would have something to say about her carefree attitude. She paid neither them nor their thoughts any mind.

When she finally settled in at her desk, and her hips grazed the sides of her high back black leather chair, she wished she had stuck to her commitment to lose more weight. Lately she had begun to hate shopping for clothes. When she last weighed herself she had come to the conclusion that she weighed more than a few professional heavyweight boxers and some of the players in the National Football League. As her size eighteen clothing had become snugger, she was determined not to go up an additional size. Boredom and stress over the last few months had taken their toll and contributed to her weight gain. Regina and Sasha could not possibly understand her plight. They were sizes six and eight respectively. When they shopped together at the major department stores such as Boscov's, Macy's and Lord and Taylor's, she often felt a bit awkward. She had to shop in the *big girls* section while they were able to get more up-to-date and fashionable outfits in smaller sizes. When trying on outfits, her frustration worsened. It seemed that most clothes that fit her were often unflattering to her figure. She found solace in specialty stores geared to plus size women such as Lane Bryant, The Avenue, and Ashley Stewart.

She lost track of the number of diets she had been on and off over the past few years. She tried Slim-Fast, the Fruit Diet, Jenny Craig, the Hollywood Diet, the Soup Diet, Weight Watchers, Dr.

Atkins, the Lose Ten Pounds in Three Days Diet, and starvation. She lost weight on each diet only to gain back the weight plus some. She absolutely hated to exercise, but decided to start a regime of walking on a regular basis. She found it relaxing and it often took her mind away--if only for a few moments. She even found herself eating less when her mind was occupied on doing something creative or out of the ordinary.

When she finally made time to dig her scale out from the storage closet in the basement and stepped on it for the first time in a while, she was pleased. She had dropped twenty pounds simply by moving more and eating less. Maybe there was some truth to using common sense for losing weight. Nevertheless, she vowed to be confident whether she wore a size eighteen or a size eight.

Beverly admired her freshly manicured nails. She felt that if she were to play the part of a lady of leisure for the next ten days, she very well could not have ragged nails. She found a nail shop a block away from The Bookworm. Once she arrived, she decided to go for the works and included a pedicure and facial. She got a paraffin dip for her hands and feet, and acrylic nail tips with miniature palm tree designs on her ring fingers. At first she thought the designs were not exactly her style, but they eventually grew on her.

She continued going though her list, checking off stopping the mail, calling her parents, and paying the car insurance. She dialed Regina's number at work, got her voice mail and left a message. She then decided to call Sasha. Sasha picked up on the second ring.

"Galaxy Human Resources. This is Sasha. May I help you?"

"Hey girl. I just had to call before I flew out this afternoon."

"Oh, girl, I wish I could go with you," Sasha exclaimed. "I need a vacation bad before I kill one of these employees. There is just too much drama going on in this place."

"Now what's going on and why is there so much drama there? Does anybody do any work around there besides you? Who's steering the ship?" Beverly asked.

"Well, to start off, one of my clients wants to hire another employee from another department. The problem is that it is rumored that they are sleeping together. These rumors have been brewing for months. Of course I can't confront them without any evidence."

"Has anyone seen them together?"

"A few people have, but no one wants to go on the record. If she gets the job, there will be uproar in the department."

"Well, if I were you, I wouldn't say anything. You risk losing quite a bit. You know he's probably not the only one doing it. With the stories you've told me about that company, I wouldn't be surprised if all of your clients had extracurricular activities on a daily basis," said Beverly dryly. "Just stick to doing your job and plead the fifth. So, what's up with you and the guy you met in the bookstore?"

"We went out last week. I really had a great time with him. He's almost too good to be true. I'm just waiting to find something wrong with him."

"Here we go again. Why does something have to be wrong with him? Sasha, why don't you just try living for the moment every once in awhile? He doesn't necessarily have to be *the one*. If he isn't, so be it. That's what wrong with some of you single corporate women who supposedly have these wonderful lives, yet no man. You want a perfect man to one day knock on your door and proclaim he's the one. News flash, Sasha, there is no such thing as a perfect man. You have to take the good with the bad and the bitter with the sweet. I'm sure Marian has told you that at least a time or two."

"Bev, I don't totally live under a rock. I don't expect the perfect man to one day knock on my door and proclaim he's the one.

I don't want to deal with a lot of unnecessary baggage. What's wrong with being a little cautious? I just don't believe everything and everybody."

"How old are you again?" Beverly quizzically asked. "Once you get past thirty, what do you expect? I think you'd better start scooping out high school seniors."

"Ha...ha...ha. Very funny, Bev. Don't start jumping to conclusions." Sasha shifted gears by promptly changing the subject. "Have you heard from Gina?"

"She called me last night. She said she tried to reach you at home, but your line was busy. Were you on the Internet? When on earth are you going to get DSL?" Beverly continued to fling questions without allowing Sasha to answer. "She said her boss was beginning to act a bit strange. They have been working late nights for a project and he got a bit too touchy. She also had noticed that his eyes have been roving."

"Did she tell him to stop?" Sasha questioned.

"She basically tried to shake it off as just an isolated incident."

Sasha sighed. "She really should report it. The company is responsible whether or not they know about it. The law says they should have known. I'll call her today. I certainly don't want her to go through what I went through. I still shudder every time I think about how that idiot got away with what he did to me."

"Excuse me Beverly," interrupted James. "Our temporary from the agency has arrived. I'll get her started."

"Thanks, James. I'll be out in a moment to meet her." Beverly flipped to the page in her planner to recall the name of the temporary worker the agency had promised to send. "Well, Sasha, I need to run. I have a few more things to tighten up before I head to the airport."

"Okay, girl. Have a safe and fantastic trip. Don't do anything, I wouldn't do," Sasha chuckled.

"I'm going to have a great time. I'll be doing exactly what you wouldn't dare do. I'll talk to you when I get back. See ya."

Beverly's attention reverted back to the tasks at hand. She planned to head to the airport in exactly one hour. She once again pictured herself on the beach with a fresh strawberry daiquiri topped with a skewer of cherries, orange and pineapple slices crowned with whipped cream and a miniature pastel colored tropical umbrella. She planned to get more than her groove back.

Chapter 19

It is what it is.
-Terri Dean

"*L*adies *and gentlemen, the captain has illuminated the fasten seatbelt sign. Please fasten your seatbelts and put your tray tables in the upright position. We will be momentarily landing in Aruba.*"

The announcement of the pending arrival in Aruba was like music to Beverly's ears. She took a long gaze out of the window of the 747 and saw the gorgeous aqua blue waters off the coast of her vacation haven waiting to happen. At times, she still was a bit apprehensive about vacationing alone, but since she had done it several times before, it really wasn't a big deal to her. At one point, she was willing to pay for someone to vacation with her and let them pay her later. She decided she wasn't quite that desperate. She had certainly learned a lesson and vowed never to pay for someone else's vacation again. Evelyn was a former friend because she swore she would pay her back for the vacation they had spent together in Las Vegas. After the vacation was over, the payment never came. It dawned on her that during the trip that Evelyn seemed to have plenty of money to play the slots and the black jack tables, but could not pay for her own trip.

After the trip was over and it was time to pay up, Evelyn's calls to Beverly became less frequent. Each time she tried to call her, she was either on her way out of the house or not at home. Beverly had serious thoughts about taking her to small claims court or even more embarrassing to Judge Judy. In her heart of hearts, she knew that the case would have been a little difficult to prove since the agreement was made verbally. After heavily contemplating her dilemma, she finally decided to write the money off when she came to the realization that you can't get blood from a turnip. The disagreement ultimately ended their friendship.

The older couple sitting in the middle and aisle seats next to Beverly dressed in his and her royal blue Bermuda short sets seemed so excited about the trip and each other. They held hands and occasionally exchanged conversation throughout the flight. At one point Beverly was feeling a bit shamelessly jealous, but then became happy for them because it was obvious that they were in love and probably had been that way for sometime. It made her wonder about their secret. With the divorce rate over fifty percent, she figured it had to have been something very special that kept them together.

Beverly could feel the plane's descent. Flying had always made her a little nervous. What used to get to her was that all the people around her were always so calm. She knew that they were just as scared as she was. To her, there was no comparison to the feeling that your plane was going down. Anytime she flew, she reminded herself of what her friend Ella used to say about flying—*once you are in the air, there are no options.* Before each flight, she prayed for a safe trip and a healthy flight crew.

As the plane continued its descent into Queen Beatrix International Airport, Beverly tilted her head back on the headrest, closed her eyes and tried to think back to when she was that happy in a relationship. Every time a pleasant thought came to her, she immediately thought about a painful, negative memory. Each thought gave her an "ah ha" towards her theory why some women suddenly become lesbians—they were wronged by one man too many. She knew she was no where near that type of change in her life, but she felt a little comfort in feeling that she had figured out a mystery.

Beverly opened her eyes and began thinking of how she would spend her time in Aruba. She smiled and marveled at the fact it was a good thing she enjoyed her own company and would have no problem meeting other people. She figured that most folks would be coupled up, but she knew that island men were always quite friendly. As the plane taxied down the runway towards the gate, she readied herself. She briefly powdered her nose and applied a fresh touch of orange sunburst lipstick to her lips.

The wife sitting next to Beverly asked, "Don't tell me you are going to this beautiful island alone, honey. Are you meeting someone in Aruba?"

Beverly felt her expression go awry for a moment and then decided to be polite. She noticed out of the corner of her eye that her mate had taken the opportunity to close his eyes for a moment.

"Well, I couldn't find anyone to go with me this time around and I really needed some R and R."

"A nice pretty woman like you couldn't find anybody? My daughter has the same problem. She say's there are no available men left. They're either married, gay, in jail, or got too much baggage.

They don't make them like they made her Daddy. I guess I am lucky to have found him when I did." The woman's Baltimore accent became more apparent.

"Well," huffed Beverly. "I just try to go with the flow. I decided I wasn't going to actively look anymore. In fact, I'm too busy to look. If it happens, fine, if not, that's fine too."

"I hope you enjoy your visit, sweetie. Who knows, you might just get lucky like that Stella woman."

Beverly smiled. "Thank you. I hope you enjoy your stay as well." She figured the woman had not heard that "Stella" had discovered that her husband was gay. She decided to keep the thought to herself.

The fasten seat belt light no longer illuminated. The clicks of seat belts being unfastened followed by passengers hurriedly removing their luggage overhead made her anticipation of the beach, a cool breeze, and a tasty frozen concoction heighten even further. She instinctively knew this would be the best vacation she could possibly ask for.

The ride from the airport to the resort was brief, yet scenic. It gave Beverly a brief hint of what to expect. Once she arrived at the resort, bellmen were readily available and quickly escorted new guests to their rooms.

"Welcome to the Aruba Grand Beach Resort and Casino," greeted the front desk clerk. His burgundy and gray uniform made him look official. How may I be of service to you?" The smoothness of his Caribbean accent was like a breath of fresh air.

Beverly grimaced, "Reservation for Beverly Brown." She began reaching into her purse to retrieve her MasterCard and driver's license.

"Miss Brown, I see you'll be stayin' ten days with us. I need for you to fill out this card and I will present you with your room key. Will you be needin' any assistance with your baggage?"

"Yes, I'd like that," replied Beverly. She instinctively knew she was going to enjoy her stay. The bright tropical colors of the lobby spontaneously made her feel truly welcomed.

He handed Beverly two duplicate room access cards. "Enjoy your stay, Miss Brown. And if you be need anythin', I mean anythin' at tall, you just let us know." A bellman was readily available and began loading Beverly's bags onto the luggage cart.

"Right this way, please." Beverly noticed a handsome mocha colored face with dramatic brown eyes and a perfect sensual smile. He had a somewhat muscular build, but it was a bit difficult to distinguish under his bellman's uniform. He looked to be in his early thirties. They began walking towards the elevator.

Beverly flirted, "What's your name?"

"My name is Jonah. Is this your first time visiting our beautiful island?"

"Yes it is," Beverly beamed. "I plan to have the time of my life. So far, I'm enjoying the scenery and I can't wait to really explore."

"Tis a shame a nice lady like yourself be travelin' alone."

Beverly was growing weary of the traveling alone comments. "Well, I really needed a break and I don't mind. All I want is some peace and quiet for the next few days."

"Our island offers so many beautiful tings to see. If it was not for the rules, I would show you what the island has to offer."

Beverly's brow was raised. "Well, if you don't tell, I won't tell."

"Tis is worth me losin' me job," asked Jonah as he flashed an enthusiastic smile with a hint of a plea in his eyes.

Without hesitation, Beverly said, "We'll be very discrete. You won't lose your job. Why don't we meet a little later at another location after you get off work?"

Jonah agreed. "I finish at 5:30. Give me some time to go home to change into something a bit more comfortable. We can meet at 7 o'clock at Chili's Bar just up the road a bit."

"I'm looking forward to it," beamed Beverly.

"Me too, pretty lady."

At times, Beverly's "wild child" side as she had called it, reared its head and surprised her. She was not one to settle for the everyday life. As far as she was concerned, life was for the living. After her six months of therapy with Dr. Quincy after Carl's death, she had come to the realization that she was her biggest critic. Through therapy, she was able to focus on her needs as an individual. Sometimes she felt guilty for placing her needs above others, but she figured if she was not good to herself, she could not expect anyone to be good to her.

After unpacking her bags, she drew open the glass doors to the balcony of the suite and gazed dreamily at the ocean view. The scenery was filled with a white sandy beach, coconut trees and the sound of the waves nakedly crashing into each other. It made city life a mere remembrance. She cleared her mind of all outside interferences. She allowed herself to drift to simpler times when she had no worries and time and space had no boundaries.

Her daring side had once again emerged. Sasha and Regina often told her she was crazy for some of her antics. Once she had dated fraternal twin brothers, Jonathan and Jason. Jonathan was an attorney and Jason was a software engineer. Jonathan lived on the East side of town while Jason lived on the West side.

While at Jonathan's on a Saturday evening, he showed her pictures of his family and pointed out Jason as his twin. After the discovery, Beverly decided she was not going to give up a good thing. Deep within her, she knew it was wrong, but she figured neither one of the relationships was serious, so it was fair game.

Granted she had been seeing Jonathan two months longer than Jason, neither one would suffice for the long haul. Jonathan was a homebody while Jason could not get enough of hanging out at Diamond's, a local club in the heart of the city. It dawned on her that it was possible for the three of them to be at the same place at the same time. Baltimore was small compared to other major cities. Frequently, she ran into someone she knew while out shopping or on an outing with Sasha and Regina. They insisted that she would be "busted" for her lack of morals when she least expected it. They were right—it happened when she least expected it.

Jonathan had invited her over for dinner. He planned to put a couple of steaks and marinated chicken breasts on the grill. While they were about to dig in for a succulent meal, Jason appeared out of nowhere. He had decided walk to the back of the house after not getting an answer on Jason's cellular phone and front door and seeing his car in the driveway.

The sight of Beverly startled Jason. His glare at her could have cut through her like a hot knife slicing butter. Jason remained calm and introduced himself as Jonathan's twin. Beverly intensely searched his face to get a hint of what was racing through his mind and wondered if he would disclose her deception.

Jason left after about an hour with Beverly's *secret* in tact. As she surmised, she never heard from Jonathan or Jason again.

Beverly found herself slowly drifting off to sleep as she lounged on the chaise chair and allowed the warm ocean air to gently caress her face. She relished the thought of spending the evening with a younger man. She did bring protection—just in case. Whether something happened or not, she intended to enjoy her vacation one way or another.

Chapter 20

You cannot belong to anyone else, until you belong to yourself.
-Pearl Bailey

Sasha's meeting with Jessica Connors had lasted longer than she had expected. Jessica was the Payroll Manager at Galaxy and had been experiencing issues with one employee who had been habitually late and another employee who Jessica believed was an alcoholic. Both employees had been at the company for at least three years. Although Jessica was new to the organization, she had quickly developed a reputation for being quite stern and strictly followed the book. Any deviation from "the plan" was not acceptable in Jessica's eyes. Jessica stood a petite five feet tall, yet her personality was as bold as any mountain. Her short, blond, boyish low maintenance hair cut gave her more time to focus on the more important things in life.

"Let me get this straight, Sasha," said Jessica in a sarcastic tone. "Are you telling me that I can't fire those two idiots right at this moment just because I have not documented any of their behavior? It's not my fault that their former manager didn't keep good records. Hell, she didn't keep any records. All I know is that Becky can't seem to get to work on time and Rita comes in smelling like a distillery. On top of that, they're poor workers. As far as I am concerned, they are no good to me or my department dead or alive."

"Jessica, have you confronted these employees?" responded Sasha in an extremely annoyed voice. She attempted to hide her growing discontent with the situation at hand. She and Jessica had been going back and forth on the Becky and Rita issues for forty-five minutes. Sasha felt as if she had been talking to a brick wall.

"Confront them? Why should I have to confront them? When someone is an employee, my expectation is that they'll come to work on time, work a productive eight hour day, and then go home. The next work day, I expect the same and they come back the same way they left. When I come to work, I don't want to hear about anybody's personal problems. All I want to hear is that the work is done and the deadline has been met. Nothing more, nothing less. I am so sick and tired of being a professional baby sitter, Sasha. I hope that's not why Galaxy hired me."

Sasha continued to feel drained from her meeting with Jessica. It was only 9:30 a.m. The pain above her temples loudly called out for a dose of Tylenol.

"Jess, you need to talk to these employees to find out exactly what is the problem. If need be, refer them to the Employee Assistance Program, particularly in Rita's case. It's up to Becky if she wants to go. As for Rita, we can send her for drug testing. If she tests positive, she has no choice but to get treatment and go to counseling as a condition of her employment. If she refuses to go, we'll terminate her employment. As far as the performance issues, put them on a performance improvement plan for thirty days. If there is no improvement, then you can terminate them. The important thing here is that you document your conversations and any events related to their performance just in case they try to sue us if they are terminated."

"Thirty days is a long time, Sasha."

"Jess, I realize that, however, part of my job is to protect you and the company. We have to have the appropriate documentation or we won't have a leg to stand on." Sasha slipped a gaze at her watch. At that point, she had been trying to reason with Jessica for over an hour.

"Alright. I guess I'll have to deal with those two." As Jessica rose to leave, a big sigh of relief hit Sasha. Jessica's impromptu visit was somewhat expected. It seemed that Jessica had issues every since she had arrived. Jessica's military background mirrored her management style. Many of the employees had been used to doing their own thing under the management of Karen Dawson, the department's former manager. Sasha had heard through the grapevine that Karen had become quite lax in her duties during the last year of her employment with the company because she was closing in on her long awaited to retirement. Her laxness was now causing much havoc for the department and Sasha. Jessica was determined to do whatever it took to get the department back on track. If it meant firing everybody in the department and starting all over with new employees, she would do it. Sasha's biggest hope was that Jessica's determination to "clean house" would not cause any litigation to potentially add to her overwhelming workload and employee relations issues.

As Sasha reached for her desk phone, she was interrupted by another impromptu visit. This time it was Craig Lavalle. He was a twenty-seven year old computer programmer who had been with Galaxy for four months. He would stop to talk with Sasha any opportunity he could get. Sasha had begun to think that he actually had a crush on her. His six feet tall, fit, muscular frame leaned gallantly in her office doorway.

"Hi Sasha," said Craig, in his bad imitation of Barry White's deep and soothing voice. "How is your day going?" Craig impulsively licked his lips and grinned.

"As well as can be expected Craig. And how are you?" Sasha tried her best not to be annoyed by another interruption. After all, her job was to serve the employees of the company.

"Not bad. Not bad at all," said Craig as he eyed Sasha as if his life depended on it. "You know we ought to go out to dinner sometime. It will be my way of thanking you for reviewing my résumé and getting me hired."

"Craig, that's not necessary. I am just doing my job. They pay me to be nice to everybody," Sasha smiled. At the same time, she wished Craig would go on his merry way.

"No really, I want to do something nice for you."

"Craig, really you don't have to do anything." At that moment, Sasha's telephone rang. Craig mouthed, "I'll catch up with you later." Sasha felt saved by the bell.

"Galaxy Human Resources. This is Sasha Grant. May I help you?"

"Yes you may. You may help me by joining me at a basketball game tonight." It was unmistakably Darrell.

"Hi Darrell. What a nice surprise," smiled Sasha. Jessica and Craig's annoying visits were quickly forgotten. "How's it going?"

"Great. I'm not complaining. I know this is short notice, but one of my frat brothers was supposed to be going to the game with me tonight. He can't make it. I thought you'd like to go. The Wizards and the Miami Heat are playing. The game is sold out."

Sasha could not name one player from either team if her life had depended on it. She understood the basics of the game of basketball, however, that was secondary to the fact that she wanted the chance to spend some time with Darrell.

"Darrell, I would love to go. Where shall we meet?"

"Sasha, I hope you know me a little better than that. I'll come pick you up from your house. Can you be ready by 6:30? The game starts at 8."

Sasha was somewhat shocked by Darrell's response, but was pleased that she was learning about his caring side.

"Darrell. Really it's no problem. It might be easier if I just meet you at the arena."

"Sasha, you are giving me a hard way to go. I asked you out. I think it would be quite inconsiderate of me to have you meet me at the designated place for our date. Believe me, my mother raised me to be a gentlemen. She also taught my dad a thing or two."

Sasha smiled. "You win, Mr. Payson. I'll be ready at 6:30," said Sasha.

"See you then, sweetie. Bye." said Darrell.

"Bye."

Darrell's call had made Sasha's day. He had called her sweetie. That was the best thing he could have possibly said at that moment. There was something about Darrell that made Sasha forget about all of the troubles and issues of the rocky start of her day. His soothing voice was like a calming sea and his demeanor was like a smooth melody playing softly. *Hurry up 5 o'clock!*

◎◎◎

The arena was packed, the crowd was loud, and the excitement of basketball fueled the energy of the players. Sasha and

Darrell arrived at the arena thirty minutes before tip off and had just enough time to get snacks from the concession stand and find their seats.

"These are great seats, Darrell," commented Sasha.

"My client gave the tickets to me. It was the least he could do for making me burn the midnight oil for the past few weeks."

Sasha was beginning to feel more comfortable with the crowd and the euphoric atmosphere. She could not possibly sit in her seat looking prim and proper as Darrell's obvious love of the game and vocal outbursts for the Heat came alive before her eyes. The ten muscularly built bodies ran up and down the court effortlessly. Even with all of their valiant efforts, the Wizards were in the middle of being pounded by the Heat. They definitely needed some magic. Although she was an impartial spectator, she decided to cheer for the Wizards since it was a hometown crowd. The sporting event was somewhat an uneasy fit at first as she couldn't remember the last time she attended a professional basketball game. The last professional sports event she had attended was last year at Camden Yards in Baltimore for a baseball game between the Orioles and the New York Yankees. She knew she could still name at least ten players from the Orioles. She felt somewhat of a relief as the buzzer signifying the end of the first half of the game sounded. She wanted to minimize her lack of knowledge of the players to Darrell as much as possible.

"I see you are a Wizards fan, Miss Grant," said Darrell as he put his arm around her. She feared his next question. "So tell me, how long have you been a Wizards fan?"

"Oh, I have been a fan for as long as I can remember," Sasha fibbed. "You know the Wizards were called the Bullets quite a while ago. Even before that, they were in Baltimore and were called the Baltimore Bullets." Sasha grinned and wanted to give herself a pat on the back for remembering that piece of sports trivia.

"Hmmm. I'm impressed. Beauty, brains, and a sports fan. So, what do you think about Mugsy Boggs' game tonight? He's probably the best player the Wizards have at this point."

"Oh, Mugsy is the bomb," responded Sasha.

"Miss Grant, I must inform you that you have been busted. Mugsy Boggs has not played for the Wizards or Bullets, for that matter, in years."

Sasha began laughing and nudging Darrell's arm. "I'm sure that you could tell that I really don't follow basketball, let alone know some of the players. I really don't appreciate being the butt of your jokes, Mr. Payson."

Darrell replied, "I just wanted to see how far you would go with your little charade. I must admit—you are good."

Sasha gleamed and said, "Excuse me, but I take pride in my knowledge of sports. We'll have to go to a football game. I'll just have to start my research early."

"Yeah, you do that," said Darrell. Sasha's great sense of humor highlighted his comfort level with her. He had to give her an "A" for her efforts.

Sasha excused herself to go to the ladies room. As usual, the line for the ladies room was ten times as long as the nearly nonexistent line for men's room. Obviously a man had designed the arena, she thought.

While waiting for Sasha to return, Darrell reviewed his program. He was glad that she was available on such short notice. At times, she was not very vocal during the game; however, he chalked that up to her not being very familiar with neither the game nor the players. Nevertheless, he enjoyed being with her and she was actually better company than his frat brother would have been.

"Miss me?" asked Sasha as she returned to her seat. Darrell noticed that she had reapplied her sheer pink lip gloss and powdered her nose.

"Of course I did. I kept your seat nice warm for you," said Darrell, as he welcomed her back with his sensuous smile.

The second half of the game was uneventful. The Heat won as expected by a wide margin. The hometown crowd went home with hopes that the Wizards could perhaps win the next one.

◎◎◎

The drive back to Baltimore on the beltway was smooth and easy. The heavy traffic from the game quickly disappeared as the spectators went their separate ways. The comfort of Darrell's passenger seat molded Sasha perfectly. Once again, it was a great spot for her to be in--the comfort of Darrell's presence.

"The Heat is the best thing that ever happened to basketball," boasted Darrell. "Shaq is the glue that holds that team together."

"True, but he definitely has goals that go beyond basketball. Mark my words."

"Oh, are we making a prediction?"

"I guess you could say that. It wouldn't surprise me if he started another venture of his own."

"You just might be right, Sasha."

Darrell pulled easily into Sasha's driveway. She turned to him and touched his hand. For a brief second her boldness surprised her. His large, smooth, warm hand melted her like butter on a stack of hot cakes.

"Would you like to come in for something to drink? I have soda, juice, tea, and coffee."

"I'd like that."

Sasha and Darrell enjoyed a hot cup of tea while they sat on the living room sofa. Darrell sat on one end of the sofa, and Sasha sat on the other. The lighting of the living room and the smooth sounds of Bob Baldwin's latest music project provided a warm, soothing atmosphere.

Darrell reached over and picked up the copy of Susan Taylor's, *Lessons in Living*, from the cocktail table and flipped through a few of the pages.

"Did you enjoy this book?" inquired Darrell.

"I enjoyed it immensely. It helped me to put a lot of things in life into perspective. Sometimes you need to get another person's viewpoint to help you sort things out."

"I know exactly what you mean. I really miss talking to my Dad about lots of stuff. Now I primarily rely on my brother and frat brothers for advice." After taking a sip of his tea, Darrell paused for a moment. "Sasha, what makes you tick?"

Sasha was somewhat stunned by Darrell's question. The puzzled look on her face made him offer a clarification of what he meant.

"What makes you the person who you are? What are your dreams? Where do you see yourself in the next five years?"

Darrell's barrage of questions put Sasha on the spot. It had been a while since she had faced having to explain herself or her being to anyone. The look in her eyes said it all. He wanted to know about the woman behind the career.

"Gee, Darrell, you can't get any more pointed than that," said Sasha. The lighting from the room on Sasha's face made her eyes dazzle even more. Her pearly smile had Darrell temporarily hypnotized.

"To be honest, I can be a quiet person. My job requires me to be outgoing. My goal is to one day work for myself and be my own boss. I just have not figured out a workable plan to make my move."

"What is it that motivates you?"

"I know that money is a motivator for most people, but not for me. I'm motivated by having a feeling of accomplishment and making a difference."

"Hmmm. Why aren't you attached?" asked Darrell. Sasha was beginning to feel like she was on trial to explain why she existed. It wasn't an uneasy feeling, but she wanted to know his motive for asking.

"Okay. Where is your questioning going, counselor?" Sasha chided.

"I'm just trying to get to know Sasha Grant, the woman. You intrigue me. I have not met anyone in a long time that I look forward to talking to and being with. I hope my questions aren't making you feel awkward."

"No, not at all," responded Sasha in a concerned tone. She turned the tables on him. "Tell me about you. What makes you tick?"

"Well, I'm content. I enjoy being a financial planner, but the job is not my life. Over the past few years, I've gotten involved in the community and have done more activities with my frat brothers. Since my parents and sister's deaths, it really hit home to me that life is far too short. No one knows when their time is up. My goal is to make every moment worth it."

It appeared to Sasha that Darrell seemed to have it all together. He had goals and a purpose. She wondered why he had no steady girlfriend or a wife for that matter.

"So, Darrell—tell me this—why don't you have a girlfriend to share your successes? Inquiring minds want to know," said Sasha as she smiled.

"Believe it or not, Sasha, I want the same things out of life you want."

"And what is it that I want out of life, Darrell?"

"You want someone to come home to. You want someone to ask how your day was. You want someone to be there for you."

The truth was beginning to sting and she knew it.
"Darrell, the reason that I am still single is the same reason why so many other women are single. The pool of eligible good men is extremely small these days. I have far too many friends that would settle for a bad relationship rather than have none at all."

"Sasha, you are not the only woman in this world who has experienced a bad relationship," remarked Darrell.

"Darrell, in my thirty-six years of living, I have never received flowers on Valentine's Day. I have never been on vacation with a guy. God knows I get tired of always vacationing with my girlfriends. For once in my life, I'd like to experience a slow dance. Let me stop. I know I am sounding like a whining baby."

"No, you don't sound like a whining baby. You sound like a woman who has been hurt. I seriously get your drift. Men get their feelings hurt too. Women don't have a monopoly on that. The important thing is that you don't let any hurt of the past stop you from opening your heart to great possibilities."

Darrell's comments were like a breath of fresh air. Even if nothing serious came out of their relationship, he had at least begun to prove to her that some men had feelings.

"I realize that, but it's easier said than done." replied Sasha. "I don't even want to get started." The moment the words exited her mouth, she wished she hadn't said them.

Darrell gazed at his Movado watch. It was half past 11 p.m.

"I guess I'd better hit the road. Some of us have to go to work in the morning," joked Darrell.

"Indeed we do," replied Sasha.

"As usual Miss Grant, it has been a pleasure to be in your company." He stood up and grabbed his black leather jacket from the loveseat. Sasha stood as well and faced him. Darrell then gently embraced her and kissed her on her forehead. His soft lips pressed upon her skin felt like a feather brushing upon her most intimate places.

"Same here. Drive safely." Sasha walked Darrell to the door and then watched as he left the driveway and sped home.

Darrell Payson was an interesting man indeed. The more she learned about him, the more interesting and mysterious he had become. She had to constantly remind herself not to think ahead and that Darrell was no different from any other man she had crossed paths with in the past. She was determined to stay focused on her career and not allow her imagination to run wild with ridiculous thoughts of her and Darrell. His friendly kiss on her forehead was proof enough that he thought of her only as a friend. If anything, she learned that there were some gentlemen left in the world despite her horrid past experiences and that of other women she knew.

◎◎◎

"This is Mike at the front desk. I have a delivery for you."

"I'll be down in a minute, Mike," said Sasha. She hung up the telephone and briefly debated herself on whether or not to send Rosa down to pick up the package, but then she remembered she had asked her to complete some time sensitive new hire data entry.

As Sasha reached the front desk, her attention immediately diverted to the huge crystal vase with twelve beautiful, long-stemmed, yellow roses. She looked at the security guard and peered for her package.

"There's your package, Sasha," said Mike as he pointed to the large vase.

Sasha was surprised. She could not think of who could possibly be sending her roses. She thanked Mike, picked up the roses and headed for the elevator. While on the elevator, she managed to balance the vase in one arm and opened the card. Her mouth dropped. She was astonished and felt a gush of warmth in her heart. The card read: *Today is your Valentine's Day. I hope you are having a good one. Darrell.*

Chapter 21

If you are on the road to nowhere, find another road.
-Ashanti proverb

Darrell gazed at the office wall clock. It read 4:57 p.m. He was glad that the work week was finally coming to a close. He had endured a long week of meetings with clients and sales presentations to several organizations. He was looking forward to spending more time with Sasha over the weekend. In the short time he had known her, his fondness for her steadily grew with every moment they spent together. Each time they had a date, he discovered something new and unusual about her. He noticed that she had become quite talkative at times. A part of the excitement of being with her was that he never knew what she was going to say. He found her wide array of interests intriguing. He often caught himself thinking of her at the most inopportune moments. On a few occasions, he found himself not totally listening to his clients and had to ask them to repeat what they had been saying.

As Darrell was updating a file on a new client, he was interrupted by two of his colleagues.

"Hey, D," said Jared. Jared had been a financial planner with the firm for six years, married, and had a three-year old daughter. He could have passed for Darrell's slightly younger brother. "Are you rolling with me and Victor for happy hour at Don and Mike's?"

"Oh, man. I almost forgot," said Darrell. "I've been so engrossed this week. Let me tie up a few things and I'll be ready to go. I'll meet you over there in about twenty minutes."

"Alright. We'll be waiting," said Jared.

Victor stood next to Jared. His thin build, black framed school boy glasses and unassuming demeanor made him look geekish to the world.

"I can't believe the wife is letting you hang out on a Friday night. Did she kick you out or something?" joked Victor.

"Not hardly," said Jared shooting him a sly look. "Kiana and Jessi went to visit one of Kiana's friends from college in Cleveland for the weekend. Just because I'm married doesn't mean I have been sentenced to jail. Kiana and I have a great relationship."

"Yeah, right man," shot back Victor.

Victor was normally a man of few words. Unless it was business, he really didn't have much to say. He had been divorced for five years and had not dated much since that time. Darrell and Jared tried to get him back into the dating scene, but Victor had been a little resistant to change. They encouraged him to update his wardrobe and change his approach. They noted that Victor knew his stuff regarding the business world, but was clueless when it came to women. He was a long-term project in the making.

Darrell began clearing his desk. He had made quite a few notes on Erika Bellamy's file regarding her investment portfolio. If she wanted to retire before age sixty-five as she had stated during their meeting, she had a lot of saving to do for quite sometime.

He could not help but notice Erika's flirtatious actions and wondered if she was naturally that way. She was so different from Sasha and wondered if they were really friends. He could not help but notice Erika's seductive voice changes and her overstuffed bosom spilling over in her overly tight spandex dress. The red dress was at least two sizes too small. Her breasts were probably screaming, *we can't breathe*. Every time she talked, he could hear the breathiness in her voice. Throughout their meeting, she made it clear she wanted his help in other ways. He simply tried to divert her attention to her finances in a firm, yet professional manner. It was not the first time a woman or man for that fact, tried to come on to him during the course of business. Each time, he politely explained to them that he was about business. The males who approached him were immediately told that his door did not swing that way. If the behavior continued, he told them that he would not do business with them. Each time those instances occurred, he informed his manager of what had happened, just in case it came back to haunt him. He did not want to end up with a fate like his former peer, Harold Hughes.

After Harold had been secretly dating a client, she turned the tables on him and alleged that Harold had sexually harassed her. The client sued the firm. The firm decided to offer a settlement to avoid costly court costs. Harold was subsequently dismissed and had been blacklisted by every firm in the local area.

After Darrell shut down his computer, he grabbed his British tan leather portfolio and headed for Don and Mike's on the Waterfront. It was a relief to finally get some well deserved down time.

◎◎◎

Jared waved as he saw Darrell enter the bar. It had been an office favorite for happy hour for years. Darrell immediately noticed that quite a few people had the idea of spending the evening there to unwind. The crowd consisted of professionally dressed men and women in suits with drinks and relaxed looks on their faces. It was indeed Friday.

"Hey, man. We thought you had changed your mind," greeted Jared. Our man Victor is on his second drink already. He's been checking out the honey in the hot red spandex dress over there. He might be up for the challenge tonight."

Darrell glanced to the right to check out the woman who had been eyeing them. He immediately shook his head in disbelief. It was Erika.

"Damn. I don't believe this," Darrell commented. "That's one of my new clients, Erika Bellamy. She's one of Sasha's friends. She came on to me today."

Victor began to look disgusted. He often thought of Darrell as a pretty boy who seemed to attract women like bees to honey. It didn't matter—old, young, fat, skinny, married, single—they wanted him. He knew he could treat a woman right if only he had only been given a chance. His former wife Carolyn didn't know what a good thing she had. He suddenly gulped the remainder of his rum and coke.

"D, can you believe it? She's walking over here," exclaimed Jared. "Her walk has ho written all over it."

"Good evening gentlemen," said Erika as she approached the threesome. "Fancy meeting you here, Mr. Payson." Darrell figured she had overheard them briefly talking about meeting at Don and

Mike's after work and wanted to continue her pursuit. He noticed the distinct, strong, pungent odor of cigarettes, hard liquor, and buffalo wings on her breath. He also noticed that she was a bit wobbly on her feet. She immediately made room for herself at the booth with the three men. She sat next to Victor who did not seem to mind.

"So do you think you'll be able to help me Darrell?" Erika slurred. She immediately put her fifth Sea Breeze to her lips for a long swig. It was evident that she had had more than enough to drink. Victor noticed that Erika's left hand had somehow managed to graze his right leg. He could feel her long manicured nails drag across his micro knit pants. For some reason, he and his manhood did not seem to mind.

"Well, if you follow the plan and stick to a budget, you can retire somewhat in a little comfort," responded Darrell. He and Jared noticed that Victor's demeanor had changed—he appeared even more relaxed. They could not tell if it was the drink or Erika's presence.

"I haven't been here in a while. I just decided that I needed a drink before going home." Erika's speech had become more slurred. She was becoming beyond drunk.

Darrell looked at his watch. He had had about enough of Erika for one day.

"Well, I need to head home. I have quite a few things to do over the weekend." Darrell figured this was his opportunity to exit and leave Erika.

"Man, you haven't even had a drink," said Jared.

Annoyed, Darrell responded, "I really need to leave," as he threw a look to Erika.

As Darrell got up, Erika pursued him, lost her balance, twisted her ankle, and fell to the commercially carpeted floor. On her way down, she hit her head on the chair occupied by an older gentleman at the adjacent table. Darrell and Victor helped her up. Jared assisted by picking up the contents of her handbag, which had spilled on the floor and placed them back into her bag.

Victor asked Erika, "Are you okay?"

Erika put her hand to the side of her right temple. She suddenly felt a throbbing pain on the spot where she hit herself. Despite her drunken state, she instantly knew that the spot would surely become an unattractive lump.

"I'll be okay. I just feel a bit woozy. Between the drinks and hitting my head, I don't feel so great right now." Her speech was no longer breathy. She turned to Darrell. "Darrell, do you mind taking me home?"

Darrell wanted to refuse, but felt that was not the gentlemanly thing to do. It was obvious that she had far too much to drink and could not possibly drive herself home. He had no idea what kind of game Erika was up to, but he would have no part of it. He would simply take her home and make sure she got in safely. After one of his best friends from college had been drinking and killed himself by driving off of a bridge after insisting he was okay to drive, Darrell vowed never to take a drunk person's word for it. The guilt of allowing Robert to drive continued to eat at him even after several years had passed. Even though Erika was not someone he was fond of at that particular moment, he could not bring himself to just let her go by the wayside and risk hurting herself as well as others. She didn't live too far from where he lived; he figured it was the least he could do.

"Sure, not a problem," said Darrell reluctantly. Erika took the opportunity to grab Darrell by the arm to help her balance her stance. He decided to ask one of the restaurant workers for a small plastic bag just in case Erika felt the need to regurgitate in his M5. The thought of Erika's vomit on his car's leather interior made Darrell's stomach churn.

As they drove towards east Baltimore, Darrell remembered from Erika's paperwork that she lived on East 25th Street, but not the exact house number. At the traffic light, he glanced at her in her drunken stupor. It was obvious that the alcohol had gotten the best of her. Her loud snoring sounded like a symphony of fireworks on the fourth of July. Darrell tried to wake her to get her house number.

"Erika, what's your house number? I'm on your street." Darrell had become quite annoyed because Erika did not respond. As soon as she opened her eyes, they rolled back to a closed position and the symphony continued.

Darrell sighed in disgust. "I don't believe this," he mumbled to himself. It was getting close to 7 p.m. and he could not take another moment of Erika's lack of responsiveness. He felt he had no choice but to take her to his place. She could camp out in his guest bedroom and leave first thing in the morning. At that point, he wanted the Erika nightmare to end.

Darrell helped Erika out of the car. She could walk, but not without help. She leaned heavily on his arm as he escorted her into his house. On the way, one of her pumps slipped off. He did not notice she was minus one shoe until she began limping. He sat her down on the charcoal gray leather sofa in the family room while he backtracked to retrieve it.

When they finally reached the guest room, Erika collapsed on the comforter-covered mattress while trying to pull Darrell towards her. When her arms grasped the air, she began to whine to him about how sorry she was and how she just wanted to be loved. Undressing her and providing something more comfortable for her to wear was out of the question. He simply ignored her by exiting the room and closing the door behind him. When her whines turned back into a symphony of snores once again, he figured she was down for the count. First thing on Saturday morning, he planned to take her home followed by dismissing her as a client on Monday morning. He debated whether or not to tell Sasha about her friend, but immediately decided it was none of his business. He simply wanted to forget Erika Bellamy—she was truly like one of those reoccurring bad dreams with no end—they just simply pick up where they last left off.

Chapter 22

In a moment of decision, the best thing you can do is the right
thing to do. The worst thing you can do is nothing.
-Theodore Roosevelt

As the sun began to peer through the white aluminum mini
blinds, Sasha slowly began to awaken from her slumber. She
topped off Friday evening with a Seagram's wild cherry wine cooler
and a bag of microwave popcorn. She knew Marian would cringe if
she knew that had been her dinner. Nevertheless, the light snack was
just enough to knock off the hunger pangs without making her feel
stuffed. At times the wine cooler tasted like a stronger version of
kool-aid until she slowly began feeling the relaxing effects of the
concoction. Generally, one or two coolers would do it for her. Over
the years, her tolerance for alcohol never changed—she had a one to
two drink maximum.

Sasha's body clock automatically woke her up when the sun came up on the weekends. This was a habit she had maintained for years. She immediately thought of Darrell and their plans for Saturday. She had not talked with him in a couple of days. She felt a hint of disappointment, but was looking forward to spending time with him. Both had been busy with travel and meetings. She was looking forward to a fun filled day at the Maryland Zoo in Baltimore, the National Aquarium, and the ESPN Zone. She did not have to check her calendar for the time he would pick her up. Their meeting time had been etched into her mind.

As she entered the kitchen, she noted it was 6:45 a.m. and a bit early to call anyone on a Saturday morning except for her parents. It amazed her how early they would get up and for no good reason. It wasn't like they had jobs to go to on a regular basis. Both had retired early and were enjoying every moment of a life of leisure.

Sasha figured she would get a jump on straightening up around the house followed by a shower and breakfast. She anxiously decided she would call Darrell around 10:00 a.m.

After her second cup of tea around 10:05 a.m., Sasha picked up the receiver and dialed Darrell's number. The line was picked up after the fourth ring.

"Hello."

Sasha could not speak.

"Hello," the annoyed voice repeated. "Is anyone there? Hello." The person answering the phone looked at the caller ID box which displayed Sasha's name and telephone number. "Oooooo, Darrell baby," the voice on the other end of the receiver breathed seductively. "We can continue that a little later."

The voice sounded very familiar to Sasha and it was clear that she wanted Sasha to hear what was going on at the moment. The voice distinctively sounded like it belonged to Erika Bellamy.

"Well, who ever the hell you are, my man and me do not have time for your games," snorted Erika. Her poor use of the English language had become more evident.

"Who is this!" shouted Sasha.

"Excuse me, but you called here. I'm guessing you wanna speak with Darrell. Unfortunately, he is not available to take your call."

Sasha took a deep breath before speaking. She was sure it was Erika.

"Erika, why are you at Darrell's house?"

"You must be some kinda stupid, Sasha. Obviously, if you were here, you wouldn't be asking me that dumb ass question." Erika bragged, "News flash. It was the best I ever had. I could feel that thang in my chest. Too bad you'll never experience *that* with Darrell." Sasha could picture Erika's smirk.

After Erika's comment, Sasha immediately hung up the telephone. She chose to put an immediate stop to Erika's humiliation. She had had enough of Erika as well as Darrell for that matter.

As she stood in the middle of the kitchen floor, Sasha began feeling a burning sensation throughout her body. It started at the top of her head and radiated to the tips of her toes. The nauseous feeling in the pit of her stomach began to bubble. She let out a blood-curdling scream as if her life was about to end. Her first instinct was to call Darrell back and give him a piece of her mind. She was so angry she could feel microscopic beads of sweat forming across her forehead.

Her furious demeanor began to take over as she closed her eyes and began feeling light headed. She dropped to her knees, lay on the kitchen floor and began crying like a baby lost in the wilderness with no place and no one. She felt disconnected from the world and could not believe what was happening to her. The confines of home made her feel shallow and filled with gloom as she was once again left alone to wallow in her misery. She wanted to put herself out of her pain and find solace somewhere.

Sasha never thought of going the suicide route over a man, but for a brief moment she just wanted to die. She told herself to get herself together and to simply suck it up. She then tightly curled herself into a ball and began rocking on the white ceramic kitchen floor. The tears began rolling like a dam had opened up allowing the water to flow on its own. As she held herself and rocked, her spirit became solemn and broken. Her stomach continued to churn as the physical pain of rejection began to seep into her heart. She called herself stupid for believing that Darrell would treat her with respect. Her mind quickly began building up hate for him. She could taste the hate that began to boil within her. Her spirit began to wrestle with her heart.

Damn that Erika. What a bitch! Sasha began picturing Erika and Darrell together. It had only been four months since Sasha and Darrell had met. She surmised that Darrell really only wanted one thing out of their relationship—the booty—and that she was just moving too slowly. Erika was willing to go after Darrell with the rigor of a race horse trying to win the Belmont for the Triple Crown.

As Sasha continuously sobbed, her mind fought back and told her to get herself together. She picked herself up from the floor and headed for the powder room. She looked at the reflection in the mirror. Her eyes and face had become swollen and her hair looked as if she had been in a catfight. She turned on the faucet and splashed cold water on her face. As she continued to gaze into the mirror, the steady tears began stinging her face. She regretted looking forward to spending time with Darrell all week. She shook her head in disbelief that he would even entertain the likes of Erika. She figured Erika was every man's type—whore.

She could not figure out if she was angrier with Darrell or with herself. To her, he fit the typical male dating pattern: caring, romantic, and easygoing. After the intimacy, things change. The challenge is gone for them. They move on to the next prey. Luckily, he had not gotten that far.

She set in her mind that the incident with Erika would not destroy her and vowed not to let Darrell stay in her mind. She thought back to the times with Jordan. Her mind lingered on what they had before he rejected her and how the hurt made her an emotional wreck. Even after it had been months since they had spoken, she still cried at those moments when she longed to have a date or just experience some male company. Her mind still went back to him. Darrell almost made her forget about Jordan. She still wondered who Jordan was with and what she could have done differently to make the relationship last.

Sasha allowed herself to once again reminisce about another past potential relationship. Shawn came to mind. She met him through a mutual friend. He needed help with revamping his résumé in order to advance his career. She found her initial telephone conversation with him quite intriguing. He was 27, had a master's degree, earned $80,000 a year, loved athletics, was single, had no children, and none on the way.

The masterpiece Sasha created for him was one of her best revamps of a résumé ever. Shawn expressed his gratitude with her work and insisted that they meet for lunch. Since she lived in Baltimore and he lived in Northern Virginia, they mutually decided to meet conveniently in Washington, DC. Shawn emailed a picture of himself in his Air Force reserves uniform standing in front of his white Escalade. She allowed her imagination to run wild. His physique spoke that he had it all together—he was tall, had broad shoulders, and strong, masculine features. The smoothness of his mahogany skin literally left her breathless for a few moments.

Sasha and Shawn finally met a few weeks later on a Saturday at B. Smith's Restaurant at Union Station. When they met, they greeted each other with a hug. Sasha did not want to let go--it felt good to be in a man's arms after a long hiatus. Over lunch, they talked about their respective interests and their hopes and dreams for the future. Their encounter ended with a "take care" and a hug. They continued to keep in touch via telephone and email for the next few months.

Her next in person interaction with Shawn was four months later in San Francisco. She was in San Francisco on business for her former company. Shawn was there during the same time period for an interview with a software company.

She invited Shawn to dinner at a restaurant at her hotel. After dinner, she invited him to her room to share a bottle of Merlot. They drank the wine, talked, and watched TV. The more she allowed the wine to soothe her senses, the six years between them slowly dissipated. Shawn sat in the reclining chair as Sasha lay across the bed. She remembered thinking--*he is two feet away from a horny woman and a king-sized bed. What is he waiting for?* Regina had insisted that she bring some protection just in case she met someone while she was in town. Sasha told her she knew that she was not that kind of woman. Regina told her to still be prepared.

As she lay across the bed, she tried hinting by adjusting her body to say, "come hither." She then tried looking seductive. After no response, she tried arching her body to show how much it wanted to feel his touch. Still no response. Shawn was not budging. He initiated the end to the evening by stating he had to get back to his hotel room so he could be well rested for his interview. To Sasha's disappointment, their evening ended with a friendly hug goodbye.

The hug left her with memories of what could have been. Ironically, two years later, Shawn told her that he wanted to get intimate her that evening. She figured it was a little too late to recreate the "San Francisco Package" as they had nicknamed it.

She later heard that Shawn was living in Santa Monica, California with his wife and new baby. She felt her efforts to help Shawn career wise ended up assisting in grooming him for another woman. She kept telling herself that circumstances such as those are a part of life to help one grow. She considered it as another lesson learned.

Determined not to feel sorry for herself once again, she tried lifting her spirits by telling herself it was Darrell's loss, not hers. She thought back to the sermon she heard preached by Reverend Isaacs, entitled, "Living with Rejection". It was a spur of the moment thing when she had decided to attend church that day--it was one of those Sunday mornings she felt compelled to worship—things were not going right and she had felt empty inside. Bedside Baptist just was not cutting it. Bedside Baptist is what she referred to when she decided she was too tired to attend church and watched church services on TV. She had become a regular of national religious programs with Joel Osteen and Creflow Dollar as well as local Baltimore pastors.

It had been quite a while since she had attended church and it had crossed her mind that perhaps she had been removed from the church's active membership records and placed on the inactive list. After she heard "Living with Rejection" for the first time, she felt that the sermon hit so close to home that she decided to purchase audio taped copies for herself as well as a couple of her friends who had experienced bad relationships and were still hung up on good for nothing men. She searched for the tape in her cassette storage box amongst her very small collection and found it secured in its case.

She placed the tape in the cassette player, hit the play button, and retreated to the living room sofa to recline. She closed her eyes to think of good, relaxing thoughts. She wanted to forget Darrell, but she knew realistically that it would not happen overnight. As her body relaxed, she listened to the all so familiar tape that told of using rejection as a stepping-stone to something that is much better from God.

After listening to the tape, Sasha actually felt better. She decided to take a nice long shower, get dressed and get out of the house. Since it had been a while since she had spent time with Tiffany and Tyrique, she decided she would call Regina to ask if she could take them to the movies. She was sure there was some children's movie playing somewhere. They often made her laugh with their innocence and mischievous ways.

She thought and held on to hope that *this too shall pass.*

Chapter 23

There are three kinds of people in the world;
those who make things happen,
those who watch things happen, and
those who wonder what happened.
-Unknown

Erika grinned as the dial tone echoed in her ear. It was the sound and feeling she had longed for. She finally had the upper hand over Sasha. *So much for Miss I got it going on. Serves her right. Going around thinking she's better than anyone else.* Revenge was feeling awfully sweet to her.

She took a moment to reminisce. When she and Sasha worked together in downtown Baltimore, Erika was the department's administrative assistant. As a part of her responsibilities, she performed administrative duties for Sasha. At times she felt that Sasha had talked down to her when assigning her work. Sasha was very particular about how she wanted things done. She would often hand work back Erika because of typographical errors. Typos to Sasha were like a slap in the face. She vowed she never would forget the time Sasha talked to their manager about Erika's work. At the time, Erika had been having issues with her boyfriend. The stress of being in a relationship with Larry was beginning to reflect in her work. She and Larry fought just about every night. If it was not about him staying out late, it was about his babies' mamas calling at all hours of the night. She often thought she was far too forgiving to him, but she held onto him until she could do better. To her, having no man was not an option.

After meeting with the department manager and Sasha, Erika was placed on a performance improvement plan. She had exactly thirty days to get her act together or she faced termination from the company. If she thought she could have gotten away with it, she wanted to give Sasha a good old-fashioned ass whipping for not understanding her plight. She couldn't afford to be unemployed, especially with Larry's erratic employment history. She knew that she had to start seriously straightening up or start looking for a job elsewhere. Since she had already invested three years with the company, she felt that it would be in her best interest to stay despite her hate for her boss Irene and Sasha. She could fake it with the best of them. Sasha was no better than anyone else. Getting back at her through Darrell was the sweetest revenge. She wanted to savor the moment as if it was the last morsel of strawberry shortcake tantalizing her taste buds and longed for more.

The hate in Erika's mind spoke out once again. "Miss Grant, this is only the beginning of my wrath. You ain't seen nothing yet. There is more where that came from."

◎◎◎

Peace and serenity was once again his. A sigh of relief took over him. For the past ten hours, Darrell had the likes of Erika Bellamy in his home.

The thought of her invading his space made him furious all over again. He had dealt with bold women who had come onto him before, but Erika was different. It suddenly became obvious that she was calculating and had it all planned. Even after he reminded her that he was dating Sasha, she came on even stronger. She made it very clear that she wanted him and if he resisted, he was missing the best thing that could have possibly happened to him.

As Darrell stepped out of the shower to grab a towel, Erika stood before him in the nude. Her hands rested on her hips as if she were posing for a Kodak moment. Her erect nipples pointed in his direction. She startled him for a brief moment. His eyes darted to her ample breasts, covered mound and then to her bloodshot eyes.

"I know you want me, Darrell," Erika breathed.

Darrell quickly wrapped a towel around his lower torso and gave Erika a look of utter disgust. He could feel his temper rise.

"Look, Erika. For the record, I do not want you. Don't take my kindness as a sign of weakness. Believe it or not, I was trying to help you out so you wouldn't kill yourself or anybody else for that matter. I want you dressed and out of my house. I'm calling you a cab."

He grabbed her by the arm and forcefully guided her out of the master bathroom. She tried to break loose, but it was obvious that his grip was much stronger than hers.

"Get offa me!" she screamed. "You're hurting me! How can you even think about dismissing me! You know you want me!" Her body attempted to resist Darrell's strength.

Darrell tried to stay calm. "Get dressed. I want you out of my house right now."

Erika began sobbing as Darrell forced her back into the guest bedroom and slammed the door shut after exiting. She began putting on her rumpled clothes from the night before tripping over one of her pumps. She regained her balance by holding on to the mahogany bed post. She could not believe Darrell was resisting her advances. It had been quite a while since she had been rejected. She knew that most men would jump at the opportunity to be with her. She figured Darrell would come around once Sasha decided not to have anything to do with him ever again. One thing she knew about Sasha was that if a man did her wrong just once, he was history. She never understood why she was so hard on men. She figured it was from that fancy upbringing of hers and the fact that she knew the first time she met her she was a daddy's girl.

After giving Erika a few minutes to get dressed, Darrell opened the door to the guest room without knocking. His harsh stare glared at her as he stood in the door way. He looked good in his royal blue Tommy Hilfiger polo shirt and jeans. Even his angry stare made him look sexy.

"I've called a cab for you. It should be here in about fifteen minutes. I'd appreciate it if you would wait in the living room," Darrell said as he cut a look at her. He could feel the anger continue to rise in the pit of his stomach.

Erika grabbed her purse from the bed. "Well, you'll never know what you missed, Darrell," she remarked as she sashayed past him towards the stairs. She turned back to his dark eyes. "I wonder what Sasha would say if she could see you now," she smirked. "Miss Goody Two Shoes would just die. You know queen bee doesn't like being made a fool of by anyone."

"Erika, if I weren't a gentleman, your ass would have hit the stairs about ten minutes ago. You apparently took my kindness for granted. Not all men want sluts like you. I advise you to quietly wait in the living room for your cab." Darrell turned and walked away. The sight of Erika was physically making him sick. The cab could not get there fast enough.

The honking of the taxi's horn allowed Darrell to exhale a sigh of relief. He ran down the stairs to open the door. Erika appeared motionless.

"Out," Darrell spoke.

Erika slowly rose from the sofa. Her steps were shallow, slow and deliberate. As she stepped onto the exterior cement steps, Darrell stepped just a head of her and walked around to the cab's driver's side.

Darrell handed the cabbie a crisp twenty dollar bill. "This should get her home with plenty to spare. She lives in East Baltimore."

"No problem, mon." The driver's dread locked hair and West Indian accent were quite noticeable.

"Darrell," grimaced Erika. "I had a wonderful time. We must do this again."

"Don't hold your breath," Darrell replied as he slammed the cab door in her face out of disgust.

Darrell walked back and stood in the doorway, focusing on the cab as it drove away. His anger slowly subsided through deep, deliberate breaths. His thoughts went back to Sasha. He figured he would tell her the entire story before Erika got the chance to weave a web of distorted deception. He decided he would tell her as soon as he arrived at her house. This way, he would have the opportunity to set the record straight. He didn't want anything or anybody to interfere with what could possibly be the best thing that ever happened to him.

Sasha had a certain innocence. Her naivety often threw him off guard. For her age, she probably should have been more experienced. It didn't matter to him. All he knew was that he wanted a relationship with her. He wanted to explore her mind, body and soul without boundaries. This would probably take some time, but he felt that she would be worth the wait.

Promptly at 12 noon, Darrell rang Sasha's door bell. He rang it a second time when she did not answer. He saw her peer through the white mini blinds, but she still did not open the door. He then used his cellular phone to call her—his call was forwarded to voice mail after four rings. He became worried and concerned for her safety, so he walked around the back of the house to investigate. He didn't find anything unusual. He turned the knob on the white clear view storm door and discovered it was locked. He then tried to reach her again by calling her from his cellular telephone a second time. This time she picked up.

"Darrell, why are you on my property?" snarled Sasha.

"I thought we had plans for today," replied Darrell.

"I don't know what kind of game you're playing, but I'm no dummy. How dare you even come over here. You are just like the rest of you sorry ass men." Darrell was not used to her talking like that and wondered where she was getting her facts and her attitude.

She continued, "I'm not going to be a part of anybody's harem. It appears that you have women all over. I refuse to be one of them. We don't owe each other a thing. But to deal with someone I know—now that's low. I bet you want to compare the two of us, huh? Okay—let's compare. I have a better than decent job, she doesn't have a pot to pee in or a window to throw it out of because she lives off of men like you. I have morals, she has none. She lies, I don't. She's deceitful, I'm not. So, there's your comparison, Darrell. You think you're this wonderful and a great guy. As far as I am concerned you are a low down, dirty dog. Get off of my property before I call the police. I don't ever want to hear from you again. If you do contact me, I'll consider it harassment and take whatever steps I need to take to make you stop. Trust me; you don't want to go there." He could tell by her serious tone, that she meant business.

Sasha abruptly ended the telephone call with a click followed by silence in Darrell's ear. He shook his head in disbelief.

He closed his flip phone, walked to his car, started the engine and left the area. He wasn't in the mood to go toe to toe with Sasha's wrath. She confirmed his theory that some women had something mental going on upstairs. He had no idea who she was talking about and he was not going to even attempt to understand it. As far as he knew, he had not done anything wrong. He had never seen that side of her before and he wondered why he was feeling like he had taken a left hook out of no where.

Chapter 24

Nothing ever strikes without warning.

-Danny Glover

"Regina, let's say you and I have a real celebration for a great presentation!" Ken enthusiastically said as he entered the office. "The presentation went off without a hitch. They bought the idea hook, line, and sinker!"

"We did it, huh!?" exclaimed Regina.

"Yes, we did and the emphasis is on *we*," replied Ken. "You know I couldn't have done it without you. Just a little hint, but you can look forward to a great bonus at the end of the year and I plan to request a departmental bonus for you within the next week. You really deserve it. I know you have a family and other obligations. I appreciate your sacrifices to ensure a successful presentation. Your computer skills are the bomb as the kids say."

Regina was surprised by Ken's use of slang. Apparently he had been watching more than his share of Black Entertainment Television and Music TV. She figured it was his way of "being down". She savored the praise. Ken was a nice change of pace when compared with the way Michelle treated her. She very seldom received a thank you from her for working overtime or doing excellent work. For the first time in a long time, she felt appreciated by her manager.

"I already took the liberty of making a reservation at the Baltimore Gardens Restaurant and Hotel for 12 noon today," said Ken. "After lunch, we're taking the rest of the day off. I'm actually attending a conference at the hotel over the weekend, so that will give me time to check into the hotel and get prepared for the reception tonight at 6."

"What type of conference?" quizzed Regina.

"Model trains. You have to see it to believe it. They have all types of trains going back to the very beginning. I have collected model trains since I was eight."

Model trains did not interest Regina. She didn't get the connection with a miniature train heading to no where. "Ken, that sounds good. So, I guess we should leave around 11:45?"

"Works for me," replied Ken.

Regina spent the rest of the morning doing some administrative work consisting of filing, making follow up calls, arranging meetings, and responding to emails. Although some of the work was routine, she proud of the fact she did not have the type of job where she had to take work home on a regular basis. Beverly and Regina always complained that there were never enough hours in the day to do what they needed to do. Half the time they would bring work home, they ended up taking the same work back to the office. She thought it was a wasted effort. Generally, when she left work each evening, the work stayed. It was bad enough when Keith had to work on briefings at home. She didn't need to bring work home as well. At least there was some balance on that note.

Regina took a short break from her daily duties. She wrote out her supermarket list, made a hair appointment, and talked to her mother. Every since Sara retired over seven years ago, she made it a point to call Regina at work to catch up at least twice per week. She often had to explain to her that she was working and that Sara needed to find a hobby. As far as her mother was concerned, she already had enough hobbies. Between her activities at the senior center, volunteering at the Fourth Avenue Baptist Church, and occasionally babysitting the neighborhood children, she had more than enough to keep her busy.

Regina finished her morning with a second cup of coffee. She stopped in to see Ken to make sure he did not require any assistance. She patted herself on the back for being able to manage her boss. She chalked up the recent encounter with Ken as her mind being silly. After all, he had a wife and family and was probably just a bit tired. She figured the long hours at the office had finally caught up with him.

Regina stood in Ken's doorway. "Are you ready to roll?"

"Be right there. I just need to hit the send button on this email." After hitting the send button, he rose from his chair and did a slight stretch. Ken's overarching belly protruded from his brown suit jacket. "We can walk the three blocks. Do you mind?"

"Not at all," replied Regina. "I think a little walking before lunch will do us a lot of good."

On the way to the restaurant, Ken and Regina took another opportunity to catch up on their families. They traded 'guess what my kid did' stories with ease. That was one thing they had in common.

"It's not too busy in here, Regina. I'm surprised for a Friday," remarked Ken.

"Well, maybe they went elsewhere. I'm not complaining," commented Regina.

Ken and Regina ordered lunch. She dined on broiled crab cakes with chutney sauce while Ken had a sixteen ounce New York strip steak with a garden salad and baked potato with butter and sour cream. He took the liberty of ordering a bottle of Bollinger Grande Annee champagne to celebrate their success. As they toasted, he took the opportunity to tell her how very much he enjoyed working with her and how pleased he was with her work. The more he worked with her, the more he had difficulty trying to hide his feelings. She was a natural beauty and her nurturing spirit was an eye opener. The Escape cologne she wore on a daily basis made him savor her scent. He looked forward to it everyday. He had asked her what she was wearing because he wanted to buy the same scent for Doris hoping to have the scent at home as well. On Doris, it didn't quite smell the same. In fact, it stank.

"Ken, I need to run to the ladies room. I'll be right back."

Ken intensely watched her walk away until she was no longer within his eyesight. He enjoyed watching her walk. Her strides were elegant, confident and demanded attention.

Ken took the opportunity to come out of his Regina daze. He suddenly realized the opportunity was too good to be true. He looked around the restaurant to see if anyone was looking in his direction. When he felt the coast was clear, he succinctly deposited the white powder into Regina's champagne glass and refilled it. He watched the powder dissolve with raised eyebrows and a smirk on his face. He began to relish his plans taking shape.

Upon Regina's return, Ken said, "Welcome back. I have another toast. Here's to more of the best. The best is yet to come."

"Here, here," responded Regina as she raised her glass. Their glasses met in agreement then resumed their consumption of the champagne.

Ken continued to search her eyes. His research indicated the drug would take full effect within twenty to thirty minutes. They continued small talk as they sipped the last of the champagne.

"Regina, I'll be staying at the Baltimore Gardens Hotel tonight. I have early check in. I've asked the hotel staff to deliver something for you to my room. Before you go, I'd like to get it to you." Ken winked. "They are probably best admired at home."

"What is it?" Regina curiously asked.

"You'll have to wait see it," replied Ken.

After Ken paid the check and tipped the waitress, Regina followed him to the hotel reception area and patiently waited for him to check in. She then followed him into the elevator. Hesitation took over her. She began feeling nauseous and her vision had become blurred. She held on to the elevator railing.

"Regina? Are you feeling alright?" Ken said with some concern in his voice. He knew his plan would be going into effect within minutes.

Regina replied weakly, "I don't feel so well." Ken grabbed Regina by the waist to help her balance. Her purse fell to the floor. He managed to pick it up and assisted her to his room. With the patience of Job, Ken salivated as his plans continued to unfold before his very eyes.

Regina woke up in a daze. *Where am I she thought,* as she stared at the antique white ceiling. The hazy room did not look familiar and smelled of fresh roses. She noticed the huge arrangement of peach roses adorned with sprays of baby's breath and greenery. The wide neck of the vase was encircled with a large white ribbon. She then noticed what appeared to be her bra, panties, slip, pantyhose, and dress strewn across the floor. That's when she realized she was naked under the paisley gold comforter. Her black purse was atop the desk. She knew she should scream, but for the life of her she could not figure out how she ended up in a strange room with no clue as to where, why and how. She noted that her body ached with a strange pain in her lower back and abdomen. That's when she noticed the dried blood on the sheets. She began to cry as she started putting together what could have possibly happened to her. She rose from the bed and placed her unsteady feet on the dark green carpet to begin seeking some non-existent solace. She reached for the room's telephone and noticed the Baltimore Gardens Hotel note pad. At least she knew where she was. The headache and nausea were overpowering, but she was determined to get some help. The realization that some unknown person violated her made her want to vomit. She had feelings of guilt for allowing herself to be placed in such a predicament. She instantly blamed herself.

Regina continued to panic for a moment as she attempted to remember her home number. She had no idea of the time or the day until she gazed at the clock radio which read 11:13 a.m. It dawned on her that the last thing she remembered was having lunch with Ken at the Baltimore Gardens Restaurant. She slowly pressed the buttons on the telephone to dial home.

"Hello," Keith answered.

"Keith, please come get me," said Regina weakly.

"Regina, where the hell have you been!" he shouted. "I have been calling all around town looking for you. I have been calling your mother, your sisters, your friends, and hospitals. Why didn't you answer your cell? Did you forget that you had a family? What the hell is wrong with you!?"

Keith's enraged tone wasn't familiar to her.

"Keith, something terrible has happened to me! I think I have been raped!" Regina cried. "I'm at the Baltimore Gardens Hotel and I have been bleeding. I don't know when or how I got in this room."

"What?!" Keith exclaimed. His tone became less strained. "Someone raped you?" His concern grew. "Okay, okay. Take a couple of deep breaths. What do you mean you don't know how you got there?"

"The last thing I remember is having lunch with Ken."

"What room are you in? Look at the phone panel. It should be listed there. Are you at the Baltimore Gardens Hotel downtown?"

"Yes, that's where we had lunch. I'm in room 1202"

"If that bastard did this to you, I swear I'll kill him with my bare hands. I'm calling 911 for you so they can get you to the hospital. Baltimore Medical is the closest. I'll get Marcy from next door to watch the kids. I'll meet you at the hospital. I'll also call Mom Sara."

"No," sternly said Regina. "I don't want her to know."

Keith was silent. It was no time for arguing. He wanted to get to her as quickly as possible. He grabbed his cellular phone while she was still on the line.

"We'll get through this, baby," Keith said. "Somebody is going to jail for this if I don't kill them first." His voice was filled with emotional pain.

With that being said, Regina knew his word was his bond. Despite the pain, she knew he would do what he said and he said what he meant.

◎◎◎

Keith and Regina held hands as Dr. Adinlewa approached them. She was of African descent and her long braids gave her a distinctive appearance.

"How are you feeling Mrs. Webster?" asked Dr. Adinlewa.

Regina replied, "Well, I've had better days."

Dr. Adinlewa turned to the second page of Regina's chart. "Your urinalysis reveals that you have Rohypnol in your body. This drug is commonly used to facilitate sexual assault. Typical effects of Rohypnol are problems remembering what happened while drugged, lower blood pressure, sleepiness, loss of muscle control, nausea, confusion, difficulty seeing, dizziness, and abdominal pain. Detectives Mulvey and Willowby are waiting to speak with you about your assault. I'll be back once they have finished speaking with you."

Dr. Adinlewa placed her hand on Regina's shoulder. Her touch felt reassuring yet doctor like. The doctor had seen more than her share of rape victims. It was never an easy topic to discuss. Keith then embraced Regina as Dr. Adinlewa exited. He knew Regina's rape would change the woman who he loved and held dearly. Her pain was his pain. He instinctively knew she would need counseling. The pain of telling their family and friends would be nearly unbearable. He worried about the twins and Regina's reaction to them. He wondered if the incident would forever change her nurturing spirit. He looked deeply into her eyes. She knew that they had no choice but to get through the horrific incident together.

"Mr. and Mrs. Webster, I'm Detective Mulvey and this is my partner Detective Willowby." Both detectives extended their hands to Regina and Keith. We'll be responsible for investigating your assault."

Regina was somewhat comforted by the fact that the two detectives were females. They somewhat resembled a polished version of Thelma and Louise.

"Please start by telling us the series of events leading up to your assault," asked Detective Mulvey.

"Well, the last thing I remember is having lunch with my boss Ken Cunningham on Friday. We were having lunch to celebrate the success of his presentation."

"Where does Mr. Cunningham live?" asked Detective Willowby.

Regina replied, "He lives in Columbia. I have an address and phone number for him." Regina retrieved Ken's home phone number from her electronic organizer in her purse.

"Did you at anytime leave the table?" asked Detective Willowby.

"Oh yes, I stepped away for a few minutes to go the ladies room. I was away for about five minutes. When I came back, Ken insisted that we toast again." At that moment, Regina realized that Ken had the opportunity to slip the drug into her champagne.

"What type of relationship do you have with Mr. Cunningham? We found a floral arrangement in the hotel room. The card was addressed to you and signed by someone named Ken."

"He's my boss, no more, no less," remarked Regina. She wondered where the questioning was going. She wanted to remind them that she was the victim, but bit her lower lip and took a deep breath to help control her emotions.

"Has he ever shown any interest in a relationship with you beyond the workplace?" interrogated Detective Mulvey.

Regina hesitated. She had figured in her mind what she was about to say would upset Keith. "Well, once a few weeks ago, Ken touched my back inappropriately. It made me feel uncomfortable, but really didn't think he meant any harm. He's never given me cause that he would hurt me in anyway." Keith's eyes shot back at Regina.

"We'd like to speak with Mr. Cunningham," said Detective Willowby. "We'll consider him as a person of interest."

"I believe he's attending a model train convention at the Baltimore Gardens Hotel," remarked Regina. "At least that's what I recall."

"Can you describe him?" asked Detective Mulvey.

"He's white, about 5' 10", salt and pepper hair, about 275 pounds, brown eyes, wears glasses and has a moustache."

"Well, he shouldn't be too hard to find. We understand the room you occupied was registered to him and he supplied all of his contact information. Right now, he appears to be our prime suspect. Dr. Adinlewa has supplied us with some evidence of the crime. The crime lab has been sent to the room you occupied. We'll be in touch shortly."

The detectives handed Regina and Keith their business cards, told them they would follow up, and then bid them goodbye. They also provided Regina with the number to the Rape Crisis Hotline for counseling. Investigating a rape was never easy. The detectives knew the scars could last a lifetime. The saving grace was that they possibly had a prime suspect within reach. It was just a matter of making the arrest.

Chapter 25

Even if you are on the right track,
you'll get run over if you just sit there.
-Will Rogers

It had been a week since Sasha had any contact with Darrell. During that time, she often thought of him and questioned how he could be so manipulative. She shook her head in utter disgust. She spent what seemed like endless hours analyzing clues to what could have possibly happened. She finally got to the point where nothing logical could explain his behavior. For seven days, she literally shut the world out. She didn't answer her telephone at home. The only calls she returned were to her parents. She figured they would send out a search party if she did not call them back in a timely manner.

Darrell called several times to her house, her cell and her office. She praised the invention of caller ID. He left her several messages asking her to call him. He finally relented and asked her if something was wrong. She had no intention of ever calling him back. When he showed up at her front door after her encounter with Erika, she refused to open the door and told him he had some nerve. He acted as if nothing was wrong. His response perplexed her.

To add insult to injury, Erika continued to make her presence known. Sasha had received numerous calls between 2 a.m. and 5 a.m. The caller ID read "Private Number". The caller simply allowed it to ring until Sasha answered. When she answered, the caller hung up immediately. After more than a few annoying calls, she put a stop to the calls by simply unplugging the telephone. She also received emails at work. Erika wrote to her to explicitly to let her know that she and Darrell had been together. Erika described their "adventures" and told her how "so very sorry" she was that she was out of the picture and Darrell now had a real woman who could please him in more ways than Sasha could ever imagine. Sasha printed out the initial email. She was too embarrassed to let Galaxy's Information Technology department know that she was receiving emails from her nemesis. She deleted the emails from her computer and called the help desk to find out how she could block a specific email address.

Erika did not stop there. Sasha began receiving calls at home from men who stated that her sister told them to call her because she was interested in going out. The men claimed they had Sasha's picture from the Galaxy website and they were eager to meet her in person. She explained to them that she didn't have a sister and they had the wrong telephone number. After several calls from several different men, Sasha figured that no one but Erika could be behind such vicious acts. She had maintained an unlisted and unpublished telephone number to avoid such prank calls.

Sasha took a long, deep sigh before picking up the telephone to call Regina. It had been a while since they had last spoken. She was beginning to feel like her old self and she felt the time was right to get back into the real world. Regina picked up on the second ring.

"Hi Sash. Where have you been? I left you at least three messages in the past few days. Are you that busy at work? You were beginning to make me think you eloped and didn't tell anybody. You must be in love. Nobody hears from you when you're that way."

"Well, it was just another waste. I've been attending my own pity party. Darrell is seeing Erika Bellamy."

"What?! How on earth did that happen? When we all worked together at the insurance company everyone knew she had issues. How did she hook up with Darrell?"

"Your guess is just as good as mine. We were supposed to spend Saturday together. I called his house and she answered. She promptly told me that they were seeing each other. And to top it off, she's been harassing me by phone and email."

"What did Darrell have to say?" responded Regina.

"I don't know and I don't care. Gina, there is nothing that man can say to me. Men are and will always be dogs. I thought he was different. Dumb me. Things were going right along, and then bam—his true colors show. Thank goodness I didn't sleep with him."

"Why didn't you allow him to at least defend himself? There could have been a logical explanation. It could have been a relative and not Erika. Stranger things have happened."

"She identified herself as Erika. As far as I'm concerned, there is no explanation he could possibly tell me to make me believe he's telling the truth. I will just take my losses as they are. Darrell and Erika can rot in hell for all I care."

"Sash, I am not trying to defend what Darrell did or didn't do, but you need to take your own advice and get all the facts and not simply jump to conclusions. Investigate. Ask questions. Use the direct approach."

"Gina, I won't even waste my time. Darrell Payson doesn't exist as far as I'm concerned. Sleeping dogs need to lie. Every time I think about it, I just get angry all over again." Sasha decided to change the topic. She and Regina were getting no where with their debate and she was beginning to get a headache every time Darrell's name was mentioned or came to mind.

"How have you been?" asked Sasha.

In a subdued voice, Regina said, "I have something to tell you. I was drugged and raped by my boss and of course quit my job. The police have an APB out for him. He's been missing every since."

Sasha was stunned. Her woes with Darrell and Erika were minutia compared to the violation Regina had suffered. She felt guilty for even talking about her situation.

"Gina," Sasha said. "I'm so sorry. Here I am pouring my issues out on you. I'm sorry I ignored your phone calls. Please forgive me." Tears began to roll down Sasha's face. Regina could hear the emotion in her voice.

"It hasn't been easy, but Keith has been supportive. I've started seeing a therapist and I'm trying my best to feel like my old self again. Sometimes I look at the kids and I just stare at them. They keep me going. I want to feel better because of them. I'll tell them one day, but they're just too young to understand. Mama is devastated. At first, I did not want to upset her for fear that she would lose it. One day I just broke down and the floodgates opened. I thank God for Mama. She prayed for my healing and Ken's capture. My cousin Winston has been checking the progress of the case for us on a regular basis. Betty and Carolyn have been there for me too. I left a message for Beverly, but I haven't heard back from her yet. I'll catch up to her one of these days. At first, I didn't want to talk about it to anyone. I felt so ashamed and embarrassed. I have begun to open up particularly in my group counseling session. I don't feel so alone. Keith has been patient. Right now, I don't want him touching me in an intimate way. It just pains me that he doesn't see me in the same light."

Sasha was speechless. She couldn't think of any words that would bring comfort to Regina. She took a sip of her orange juice to sooth her throat and readjusted her body on the living room sofa.

For lack of something to say, Sasha asked, "Is there anything I can do?"

"No," Regina said with a sigh. "I just need some time and your prayers. Only time will help. I plan to take it one day at a time. Since I am no longer in the ranks of the employed, I have more time to devote to motherhood. It's a definite change from what I was used to. The twins are starting to get used to having me home. I've been trying to get out to do volunteer work as well while they're in school. I know I have a long road ahead of me. I just need everyone's patience and support."

"You know you've got that," said Sasha sympathetically. She still could not imagine how something like this could have happened to Regina. Her heart continued to sink.

"Well, I need to fix the twins some lunch. Maybe we can chat later."

Regina and Sasha said their goodbyes. Sasha still remained in a daze about Regina's assault. She never personally knew anyone who had been raped. She began to softly cry again for her friend. She thought about what she must have been going through, but then again she still could not fathom the thought. It was even more troubling that the rapist was still on the loose. She took a few sips of her orange juice then toasted a plain bagel and spread it with a thin layer of strawberry flavored cream cheese. With each crunchy bite, she thought about her plans for the day. She decided she needed to spend some time at home. With gas prices fluctuating upward into oblivion, she figured that the prices would be her excuse to conserve energy and stay home and watch TV. When she enjoyed her own company, she didn't have to worry about getting hurt. For the moment, that was fine with her.

Chapter 26

It's discouraging to think how many people are
shocked by honesty and how few by deceit.
-Noel Coward

Ken Cunningham knew he was a wanted man. He found comfort in his Motel 40 room watching TV and gulping his fourth Budweiser as he chewed the final remnants of his beef jerky. At that moment, he thought of Doris and how she always complained that the beef jerky stank. She demanded that he brush his teeth immediately after he ate it. She told him that the smell made her nauseous.

The motel was not the best, but it would do for now. His mind raced as he thought about how long he could be holed up in the small hotel room. He knew his cash would be running low, but he dare not use his credit or debit cards for fear he would be quickly tracked down. He knew that many of the motels on Route 40 took cash. Many one-night stands took place in the rooms along the strip. When he checked in, he used an assumed name—Charles Haskell. To elude the authorities, he attempted to change his appearance by shaving his head and his moustache. Naturally, he could not do anything with his weight in the near future. He wore dark shades anytime he had to venture outside of the motel room. He kept his head down and low, hoping his identity would not be discovered. To limit his exposure to the public, he dined alone off of fast food in his motel room. He also bought a few staples from the local supermarket in Rosedale about two miles away. He managed to switch license plates with another vehicle. Due to his limited cash, he decided not to flee Maryland. He believed he could hide from the authorities for an indefinite period of time if he played his cards right. After all, there were plenty of unsolved crimes in Baltimore. The police had their hands full with trying to solve them.

In the event he was discovered, Ken held his 357 Magnum close. It had been a while since he had fired it. The steel black handle of the weapon still felt familiar. He planned to go down fighting. He had no real plans as he finally got what he wanted—Regina. He smiled as he reminisced. He had made is mark on Regina. She would forever remember him--always.

Ken felt no remorse for what he had done. Drugging Regina was the only way he knew he would get to experience her and quench his desires. Granted she could not respond to him the way he wanted her to, but he felt powerful, as she had no choice but to be submissive to him. Her limp brown body was a treasure to behold for him. Once again he became aroused just thinking about her.

In his haste to get away, he had limited clothing. Besides the suit he wore to the luncheon, he had two pairs of jeans, two shirts, a pair of socks, and two pairs of underwear. He had been keeping the items in the trunk of his car for emergency purposes just in case he was ever stranded. He kept a small supply of toiletries in the car's glove compartment. His limited wardrobe would not get him far, but it would have to do. He spent his days and nights watching sports and HBO. There wasn't much else for a wanted man to do for now.

It was 11:00 p.m. The remote was handily in his hands at all times. He used it to change to channel 4, WZR-TV.

"Good evening, this is Vanessa Falby. Ed Morgan has the night off." Suddenly, Ken's picture appeared on the twenty inch television screen. "Baltimore has an alleged rapist at large. Baltimore City Police are on the lookout for Ken Cunningham who has been accused of raping a Baltimore County woman at the Baltimore Gardens Hotel in downtown Baltimore. Cunningham was last seen in downtown Baltimore. He is described as five feet, ten inches tall, 275 pounds, wears glasses, has a salt and pepper hair and a moustache. A reward of $10,000 has been posted for his arrest and conviction. If you see him, you are asked to notify the Baltimore City Police Department by calling 410-555-3960. In other news around the city..."

Ken stared at his likeness as it was portrayed on the news. He studied his supply of food. He knew he would have to be confined to his room until he could figure out a plan for his next move. He figured that Doris and their children were distraught and probably in disbelief. At the moment, he did not care about his children or her. He had completed his mission and nothing else seemed to matter. He went to sleep without a sane thought on his mind and he liked it that way.

Beverly's stay at the Aruba Grand Beach Resort and Casino was more enjoyable than she had planned. She allowed herself to separate from all the typical distractions the world had to offer. Once the Boeing 747 had descended and landed upon Aruban soil, she easily crept into a Caribbean state of mind—no worries, no problems.

The ten days she spent at the resort were her own. She came and went as she pleased. She basked in the sun, shopped until she dropped, and met lots of people from all over the world. She had not been worried about being alone per se, but it was comforting to be with others who simply wanted to have some fun. The bellman, turned personal tour guide, Jonah, proved to be worth her time. Beverly took a chance to get to know the island born and raised perfect stranger. His native tongue was a part of her attraction to him. Although Jonah bluntly told her he could provide an even more delightful experience, she firmly, yet politely declined. To soften the blow, she provided him with a monetary thank you for his trouble. Jonah didn't complain as he was pleased with the token of her appreciation. He had offered his address and telephone number. She accepted it without hesitation, but knew she'd probably never bother to use it. She conveniently tucked his information away in a small hidden pocket of her red leather folding wallet and would simply refer to the piece of paper as a keepsake from her trip.

As she began repacking her personal belongings, she smiled. Her impending departure from Beatrix International in route to Thurgood Marshall Baltimore Washington International Airport was near. She wanted to make it to the airport at least two and a half to three hours before the scheduled departure. With the new and ever changing aviation rules, she didn't want to leave anything to chance.

She zipped the large black suitcase on wheels with ease and placed it upright on the tan carpeted floor. She did one last walkthrough in the suite to ensure she had not left any personal effects. Once satisfied, she grabbed her purse, suitcase and carryon baggage and made her way to the registration desk on the lobby level.

The front desk clerk on duty promptly greeted her with his Caribbean accent.

"Ah, Miss Brown, it's so nice to see you this lovely mornin'. Don't tell me you're leaving us so soon."

Beverly tried to remember his name, but got a glimpse of his gold embossed name tag which read "David". She replied, "Sorry David, but I'm headed back to the States. I have enjoyed myself more than you can imagine." She continued to glow as she handed him her room access cards. He promptly began the checkout process.

"Miss Brown, there may be a problem with your credit card. It's not going tru'. Let me try again." David swiped the card a second time and input the amount of $2,061.49 once again.

"The system still says denied. Do you wish to try another card?"

"No," replied Beverly with a perplexed look on her face. It was the only card she had with her. "Before I left home, my MasterCard had and zero balance. My credit limit should more than accommodate what's due. I don't want to miss my flight. Can I use your phone to call customer service?"

"Certainly, Miss Brown." He dialed MasterCard's customer service center as she looked on. Once he heard the automated voice, he handed Beverly the telephone receiver and base. After inputting her credit card number and zip code for the automated system, she heard the greeting of the customer service representative.

"Hi, this is Sally. How may I help you?"

Beverly took charge of her thoughts, before speaking. "I'm in Aruba and I am trying to check out of the hotel. The front desk person says that my transaction has been denied. I'd like to know why." Sally verified Beverly's home address and home telephone number.

"Miss Brown, it appears that you have reached your $10,000 limit."

"That's impossible. I pay for whatever I charge each month. I don't carry a balance from month to month. There must be some mistake."

"We have quite a few transactions which were made last week. Do you recall making a purchase for $2,500 from Rims, Rims and More Rims?"

"Rims, Rims and More Rims? What the hell kinda store is that?" Beverly's tone became noticeably perturbed. She immediately knew that she'd never make a purchase from that retailer and besides she wasn't there to make it. She couldn't fathom what was happening to her.

"Miss Brown, the system says it's an automotive retailer. Do you recall authorizing someone else to use your card?"

"No, I'm the only person authorized to use my card. Obviously, there is some type of mistake."

"There are also some transactions from Victoria's Secret, Macy's and Reed's Jewelry Store made three days ago."

"I've been in Aruba for the past ten days. I didn't make those charges. Like I said before, no one else besides me is authorized to charge on my account." David tried to busy himself without her knowing his concern while simultaneously trying to keep his ears close to the conversation.

"Miss Brown, I'll close this account and get our Security Department to do an investigation."

"What am I supposed to do now? I owe the hotel over two thousand dollars. This is the only credit card I have with me. I only have one hundred dollars in traveler's checks left."

"Miss Brown, there is nothing we can do on this end until the investigation has been completed. I'm sorry." Sally then nonchalantly asked, "Is there anything else I can help you with?"

"No."

Beverly slammed the telephone into the cradle, still perplexed. David shuffled papers on the desk then turned his attention to her. She noticed his pointed gaze of suspicion. Before he had a chance to speak, she dialed Sasha with the premise of asking her to wire the money. She was the first person to come to mind who she knew had direct access to the two thousand she needed. As the telephone rang, she tried to ready her mind for Sasha's predictable line of questioning which would certainly include the five W's--who, what, where, why, and when. She planned to preface her explanation with a plea for help to minimize time consuming questions and to squash any time restraints Sasha would perhaps throw her way. She didn't want to think about missing her flight. All she could do was silently pray that Sasha would answer.

Chapter 27

No great discovery was ever made without a bold guess.
-Sir Isaac Newton

Darrell arrived home and immediately went to the kitchen to grab an ice cold Heinecken. He instinctively grabbed the bottle opener that had a magnetized base and was conveniently perched on the refrigerator door. He immediately pried the cap open and took a big gulp of the golden liquid. It hit the spot. He didn't waste any time as he took off his suit jacket and unloosened his tie. He plopped himself on the sofa and turned on the TV just in time to catch the beginning of World News Tonight.

After opening the mail, reheating and eating some leftover barbequed chicken, macaroni and cheese and spinach, he picked up the telephone to check for messages. The standard dial tone indicated there were none. Out of curiosity, he checked the caller ID and noticed Sasha's number date stamped on April 20 at 10:05 a.m.—the same date and time Erika would have been at his house.

"Damn it," he remarked out loud. It started coming together. He was probably in the shower and Erika answered the phone when Sasha called. He could only imagine what they talked about. He shook his head in disgust. His life had become nightmarish every since Erika Bellamy had entered it.

Just as he was walking up the carpeted steps, the telephone rang.

"Hey, D," said Jared. "I'm surprised you're home this early. I was just going to leave you a message to see if you wanted to come over tomorrow to watch the Bulls and the Wizards. The wife even volunteered to cook for us. Sometimes she thinks she's slick," winced Jared. "This is just her way of making sure she knows where I am. Victor, Nate, Joe, and Taylor are coming over, too."

"Man, I'll be there," replied Darrell.

"Just bring your appetite. You know my country woman can cook."

"You know I know that. Every time I think about her sweet potato pie, I just smile all over again. Tell her that's my special request."

"I'll let her know," said Jared.

"I made a discovery today. I found out why Sasha went ballistic. Remember Erika Bellamy?"

"That drunk client of yours who approached us at Don and Mike's?"

"Yes, that would be her. She answered my phone and told Sasha only God knows what while I was probably in the shower."

"That sounds logical. Ah, did anything happen between the two of you?" quizzed Jared.

"Hell, no. I wasn't about to let that happen," Darrell shot back. "That's what I get for trying to be a Good Samaritan. Granted she tried, but I wasn't about to let that happen with that woman. The thought didn't even cross my mind."

"Okay, man. I hear you. You and Sasha seemed to hit it off pretty good. So, do you plan to call her to explain?"

"She was so angry when I last saw her, I don't know. She was pretty adamant about me not contacting her again. I have lost track of the number of times I've tried to reach her. Plus, I've been having second thoughts about dealing with somebody who can get hot headed like that. I don't want to end up being a Lorena Bobbitt like victim."

Jared laughed. "Man, try another approach. This is what I do when I know I have done something wrong. Don't think this is corny or that I'm whipped, but I get Kiana a nice I'm sorry card. When I really mess up, I write her a letter."

"Oh man, don't tell me you have a feminine side," laughed Darrell.

"As a matter a fact I do and I'm man enough to admit it. D, you're still wet behind the ears when it comes to women. You have to work on matters of the heart. Man, when Kiana and I make up, it is some of the best loving any man could ask for. I don't ask any questions, but Kiana can get freaky when she wants to. She must be reading Essence, O Magazine or somebody."

Darrell belted a hearty laugh. "Hey, you just may have solved a mystery for all of mankind."

"Man, trust me. It works," Jared said reassuringly.

"Alright, alright. You may be on to something. I really enjoyed being with Sasha. She just might be worth fighting for. I'll try your little hustle and see what happens. I am not used to begging any woman to go out with me and I am not going to start. We'll see what happens. I may even throw in some roses to top it off."

"Hustle? Now that is low. Okay, man. See you tomorrow."

Darrell pondered what Jared said. It was beginning to make logical sense. Although he had not figured out exactly what he would say, he would at least say there was a definite misunderstanding. He reclined in his lazy boy in the master bedroom and watched a basketball game on ESPN then went to his home office. He grabbed the ink pen from its holder and a couple of ivory sheets of specialty paper from his stationery drawer and put pen to paper.

Dear Sasha,

I don't know where to begin other than to just come out and say it—I believe we have had a misunderstanding and I am sincerely sorry for that. Please hear me out and allow me to explain.

I recently discovered that you called me when Erika was at my house. Trust me, she was not here because I wanted her here. On the previous Friday afternoon, she and I met at my office to discuss her financial situation and retirement planning. Yes, she did try to come on to me at my office, but I told her under no uncertain terms that I was not interested in her in that way and that our relationship would be strictly business.

After she left my office, a few of my colleagues and I went to Don and Mike's for happy hour. She was there when I arrived. When she approached the group, she was quite drunk. She was so drunk to the point that she fell and hit her head. For fear of her safety and the safety of others, I attempted to escort her home. Because of her drunken state, she could not tell me her exact home address. I remembered the street from her paperwork, but not the number. I then decided to take her to my house with the intention of letting her sleep it off in my guest room and getting her home the next day. I was simply trying to be a gentleman. She attempted to come on to me once again; however, I told her bluntly that I was not interested in her. Nothing sexual occurred. I have no idea what she said to you exactly, but I have never had any interest in her or dated her for that matter. She's not the type of woman I would date even if I had not been seeing you.

I know my explanation may not be believable, but it is the God-honest truth. You are such a wonderful woman with so many fine qualities. A man would be a total fool to deliberately disrespect and hurt you. I want to make things right between us. I sincerely miss your beautiful smile, great sense of humor, and company. Can we at least talk? Up until this point, I pondered whether or not to try to contact you after our last conversation. I have thought long and hard about you. I don't want our relationship to come to a crashing halt over what I believe is a terrible misunderstanding. I would like the opportunity to see you face to face and talk about what happened and come to a true understanding. I know you have had some not so great relationships in the past. So have I. I don't want this unfortunate incident to make you bitter where I am concerned. I just want the opportunity to show you that I am worth your time and energy. I want us to continue to get to know each other. If it sounds like I am pleading my case to you, well, I am. You are a quality woman and I hope that you think I am a quality man.

Sasha, please say yes. I promise you it will be worth your while. I hope the dozen of red roses I am sending will help soften your heart. I have never written a letter like this to any woman and I want you to know how very sorry I am that you have been hurt. I know I can't automatically wipe away all the pain and tears you may have suffered at the hands of men from your past. However, I'd like to try. Won't you please give me that chance?

I will understand your position if I don't hear back from you, but I am hoping that you will open up your heart to the possibility of continuing us. Please give us the opportunity to experience good times, laughs, and great conversation once again. I will patiently await your answer.

Peace and blessings,
Darrell

Darrell reread the letter and was pleased with its contents. He was surprised at his level of expression and didn't know he had it in him. He planned to get to the florist down the street from his office the next day with the letter in hand sealed in an envelope for delivery with a dozen long stemmed roses to Sasha's job in hopes that Jared's advice had some validity. Even if she still refused to bend, he figured at least he tried. He wouldn't know whether or not she would have opened her heart again, but he concluded under any circumstances it was worth a try. He did not want to pressure her into an immediate response even though she could not answer quickly enough.

Satisfied with his prose, he folded it into a tri-fold, placed it in an envelope, sealed it, penned her name on the front, and placed it in the pocket of his portfolio. This could be either another beginning or the end for them. Either way, he would be a man about it and would accept the consequences.

Chapter 28

Don't let anyone steal your spirit.
-Sinbad

Beverly returned to Thurgood Marshall Baltimore Washington International Airport feeling like a brand new one hundred dollar bill. She had taken an 11:35 a.m. flight from Aruba and had plans to stop at The Bookworm first to begin to get back to her reality. She was able to avoid disaster at the resort. Sasha came through for her with the two thousand she needed. Surprisingly, she did not ask as many questions she was sure she'd have to answer. Once she got back to The Bookworm, she planned to immediately pay Sasha her money. She never knew when she'd have to reach out for her help in the future. She also planned to immediately follow up with the bank.

After getting her luggage from baggage claim, she whisked herself to the shuttle bus stand for satellite parking. Once she arrived at the lot, it took a little time for her to remember exactly where she had parked. After finally finding her car, she opened the trunk, placed her luggage inside, secured it and drove to the exit to pay the parking fee. That's when she realized she was truly back to her reality. Not a bad reality, but back to being a responsible adult.

Beverly arrived at The Bookworm and found James in the midst of ringing up a customer's order and Sharon stocking the shelves with books.

"Hey Bev!" shouted James. "I must say you do look divine! I guess Aruba did you some good." Sharon stopped what she was doing and walked in Beverly's direction. Beverly's Aruban escapade boldly showed on her tanned face.

"Welcome, back. You do look great," jumped in Sharon. "We have been holding down the fort pretty good if I must say so myself."

"Fantastic," Beverly said. "I appreciate that." Depending on the state of the business, she planned to give them small bonuses at the end of the next pay period for managing while she was vacationing.

"Well, let me get back to business," said Beverly. She abruptly broke up the brief chat and headed to her office. As far as she could see, it was exactly as she had left it.

She checked her office voice mail first, then her home voice mail, followed by U.S. regular mail. She returned calls to her parents and some vendors. She decided to call Sasha to begin catching up. Sasha always had some man or work drama going on. She would often joke and tell her to hold on while she went to get her popcorn.

"Good morning, this is Sasha."

"Hey, it's Bev. I'll bring you a check for the loan this evening. Girl, I can't thank you enough. I don't know what I would have done without you."

"It's no problem. I know you're good for the money. Has the credit card company finished the investigation?"

"No, not yet. They just started. I'm still trying to figure out what the hell happened. The account is closed and I called the credit card companies about my other accounts. They say I won't be held liable for fraudulent charges which is a good thing."

"Other than that, how are things?" Sasha inquired.

"Well, I'm back in the saddle again."

"Ooooo. You are sounding a bit vibrant," Sasha swooned. "I trust Aruba was just what the doctored ordered?"

"You know it. Girl, I had an absolute blast. If you and Gina can pull yourselves away for a moment from your busy lives, the three of us need to go down there. I met so many nice people. I even hung out a bit with an island guy. I can't wait to go back."

"Okay…spill it," demanded Sasha.

"Oh, Sasha," huffed Beverly. "Sometimes you act like you are a thirty-six year old virgin. I met a younger guy. We had a great time and that's it. If you must know, I didn't do him. It crossed my mind for a second, but I didn't. I was not about to take any chances. The same way I went to Aruba is the same way I intended to come back— healthy." Beverly began laughing. Sasha's naivety never ceased to amaze her.

Sasha chose to ignore Beverly's remark and changed the subject. "Have you spoken to Gina?" she said in a serious tone.

"No, but she's on my list of people to call. I had good intentions of calling her before I went to Aruba. I just ran out of time. Is everything alright?"

"Um, I'll leave that up to her to discuss with you," Sasha said hesitantly. The line suddenly became dead silent.

"Sasha, we've been friends for years. What's going on with Gina?" The silence continued.

"Bev, I don't know how to tell you this, but she was raped by her boss, Ken Cunningham. The police are still looking for him. It's been on the local TV and radio stations."

Beverly gasped. "What?! Tell me this is some kind of joke Sasha. That is so unreal. What happened? How is she?"

Sasha rehashed the series of events. "I wish it weren't true," she said. "Gina called me, but I was in one of my funks, and didn't call her back right away. I feel so guilty about that. He put a date rape drug in her drink and raped her at the Baltimore Gardens Hotel."

Beverly was still in disbelief. Her heart ached for Gina. She couldn't imagine anyone having to go through that type of pain and mental anguish. Her only comparison was when Carl tried to force himself on her one evening. When she was able to get up, she pulled out the 22-caliber gun she had been stashing in the nightstand. She told him that that was the first and last time he would ever do something like that to her again. There was no mistaking that he understood that his actions would not be tolerated. Otherwise he'd pay the ultimate price.

"Oh, that's just awful. I still can't imagine that. That man has got to be crazy to think he could get away with something like that. Do you think she would want to have a little get together with us? It might be a nice change of pace for her. How are Keith and the twins handling it?"

"We can certainly ask. I don't think she has ventured out much. I know she's been getting counseling. I guess Keith and the kids are handling it the best way they can. She hasn't explained much to the kids since they probably wouldn't understand at this point anyway."

"I am free on Saturday afternoon. If you're free, we can ask Gina about a get together. The two of you can come over to my place."

"I just checked my calendar. Saturday is good for me, too."

"Why don't I conference Gina in? That will save a little time," said Beverly. Sasha agreed. Beverly put Sasha on hold, dialed Regina's number, and then hit the conference button. Gina answered after two rings.

"Gina, it's Bev and Sasha."

"Hello ladies. Long time, no hear." Gina tried to sound upbeat.

"We were wondering if you'd like to get together on Saturday for lunch at Bev's. I think her culinary skills have shown significant improvement. She just wants to show us what she's working with," said Sasha light heartedly.

"I'd rather not be out driving by myself right now. Maybe some other time," remarked Regina. She still felt she was not up to much socializing.

"I'll swing by to pick you up," volunteered Sasha. "We haven't seen each other in a long time. We'd really like to see you, Gina."

After slight hesitation, Regina relented. "Okay. I can do lunch on Saturday."

"George and I will do the cooking," announced Beverly.

"Who's George?" Regina and Sasha said in unison.

"I named my George Foreman grill George," laughed Beverly. "George will grill the salmon, and I'll sauté the mixed vegetables and steam some rice. Hamilton will mix our drinks."

"Okay...she's baaaaaccccckkkkk!" sang Sasha. The three women were beginning to look forward to their get together. So much had happened over the last few weeks. A little girl talk is just what the three of them needed.   To them, there was nothing like a good old-fashioned Cinnamon Girls reunion.

◎◎◎

James walked to Beverly's office and peered in at the doorway. "Bev, can I interrupt you for a moment?"

Beverly looked up from her computer screen. "Yes, James, what is it?"

"I want to tell you about some things that happened while you were gone." James had a concerned look on his face. Beverly had never seen him look so serious.

"I would sit down, but I don't want to look suspicious. Sharon has three customers in line so I figured I could talk privately with you while she's busy."

"Okay...what's going on?"

"Last Sunday I decided to go to the Patapsco Flea Market on Annapolis Road. I saw Sharon there. I'm pretty sure she didn't see me. She and some guy had a table and they were selling hardcover books for ten dollars. I asked my friend to go to Sharon's table and pretend she was a customer. The titles were pretty new. I think she has been getting her stock from you. Another thing is that I don't think she has been ringing up all the sales. I took a lunch break and one of our regular customers saw me in the food court and said that he hoped that the cash register would be fixed soon. I asked him what he meant and he said that Sharon said the cash register was broken so she used a calculator to add the cost of the book and tax, wrote down the name of the book in a notebook, took his cash and gave him change from her purse."

Beverly was shocked. "Are you sure about this, James?"

"I'm pretty sure, Bev. There's no mistaking what's going on."

"Thanks, James. I'll look into it. Can you shut the door behind you?"

Beverly pulled the surveillance videotape from the last week. She fast-forwarded it to look for anything suspicious. Within a few minutes, she noticed Sharon at the checkout area doing exactly what James had mentioned. Her mouth opened in disbelief. She mentally pinned her credit card theft on Sharon as well.

"I'll be damned," she said out loud. "She's going down." For a moment, she thought about handling it *her* way, but then stopped. She placed the tape in her brief case and headed to the police station.

Chapter 29

There must be inner healing for the broken vessels.
-Reverend Linda Hollies

It had been awhile since Beverly had entertained in her split-level rancher. The four-bedroom house was more than enough for her. It had been the home she and Carl shared and had hoped they would start a family. Despite their failed relationship and his ultimate demise, she decided to keep it. After Carl's death, she had the entire house redecorated because she did not want any reminders of their past together. She had everything redone from painting the walls to buying all new furniture. She gutted the kitchen and the three bathrooms. She felt her project was another good use of some of the insurance proceeds from Carl's life insurance policy.

The glass and Kelly green wrought iron table and three floral cushioned chairs were classically arranged around the canary yellow linen covered circular table on the wooden deck. Beverly decided to use china, sterling silverware and crystal goblets for the occasion. She planned to grill the salmon once Sasha and Regina arrived. She once again thought about Regina and couldn't imagine what she had been going through. Her heart continued to ache. She felt guilty for being jealous of Regina and Keith's relationship. She was genuinely happy they were together and that Keith was probably the support Regina needed to help see her through her terrible ordeal.

Beverly did one last inspection of the house. She lit a mulberry scented candle in the guest bathroom and an apple cinnamon scented candle in the living room. She retrieved the spiced Bacardi rum and Dailey's strawberry daiquiri mix from the kitchen cupboard and filled the ice bucket with ice from the automatic icemaker on the refrigerator door.

She heard the doorbell ring. She took off her apron and placed it on the oven door rail. She opened the door to greet her guests. The trio embraced in the foyer.

"Oh, Bev, I love what you have done to the house. I don't even recognize it," chimed Sasha.

"Did you do an out with the old and in with the new?" Regina added.

"I got a new house without having to move. I hired a contractor to redo everything," gloated Beverly. Sasha and Regina exchanged glances and raised eyebrows as if to say "Carl".

"I'll give you the grand tour," said Beverly

Beverly proceeded with the tour. Sasha and Regina could tell she had spent a mint between the refinished hardwood floors, high quality furniture, oriental rugs, cabinetry and ceramic floors in the kitchen, and other expensive enhancements. They surmised the house had probably increased in value by several thousand dollars. Beverly escorted them through the lower level of the house into the patio area then returned to the kitchen to make a pitcher of strawberry daiquiris. She poured the frozen concoction into the goblets and handed each of them a straw. The first sip was telling. They each marveled at how good the drink felt going down. Beverly also served an appetizer consisting of spinach dip and assorted tortilla chips.

Beverly got the ball rolling. "So, Sasha," she paused as she dipped a tortilla chip into the spinach dip. "What's going on with you and the infamous Darrell? Inquiring minds want to know."

"He's trying real hard to get back on track. He sent me a dozen red roses and a hand written letter." Sasha pulled the letter from her purse, took it from the envelope, unfolded it and handed it to Beverly. Beverly read the letter out loud.

"Girl, if you don't take that man back, I will," exclaimed Beverly. "This letter is a masterpiece. You could probably sell this letter on eBay to the highest bidder. If this letter doesn't win a woman back, nothing will."

Regina added, "Sasha, can't you see he's sorry for what happened? It's just a misunderstanding. You remember how Erika operated. Do you think Darrell would honestly be interested in somebody like Erika? You remember how she was. Every week there was some drama going on with her. Drama doesn't disappear overnight and you know how much that woman enjoyed drama. I wouldn't be surprised if she is on some type of prescription medication. It won't hurt to just talk with Darrell. Give him a chance," Regina pleaded.

Sasha heaved a sigh. "His story sounds a little suspect to me. Erika has been harassing me every since I talked to her when I called Darrell's house. Between the phone calls in the middle of the night, the strange men calling and the emails, I don't know what to believe."

"Why don't you confront her?" questioned Beverly. "What is it you keep preaching? Don't avoid conflict—face it head on."

Sasha shot a blank look in Beverly's direction. "I would classify this as a different kind of conflict, Bev. I am not fighting over a man. She can have him."

Regina said, "At least respond to him. That letter says he cares. Do you think he would take the time and effort to write a letter like that if he didn't care?" Regina reached for the letter from Beverly. "That is the most romantic letter I have ever seen. Keep in mind we know your track record."

"Okay, okay," Sasha relented. "I'll at least talk to him. He's not off the hook yet. He's gonna need more than roses and a letter to impress me."

Regina inquired, "So, are you going to give us more details on your Aruba escapades, Stella? I mean Bev." The three women laughed.

"Don't get so excited. There is really nothing extra to tell especially if you are referring to Jonah. It wasn't that kind of party," said Beverly dryly. "We went out a couple of nights. He gave me a private tour of the island. There was no connection in a romantic sense. He was just something to do. The last thing I need is to have some youngin' get attached. And you know I ain't taking care of no man." Beverly's diction frequently changed once she expressed her passion on a topic of conversation. She cut the conversation short.

"On that note, I'll put the salmon on the grill," Beverly said as she excused herself to head to the kitchen.

Sasha and Regina talked in a lowered tone among themselves. "I guess we'd better not bring up that topic anymore. Maybe it's me, but Bev seems a bit touchier these days," said Sasha.

Regina said with concern, "I agree. Maybe the stress of running that store is getting the best of her. I don't know. Better safe than sorry."

Beverly returned with a platter of grilled salmon seasoned with cilantro, mixed spring vegetables sautéed in ginger and butter and steamed white rice. After saying grace, the three women dived into the meal.

Beverly said," I had Sharon arrested."

Regina and Sasha looked at each other in surprise. "For what?" asked Sasha.

"She was stealing money and books. I caught her stealing money on a surveillance tape and James witnessed her selling my books at the Patapsco Flea Market. The police got a warrant and searched her apartment. They found boxes of books addressed to the bookstore. I was beginning to wonder where my inventory was going. She bought stuff using my credit card for herself and her boyfriend. For once I really listened to that accountant of mine and installed a surveillance camera. He's earned his keep for another year."

"I never would have suspected Sharon," said Sasha with a bewildered look on her face. If anything, I would have suspected James."

"Well, if it wasn't for James, it would have been a while before I would have found out what she was doing. They don't make them any slicker than her."

"Bev, this meal is divine. Your cooking skills have certainly come a long way," Regina said as she put a forkful of the mixed spring vegetable medley in her mouth.

"Thanks. That just goes to show you that we have a tendency to get better with age in a lot of respects," said Beverly. "Would anyone like a daiquiri refill?" Sasha and Regina eagerly raised their glasses.

"I'll take that as a yes," said Beverly. She filled each of their glasses.

"Beverly quizzed, "Sash, any wild human resources stories you want to share with us?" Regina and Beverly eagerly waited her response.

"Where shall I start? The latest issue is that I have a male employee who wore a business suit to work on Monday."

"What could possibly be wrong with that?" asked Regina. She raised her eyebrow awaiting Sasha's answer.

"It was a skirt, blouse, jacket, pantyhose and high heels," replied Sasha.

Beverly and Regina opened their mouths and had surprised looks on their faces. They couldn't decide whether or not they should have laughed or gasped.

"He was dressed in appropriate business attire. It's the productivity of his co-workers that's suffering. They pay more attention to him than their own work. I couldn't tell him to go home to change."

"Now if he were in Scotland he'd fit right in. The men wear skirts and it's accepted. Besides, we wear pants. What's the problem? Let that man wear a skirt if he wants to," admonished Beverly.

"I don't know how you do it," said Regina. "You ought to write a book. You couldn't make that stuff up if you tried." They shared another hearty laugh.

Sasha and Beverly shifted to Regina. She stared back. She broke the eerie silence that had drifted in between them.

"Just in case you are wondering, I'm doing fine. I know that you have been wondering how I have been coming along. I just take one day at a time. Trust me, it has not been easy. I still feel dirty, no matter how many showers I take. Thank God none of my tests have come back positive. I feel Keith's frustration. We have not made love since I was raped. Ken is still out there. Until he is caught, I can't begin to have closure. I wake up in the morning thinking about what happened. I go to sleep with the very same thoughts. I'm sure I'll be in counseling for quite some time. For the sake of my family, I need to feel better. And ya'll know I got a praying mama who keeps me on track."

"We know that's right," replied Sasha. "One way or another, he'll be caught. Is there anything we can do for you?"

"I just need for the two of you to continue to be the great friends you have always been. When I am feeling sorry for myself, I need for you to snap me back into reality. When I am feeling like I have no blessings, I need for you to remind me of how very blessed I am. That's all I ask."

Beverly and Sasha nodded in agreement and embraced Regina. Sasha smiled. "I for one will keep you entertained with my office stories." She managed to get a slight grin from Regina.

Beverly said, "I'll keep you laughing, too. I can't promise you I can entertain you with stories like Sasha's, but I'll do my best."

"Thank you so much," Regina said as tears began flowing from her eyes. "You just don't know how much the two of you mean to me. I appreciate all of your love and concern. You're the best."

The ring from Regina's cell interrupted the moment. It was Keith.

"Hey baby. I got some good news. Ken Cunningham is in police custody. They found him in hiding out in a seedy motel room on Route 40."

Chapter 30

Our greatest problems in life come not so much from the situations we confront as from our doubts about our ability to handle them.
-Susan Taylor

It was nearing the end of a horrific Monday for Sasha. She had spent most of her morning on endless and meaningless conference calls. The afternoon consisted of resolving what she felt were petty conflicts between managers. She finally halted her procrastination and decided to take a break to call Darrell in response to his roses and letter.

"Good afternoon. This is Darrell Payson."

"Hi Darrell. It's Sasha."

Darrell was pleased and relieved that she finally decided to call. "Thanks for calling me. I trust that you received the roses and the letter."

"Yes, I did. So, you weren't seeing Erika?"

"In a word, no. In two words, hell no. She's not my type by a long shot. You are," Darrell stated as a matter of fact. "I missed you, Sasha. The many times I called and didn't get a response from you were hard on me. A man would be fool to lose you." His tone became more serious. "Can we talk over dinner? Please? How about tomorrow night?"

"Tonight is actually better for me. How about 7:30 at City Sights on Security Boulevard? I can meet you there."

Darrell wanted the pleasure of picking her up from her home. He decided not to chance it by being demanding. "Okay, 7:30 it is at City Sights. I'm looking forward to seeing you."

"See you then."

Sasha left the office promptly at 5 p.m. With traffic, it would take her about thirty-five minutes to get home. Once she arrived, she showered, brushed her teeth, moisturized her body with mango body butter, and placed a hint of Eternity behind her ears, on her wrists, and on the back of her legs. She decided to wear a black halter-top dress. The three-inch spiked black heels tied her look together. She applied her make up with expert precision for a sophisticated natural look. She pinned her hair up in a chignon shadowed with tiny tendrils which framed her glowing face.

On the way to City Sights, she started to look forward to seeing Darrell. She had to admit that she perhaps was hasty in her decision to not allow him to explain. After replaying his explanation from his letter, she could see how a misunderstanding could have occurred. She had not heard anything from Erika lately, so she figured she had finally given up. This could not please Sasha any more. When she arrived at City Sights, Darrell greeted her with a hug.

His familiar cologne instantly mesmerized her. She felt warm in his brief, yet welcoming embrace. His newly formed beard made him even more handsome and gave him a distinguishing look.

"You look great!" exclaimed Darrell. Sasha thanked him for the compliment. At that moment, her beauty was reminiscent of the first time he saw her at The Bookworm, but only better. He took her well manicured hands into his. They felt as soft as fresh rose petals. "I reserved a nice table for two near the back for us." Darrell escorted her to their table and seated her. The waiter gallantly greeted them then took their drink and appetizer orders. Darrell ordered a Heinecken and Sasha ordered a glass of peach-mango flavored iced tea. They ordered an appetizer of artichoke dip and crackers.

Darrell stared at her. She was prettier now than he remembered. He realized even more how much he missed admiring her beauty.

"Is something wrong?" she asked.

"No," he replied. "I'm just glad you're here. So, what have you been doing with yourself?"

"Working, going to the gym, visiting friends in town and out of town. Nothing out of the ordinary. I wish I had more to report."

Darrell wanted to know if she was seeing anyone, but he decided not to go there. Of course he would be disappointed if she were. He was not ready to hear that she was seeing someone else. If she was, he'd give the guy a run for his money.

"Well, that sounds pretty busy to me. Sounds like the work-life balance is working for you."

She smiled. "Let's just say I am making more of an effort to make it work. No matter how much I love my job, it will never love me back. At least that's what my mother says. So, what have you been doing with yourself?" she asked.

"Besides the usual of work, I've been volunteering as a big brother. My little brother lives in Edmondson Village. So far it's been great. It makes me really appreciate my dad's influence in my life even more."

"That's wonderful Darrell," remarked Sasha.

"My little brother, Tony, has had some tough times for a ten year old. His mom is raising him with his two younger sisters. His father was gunned down two years ago on the east side of town in a case of mistaken identity."

Sasha's heart immediately sank. "Oh, that's awful for him to lose his father—especially like that."

"He talks about his dad quite a bit and the father-son things they used to do together. Of course, I am not trying to replace his father, but I'd like to help guide him."

"That's very admirable. Tony is very blessed to have you in his life." Sasha suddenly remembered how much respect and admiration she had for Darrell. She had not met anyone like him before and became settled with the fact that he was probably one of a kind.

The waiter approached them to take their dinner orders. Sasha ordered the jumbo lump crab cake, fresh garden salad with honey mustard dressing and string beans almandine. Darrell ordered stuffed rockfish with steamed broccoli and cauliflower and a baked potato with butter and a heaving serving of sour cream with chives.

"Sasha, hopefully it's water under the bridge, but I am truly sorry for what you experienced with Erika. She became a loose cannon. After I sent her home in a cab, she was calling my job and home constantly. She called my co-workers and told them lies about how I had dogged her. She even called my boss. It was so embarrassing. I'm glad I told him about her flirting with me during our first meeting. It saved me even more embarrassment. She was coming to my house all hours of the night. I finally got a restraining order to get her to stop. She stopped for a few days, but started right back up again. I had to make sure Myrtle was ready for action." He tried to add a little humor to the situation.

"Who's Myrtle?" asked Sasha.

"Myrtle is my licensed revolver," he replied hoping to get a smile.

Instead, Sasha gasped. "She did her share of harassment with me as well. I got phone calls, strange men calling at work and at home, and explicit emails. I was beginning to think my personal information was in some horrid men's restroom. I figured she got tired since she made it clear that the two of you were together. Let's just hope she's gone forever. I thought that kind of stuff only happened in the movies. If one of my friends told me that they experienced something like that, I don't think I would believe them. I'm tired of talking about her. Let's talk about something more pleasant," Sasha pleaded.

"I agree," replied Darrell. "I'd rather talk about us." He reached for her hand. His large hands engulfed hers. His touch was warm and memorable. He gently placed a kiss on the back of her right hand.

"Ms. Grant, will you allow me the pleasure of continuing our relationship?" he deeply whispered.

Sasha grinned. "Yes, I'd like that Mr. Payson. I'd like that very much." Darrell continued to admire her smile.

After Darrell paid the check and tipped the waiter handsomely, he escorted Sasha to her SUV and asked her to call him once she got in. He continued to hold her delicate hand in his. As he faced her, he gently lifted her chin and placed his sensuous lips upon hers. The familiar touch delighted her senses. His kiss became deeper and she responded accordingly. She placed her arms around his waist as he drew her nearer. He teased her lower then her upper lip with wanton pleasure. They ended the kiss with three quick sweetened pecks.

"Well," Sasha breathed. She was beginning to feel a bit tingled. Darrell experienced the same feelings.

"I can't wait until we get together again, Miss Grant."

"Me either," said Sasha as she tried to control her heartbeat. Darrell opened her SUV door and ensured she was comfortably seated. He closed the door and waved goodbye as he walked back to his car.

During the drive home she listened to 95.7 FM's Quiet Times and smiled as she thought of Darrell. She had to admit that she missed him too. She pulled into the driveway, put the SUV in park, applied the emergency brake, turned off the lights and then the engine.

"Fancy meeting you here," shouted a voice that appeared to be coming from the back seat. Sasha turned around to find Erika at the end of a gun pointed in her face.

"Don't bother saying anything. I want you to very slowly, and I mean very slowly, get out. And don't bother screaming or drawing attention. If you do, I'll kill you right here on the spot. Don't even think about trying me. This gun is fully loaded and I won't hesitate to use it." Erika's eyes conveyed that she was more serious than she had ever been. Her mouth was taut and deliberate.

Sasha followed Erika's demands. She could feel her heart pound rapidly in her chest and her nerves heighten in response to her predicament. She looked around to see if any of her neighbors happened to be watching. She noticed no activity. It was quiet as usual. The one time she needed one of them to be nosey, they weren't. There was no escaping for her at this point. The gun met Sasha's back at the clasp of her bra. It felt like a metal pipe had been lodged in her back. She began perusing her immediate surroundings hoping her fate would suddenly change for the better.

"I don't know who you're looking for. No one can help you, Miss Grant almighty. Open that door and don't try anything. If you do, trust me, you'll be sorry."

Sasha opened the door, and the warning tone for the house alarm sounded. She had forty-five seconds before the alarm would send a signal remotely to the alarm monitoring command center indicating that there was a potential problem.

"You'd better turn that alarm off," Erika said as she grabbed Sasha by the hair and moved the gun from Sasha's back to her right temple. The feel of the steel barrel against her temple made her cringe forcing her to oblige. Erika then forced her to sit on the sofa in the living room.

Sasha said nervously, "Why are you doing this, Erika? I haven't done anything to you. What do you want from me?"

"You think you're something else, don't you? I am here to tell you that you ain't better than anybody. So what, you got that fancy job, a big house, and little bit of college. That doesn't make a woman, you bitch. You're not every man's dream. I want to teach you a lesson that you shouldn't go around thinking you're better than us common folks."

Erika began pacing heavily on the carpet. Her footprints left a trail. She swallowed hard. "You made me lose my job, Sasha. Because of you, I lost a good paying job. In fact, it was the best job I ever had. I was finally getting on my feet. I know I have made lots of mistakes. I bet you didn't know I over heard you talking about me and Larry to one of your girlfriends. I'm not as stupid as you think I am. Just because you grew up with two parents, that doesn't make you perfect. You were always talking about how great your parents were, Sasha. You never bothered to ask me about mine. For your information, growing up, my mother was an alcoholic and my father was on lock down. He'll spend the rest of his life in Jessup. Oh, and now my mama claims she's born again after the way she treated me. She acts like I'm supposed to forgive and forget. She can forget about that ever happening. What a childhood I had. It's the type of childhood you deserved to have. And now you have the man of your dreams. Sorry, but your dreams are gonna be short lived."

Sasha hesitated before speaking. "Is this about Darrell?" she inquired. She paused two more seconds. "Why would you want to kill me over a man, Erika?"

"Sasha, this goes deeper than Darrell." Erika pointed the gun at Sasha and fired with distinct aim.

Chapter 31

We have learned that power is a positive force
if it is used for positive purposes.
-Elizabeth Dole

The sound of the bullet exiting the barrel made Sasha freeze for a millisecond. The bullet grazed the top of her left shoulder. She screamed from fear and pain. She closed her eyes tightly and willed herself that what she was experiencing was just a dream. She opened her eyes which forced her back into reality. She was afraid to look at the wound.

"I want to you know what if feels like to be rejected by a man. Oh, I guess you have never had that issue, Miss Grant. Well, let me tell you what it feels like. It feels just like a bullet going through your heart—especially when you try to make a good impression and he's just not interested." Erika's voice became somber and flat. "Does it hurt yet? I am here to tell you that the pain is only gonna get worse. Do you know what it's like to have the kids at school tease you because your mama's an alcoholic and had three teeth in her head? My daddy is serving a life sentence for being stupid and getting caught. He killed a man. He killed somebody's father. I hate the holidays. They were never fun for me. Not once do I remember a time when my mama and daddy sat down and had a meal with me. I didn't grow up with a real family." Erica paused in the middle of her rambling tangent and allowed the resentment to engulf more of her being.

For a brief moment, Sasha felt sorry for Erika. She felt ashamed that she had laughed at her behind her back. It was true that Erika's performance at work had rolled down hill fast, but she began rethinking the fact that she had not given her more of an opportunity to improve herself and her predicament. She steadily focused on her parents' fortieth wedding anniversary picture which was attractively framed and sat upon the end table. Sasha mustered the courage to speak.

"There are plenty of people who didn't have a so-called perfect childhood. I was an only child and wanted brothers and sisters. My dad was in the military so we moved around a lot. It wasn't easy making friends that you would have to eventually leave behind. I have friends who were abused as children. Despite their circumstances, they overcame their childhood obstacles and became successful adults." Sasha hunkered down on the sofa in anticipation of Erika's negative response.

Erika enjoyed Sasha's submissiveness. Sasha grabbed her shoulder in attempt to stop some of the blood flow. She hesitated before grabbing a handful of tissues from the end table.

Erika let out a belting laugh, and then ignored Sasha's reasoning. Her psychotic mind told her that Sasha wasn't making any sense and was simply trying to talk her out of what her mind had planned to do.

"How was your date with Mr. Payson?" Erika sarcastically asked. "Did you notice me in the restaurant? I bet not. The two of you were gazing in each other's eyes as if you were Romeo and Juliet. I have always longed for someone to treat me like that." Erika's eyes became noticeably glassy. "What do you think Darrell would say if he saw you in this predicament, huh? I tried to give him a little taste of what he could have had on a regular basis, but he continued to be the so called perfect gentlemen. Can you even imagine how many men would not have turned me down? Take a wild guess, Miss Grant."

Before Sasha had a chance to answer, her telephone rang.

"Who could be possibly calling you at this time of night?" asked Erika.

"It's probably Darrell, checking on me to make sure I got home okay."

Erika looked at the caller ID. "It's him," she said. "Pick up the phone and tell him that everything is okay. Don't try anything funny or you will get it again, but this time a little closer to the heart." Erika enjoyed the upper hand. Sasha picked up the telephone as she was told.

"Hi Darrell. I got in okay. Thanks. I had a nice time." Sasha quickly said.

"Good. Glad you made it in okay. I really enjoyed dinner with you."

Erika nudged Sasha and mouthed, "Tell him you don't want to see him anymore." Sasha did not respond. Erika nudged her again, this time the gun was more squarely inserted into her side.

"Darrell," she hesitated. "I don't want to see you anymore."

Darrell was silent and at a loss for words. "Is something wrong? What could have possibly happened between the time we left City Sights and now, Sasha?" He twitched his left eyebrow. He was unmistakably confused about what he was hearing. "Did I do or say something that offended you?"

There was loud knocking at the door. "Baltimore County Police! We have a report of a gunshot being fired! Open the door!" Darrell heard the police shouting through the door. The police cruiser's flashing lights were peering through the sheer ivory curtains and white mini blinds.

"I'm on my way, Sasha," Darrell said before abruptly hanging up. Sasha heard dial tone on the other end of the line.

Erika became miffed. "It seems that one of your nosey neighbors doesn't know when to mind their damn business. That's a shame when nosey neighbors get involved. This is the last thing I need." She grabbed Sasha by the arm and forced her to walk with her to the front door. She dropped the receiver on the floor. The battery pack spilled its contents. Sasha did not dare look to see where the contents of the cordless telephone landed.

Erika spoke in a hushed tone. "I am going to open this door. You tell them that you just had your stereo up a little too loud. Do you understand me?" Erika didn't wait for Sasha to answer.

"And don't try anything funny," Erika hissed. She draped a jacket from Sasha's closet over Sasha's shoulders to cover the blood from the wound.

Sasha opened the entrance door and then the storm door to greet the two officers standing before her. Erika had the gun pointed directly into Sasha's left side as she stood directly behind the steel door. She tried to remain close but out of the sight of the officers.

"Good evening officers. Nothing is wrong. I probably had my stereo up a little too loud," Sasha said with no emotion. For a brief moment, Sasha thought of screaming, but squashed the thought out of pure fear. She imagined she had a better chance of avoiding a more life threatening wound if she cooperated with Erika a little longer and tried to reason with her. She suddenly remembered that Marian told her that you can't always reason with a crazy person. And Erika was indeed crazy.

One of the officers noticed a streak of blood rolling down Sasha's left hand. He tried to read her eyes and then looked at his partner. He winked at Sasha as a signal that they were about to move in.

"Okay, Ma'am. When we get reports like that we have to check it out. Sorry to have disturbed you. Have a good evening."

The two officers then drew their weapons from their holsters and forced their way into the house. The shock of the two storming in with their service weapons drawn startled Erika and she backed away from the door and fell onto the steps leading to the second level. The gun she had been tightly holding escaped from her embrace and was halted by the plush ivory carpet. She put up a brief fight, but the officers were able to quickly place her on her stomach to handcuff her. They read the Miranda rights to her and walked her to the squad car. Sasha's neighbors stood in their doorways to get a glimpse of the action. About five minutes later, Darrell drove up into Sasha's drive way and ran to the ambulance where she was being treated. A police officer stopped him in his tracks.

Sasha said, "It's okay. He's my boyfriend." Darrell smiled in response to her statement. The officer let him through.

"Well, you are my friend and you happen to be of the male persuasion."

"Are you okay? What happened?" he asked.

"Apparently Erika hid in my backseat while we were at City Sights. I didn't realize it until she made herself known. That tells you where my mind was. She's been harboring ill feelings about me from when we used to work together. The bullet grazed my shoulder. The paramedics said it's just a flesh wound and I'll be alright."

Darrell held her hand and kissed her forehead. "I'm sorry this happened to you. I'm just glad you were not seriously hurt. Erika should be out of our lives for quite sometime."

"I hope so," responded Sasha. "She'll probably try to cop some type of insanity plea."

"Excuse me folks. I need to get a statement from you Ma'am," the arresting officer said. "I'm Officer Tolson."

Sasha gave her account of the events as Officer Tolson took notes while Darrell stood beside her and held her hand in an attempt to offer comfort. His presence helped somewhat ease her trauma. She was glad he was there and couldn't imagine if he had not been with her. After Erika had been transported to the police station, the potential witnesses had been questioned, and the crowd of neighbors had dispersed, Darrell and Sasha sat in her living room.

"I haven't had this much excitement in a long time, Sasha," Darrell said attempting to lighten the atmosphere.

"Sorry to have gotten you into this," she remarked. "This is the kind of stuff that happens only in the movies and on TV. It's larger than life until it happens to you."

"I'm just glad I'm here with you. It's not your fault. It's obvious that Erika has some serious issues that require immediate professional attention."

"I think I should call my parents."

"How about calling them first thing tomorrow?" Darrell suggested. "They may be worried more if you tell them now. I'll stay with you tonight."

"Do you mind?"

"Are you kidding? I'm not leaving until you tell me to. I can stay in your guest room. If you need anything, you just holler."

Sasha hesitatingly asked, "Darrell, do you mind staying with me in my bedroom? I promise I won't touch you," she tried to grin. "I'm just still a little jumpy from tonight."

No words were spoken. His discerning gaze and strong embrace were enough to make her feel safe. She whispered a silent prayer thanking God for Darrell.

Epilogue

One Year Later

The reception hall at Martin's West in Woodlawn was filled with lively chatter, live jazz, libations, an assortment of pleasures for the palate, and over 200 family members and friends. Ladies were dressed in a vast array of evening dresses and the men were decadently dressed in tuxedos and suits. The music suddenly stopped as the master of ceremonies got everyone's attention by tapping a sterling silver knife against a crystal clear goblet. He was dressed in a black tuxedo and had been fitted with a wireless microphone. He began speaking once the hall had reached a reasonable level of silence.

"Ladies and gentlemen, I would like to introduce to you for the very first time, Mr. and Mrs. Darrell Payson!" The bride and groom entered the hall to the sounds of whistles, cheers and applause.

Sasha's wedding gown was made of pure white satin with a lace bodice and a full long skirt. Her short veil rested atop her spiral curls. Darrell's white tuxedo made him more than handsome.

The guests stood on their feet. Marian and George had tears in their eyes as their only daughter and new son-in-law danced to Stevie Wonder's *Ribbon in the Sky* as husband and wife. They were mentally counting the months to what they hoped would be the arrival of their first grandchild. Moments later, the wedding party joined in—Regina and Keith, Beverly and James, Jared and Kiana, and Darrell's brother David and his wife Pam. Even Tyrique and Tiffani joined in as the ring bearer and flower girl. The guests who wished to join them on the dance floor in their first official dance were also invited.

Sasha winked at Beverly and mouthed, "You and James just might be next." Beverly smiled and embraced James tighter and he obliged.

Sasha then looked at Regina. "Thank you for being my matron of honor."

"I've been waiting for this day longer than you have," said Regina. Keith held her close. She closed her eyes and cherished his touch. Ken's capture and confession were the catalysts she needed to start feeling like her old self.

Darrell looked at his beautiful bride and then gently placed his lips upon hers for an enduring and passionate kiss. He temporarily forgot about the people around them.

"Mr. Payson, I promise I will be good to you all the days of your life."

"Mrs. Payson, I promise you that and much more."

ABOUT THE AUTHOR

Wilma Brockington is a native of Baltimore, Maryland. She holds a Bachelor of Science degree in Business Administration from Towson University, a Master of Science degree in Management and a Master of Business Administration degree from University of Maryland University College.

Visit her website at
www.wilmabrockington.com
or email her at wilma@wilmabrockington.com